Jade Lee has been scripting [...] first picked up a set of pape[...] rakish lords were her first loves, which naturally led her to the world of regency romance. A *USA TODAY* and Amazon bestselling author, she has a gift for creating a lively world, witty dialogue and hot, sexy humour. She earned an MFA in screenwriting from USC, published seventy novels, and won several industry awards, including an RWA PRISM Award for Best of the Best, an RT Reviewers' Choice Best Book Award, and Fresh Fiction's Steamiest Read award. Check out her devilishly clever historical romances at www.jadeleeauthor.com. And, lest you think *Bridgerton* is her only fave fandom, she's got a few other fancies. She adores shifters, and writes them as Kathy Lyons: www.kathylyons.com. But her biggest love is for her grandkids. They inspired her foray into picture books as Kat Chen: www.kat-chen.com.

Check out Jade Lee's previous installment
in the Daring Debutantes series:

The Duke's Guide to Fake Courtship

Look out for more books from **Jade Lee**
coming soon!

Discover more at millsandboon.co.uk.

A LORD IN WANT OF A WIFE

Jade Lee

MILLS & BOON

All rights reserved including the right of reproduction in whole or in part in any form. This edition is published by arrangement with Harlequin Enterprises ULC.

This is a work of fiction. Names, characters, places, locations and incidents are purely fictional and bear no relationship to any real life individuals, living or dead, or to any actual places, business establishments, locations, events or incidents. Any resemblance is entirely coincidental.

Without limiting the author's and publisher's exclusive rights, any unauthorised use of this publication to train generative artificial intelligence (AI) technologies is expressly prohibited. HarperCollins also exercise their rights under Article 4(3) of the Digital Single Market Directive 2019/790 and expressly reserve this publication from the text and data mining exception.

® and TM are trademarks owned and used by the trademark owner and/or its licensee. Trademarks marked with ® are registered with the United Kingdom Patent Office and/or the Office for Harmonisation in the Internal Market and in other countries.

First published in Great Britain 2025
by Mills & Boon, an imprint of HarperCollins*Publishers* Ltd,
1 London Bridge Street, London, SE1 9GF

www.harpercollins.co.uk

HarperCollins*Publishers*, Macken House, 39/40 Mayor Street Upper, Dublin 1, D01 C9W8, Ireland

A Lord in Want of a Wife © 2025 Greyle Entertainment, LLC

ISBN: 978-0-263-34535-3

09/25

This book contains FSC™ certified paper and other controlled sources to ensure responsible forest management.

For more information visit www.harpercollins.co.uk/green.

Printed and Bound in the UK using 100% Renewable Electricity at CPI Group (UK) Ltd, Croydon, CR0 4YY

Some books flow. Others are a fight.
This book did both in fits and starts.
Thanks to Rachael Nazarko for helping me through it!
And as always, Brenda, Kim and Nicole,
you're the best!

Prologue

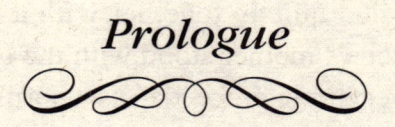

Lucy loved Almack's.

She shouldn't. It was the site of her greatest humiliation thanks to the deceitful Cedric, Lord Domac. Two years ago she'd trusted him with her biggest secret—that her father wasn't the biological father of either her or her sister—and he'd revealed it in front of the entire *ton*. She'd been so angry that she'd slapped him across the face and damned him in front of everyone.

She'd spent a long time afterwards cursing his name. Now the memory just made her sad.

Either way, she ought to hate being here, but she didn't. She loved Almack's. She loved the desperate, defiant hope that all but dripped from the walls. Girls came here praying to meet their future husbands, respectable men of the *ton*. Women ruled here in defiance of a world dominated by men. And debutantes like her gathered to be seen and to be heard by each other.

After all, in a generation, it would be they who ruled this place, and they had to decide on what they wanted.

At least that was what they told each other. In reality, every girl here just wanted to meet the man of her dreams.

Lucy was no exception. Tonight, she and her friend Phoebe giggled quietly together with a few of their friends. Phoebe's mother stood with the other chaperones, and everything proceeded as a normal Thursday night at Almack's.

Lucy danced. She drank tepid lemonade. And she found fault with every man who approached her. They were good men, for the most part. Anyone who danced with Lucy was a good man merely from the fact that he was willing to be seen with a half Caucasian, half Chinese bastard with a massive dowry to make her acceptable.

It helped that her equally mixed-race sister, Grace, was now the Duchess of Byrning.

And though the gentlemen were invariably polite, she found that their attention was focused on the size of her dowry, not herself. Phoebe had a similar problem. She was fully Caucasian, but she was a banker's daughter. She was considered a cit, and that made her only marginally acceptable to the titled elite.

'Good God,' Phoebe moaned. 'I never thought that Almack's would become dull. It's the same people every time, and none of them want to hear a thing I say.' Phoebe had lately discovered an interest in science. Medicine, to be exact, and she was spending a great deal of time in study. And what Phoebe studied, she talked about incessantly.

Her friend saw Lucy's arch look and sighed dramatically.

'I know I go on and on,' she said, punctuating the words by drawing circles in the air with her fan. 'They could at least pretend to listen. It's about their health!'

Lucy didn't answer. She didn't speak much in public. At first it was because she didn't feel comfortable enough—or safe enough—to venture her opinions out loud. Now it was because those who mattered already knew what she thought.

'Fine,' the girl huffed. 'I'll try to be interested in *them*.'

Lucy chuckled while Phoebe looked about the room. The musicians were taking a break and so everyone milled about sipping lemonade and gossiping. Except there was no good gossip to be had this evening. 'Tell me about the musical evening at Lady Bowles's home,' Phoebe suggested. 'Was it exciting?'

A musical evening exciting? Was the heat getting to her friend?

'As dull as that?' Phoebe asked.

'No,' she said. 'It was fine. I'm just not used to your music.' She'd been raised on the Chinese music of a Buddhist temple in Canton. But she'd gone to the event anyway for the same reason she was here. She hoped that someone would at last tempt her heart out of its shell. Someone, somewhere would intrigue her enough to make her feel him even from across the room.

'You can't keep pining for Lord Domac,' her friend chided in a low whisper.

'I'm not pining!' Lucy said. 'Until you brought him up, I'd completely forgotten that annoying man who can't keep a secret.'

'Hmmm,' her friend said.

Lucy shook her head. 'I'm ready to fall in love,' she said, meaning every word. 'I want my heart to flutter again, my blood to pound and my every thought to be consumed with feeling.'

'At least you had that once,' Phoebe said.

She had, and it had nearly broken her. 'He didn't deserve me,' she said flatly. 'I've ceased thinking about him.'

Thankfully, the musicians started up again, saving her from further conversation. Better yet, Phoebe took the hint and changed the topic. 'Do you want to come over tomorrow afternoon? I could tell you about the newest experiments in electricity. They're fascinating! I'm not sure if I truly believe them.'

'I would love to,' Lucy said.

Her friend frowned at her. 'You're not just saying that, are you? I know I can be a bore—'

Lucy gripped her friend's hand. 'I don't lie to you,' she said. 'Ever.'

Phoebe brightened. 'Well, that's it then. Come over

whenever you like so long as it's after one. A girl needs her beauty sleep.'

'You don't. You're stunning.' And Phoebe was. She had blond ringlet hair, bright blue eyes, and rosy cheeks. She embodied English beauty as if she were painted on canvas by a royal artist.

Lucy, on the other hand, had straight black hair, dark brown eyes, and slightly flattened features. Her skin didn't blotch, thank Heaven, but that was her only nod to classic English beauty. Fortunately, such things weren't required when one was an heiress. And so she pulled her unblotchy face into a smile as her next partner arrived.

She greeted him warmly. Perhaps he would finally coax her heart out from behind its wall. And as soon as Phoebe's partner arrived, the four of them took their places for the dance.

They were only halfway through the reel when the commotion began. Lucy had been calculating the prices of various gowns—at least the raw materials—as a way to keep herself entertained. Her partner was not a scintillating conversationalist. She'd been thinking about the price of carved ivory buttons when something strange caught her attention, but she didn't know what. A moment later, she noticed the murmurs.

The music had come to a stop, and she was curtsying to her partner only to realise that he wasn't looking at her. His attention—as well as most everyone else's—was aimed over her shoulder to some place behind her.

She turned, feeling a step behind everyone else, only to blink repeatedly as she tried to fix her vision. Something must be wrong with her sight. Because there, standing on the edge of the dance floor as if awaiting her hand, was none other than the perfidious, missing-and-feared-dead, Cedric, Lord Domac.

He was dressed in finery that was ill-fitting thanks to new muscles that pulled the fabric tight in places and hung slack where he had no fat. Indeed, his bones were prominent in hard juts that gave him a chiseled look. Compared to the soft fops in the room, he stood out like a Greek god.

But he didn't seem healthy. The man she remembered had always been animated. Now he appeared statue still as if holding himself together by sheer force of will.

She searched his eyes, looking for his telltale twinkle. She'd always loved his eyes, but tonight they seemed bright with fever rather than joy. Everything in her urged her to go to him. Something was clearly very wrong. But she could not force her feet to do so.

'Miss Richards,' he intoned without moving closer. 'May I have the honour of this dance?'

And her damned heart began to flutter.

Chapter One

China—Three years ago

Lu-Jing was sweeping up spilled rice in the temple storeroom when Nayao found her. They both slept in here, so she liked to keep the vermin at a minimum. That meant keeping the floor clean and the feral cats close.

At the sound of her sister's footsteps, Lu-Jing felt her breath ease. She wasn't abandoned…today. Every day Nayao went out searching for work as a navigator on a ship, and every night she came back defeated. No ship's captain wanted a girl on board, even if she was an accomplished sailor.

Lu-Jing's ugly secret was that she liked that Nayao couldn't find work. That meant they both remained here, hidden away. The oldest two half children in the temple. Ah-Lan had been older, but he'd left a year ago in search of his fortune.

That was the way for orphans like them. As half Chinese, half foreign bastards, they were brought to the temple as infants. They were raised until they could be apprenticed, only returning to the temple if they failed in their jobs. Nayao returned when she was exposed as a woman and no captain would take her. Lu-Jing returned bleeding and half-dead when she was discovered by the authorities in the Thirteen Factories district.

It was the only place in China where trade happened with foreigners, and no female was allowed there. Nevertheless, Lu-Jing had made a name for herself there—as a boy. She was an expert negotiator who was willing to take risks making illegal trades after dark. But like Nayao, the moment her disguise was exposed, she'd had to run for her life.

She ran back to the temple. As had Nayao.

And now they lived the half life of a half person, doing work for the temple and rarely venturing outside. Eventually, they would become nuns. There was no other safe possibility for them. At least that's what Lu-Jing believed, but Nayao wanted more. She always wanted more. Lu-Jing didn't even look up as footsteps entered the storeroom. No one else came here at this time except Nayao.

'I've saved an extra portion of rice for you,' she said. When there was no answer, she looked at the door in confusion only to recoil in shock. There were two people entering the storeroom: Nayao and the head of the temple.

'Abbott!' she said, dropping her broom quickly in order to bow. 'Are you hungry? I can find—'

'Lu-Jing!' the man snapped. He was a kind soul at heart, but he was very busy. And the orphans learned early not to bother him with anything. That made it triply shocking—and scary—that he had sought her out. 'You are twenty years old now, Lu-Jing. Do you become a nun?'

'What?'

He tsked as he looked down at her. 'Do you stay for life? Or do you seek elsewhere?'

'You are throwing me out?' she whispered. 'But I have served the temple well! I—'

'You are not thrown out.' He sneered the words. 'But a woman of twenty must decide. Do you dedicate yourself to the path here?'

Life as a nun was an honourable path. One she had accepted as her future. And yet, she had not committed to it. In her secret heart, she still held out hope for a husband who loved her and children of her own.

It was a ridiculous dream. No one in China would marry a half child except—perhaps—another half child. But the only man who had interested her had left. Ah-Lan had gone north to find his fortune. Which left her here to become a nun.

'Abbott,' she began, her tone reverent as if she truly wanted to remain. 'I wish to stay—'

Nayao interrupted her. 'There is a man who wants us.'

'What?' Instinctively she shrank back. She knew

what became of concubines married to old merchant men. They were used as prostitutes to the foreign captains. She would rather be a nun.

'Not that!' Nayao was quick to say. 'A white man who looks for his daughter.'

'One daughter,' the Abbott said loudly. 'Of your age,' he said, looking at Nayao.

'Our age,' Nayao said as she took Lu-Jing's hands. 'He does not know which of us is her.'

'But...' She shook her head. 'You believe this? That he searches for a daughter who is a woman now?' She couldn't keep the scorn from her voice. No man was that good.

Nayao sighed. 'I have asked about him. I am told he is honest. And he has spent a great deal of money to find us.'

'Not *us*,' the Abbott repeated. 'One.'

Nayao lifted her chin. 'He will take two or none.'

'You're going?' Lu-Jing gasped. 'You would leave me?'

'No!' Nayao tugged Lu-Jing forwards. 'We go together. I had to leave you before when I was young. But now we go together.'

'To a white devil?' It was not the proper term for a Caucasian man, but it was the term everyone used.

'You know as well as I that there are good men among the foreigners.'

'And bad ones!'

She nodded. 'I don't speak English, but you do.'

'Trade language!' And she hadn't used it for several years now. Not since her breasts had grown to their full size.

'Meet him with me. Help me find out if it is safe.' Nayao was pleading with her. Neither of them wanted to be separated again. It was too lonely as a half child. They only had each other.

'Or,' intoned the Abbott, 'remain here and walk an honest path.'

As a nun.

Nayao's eyes pleaded with her. She had faith that she could forge a future outside of China. Out there among the ships where there were people of every race. She had not been stabbed while taking risks with the white men.

'What do you want?' Nayao pressed. 'What future do you long for?'

She didn't need to ask the question. Nayao knew she wanted a family of her own. 'B-but among the whites?' she stammered.

'Will you find a husband in China?'

No. Not since Ah-Lan had left. But the danger was overwhelming.

'Do you hate it here so much,' she asked Nayao, 'that you will risk everything on a foreigner's word?'

'Do you love it here so much,' her sister returned, 'that you will give up everything you want to sweep floors in a storeroom? For the rest of your life?'

That wasn't a fair question. Of all the possible futures, she had built a safe life here. She had charge of the storeroom, a position no half child had ever had before. Certainly not a woman. She managed the accounts for the monks, and that was no small task. She had worked hard to gain such a position at the temple. And it was a good one.

Well, it was a safe one. But could she do this for the rest of her life? Stay in the temple, sweep floors and click-clack with her abacus as she maintained the accounts?

What an empty life that would be. Especially without her sister beside her.

'Take the risk with me,' Nayao pleaded. 'At least meet the man. Tell me if you think he is honourable.'

Lu-Jing had no faith in her own judgement. Not since she'd been exposed in the Thirteen Factories district because she'd trusted a liar. But she also couldn't let Nayao leave without fighting to stay together. They had grown up here, each protecting the other. Two half-Chinese girls surviving as best they could. Most souls in Canton cursed the half children. Some of the monks did, as well. But to be a girl half child was to be the most reviled of all.

Neither would have survived without the other.

'There is no more time,' the Abbott snapped. 'Decide now.'

What else could she do? Though the thought of leaving the temple terrified her, being a nun here without Nayao frightened her more.

'I will come with you,' she said softly. 'If only to tell you that generous white men do not exist.'

Except, apparently, they did exist. They met him in a dark corner of the Thirteen Factories district. A place Lu-Jing knew well. Lord Wenshire was an older man with kind eyes and a cough that he tried to cover. Through a translator, he told them a tale of a Chinese woman he'd loved and of their daughter together.

The woman was dead. He had verified that. But the child? He searched their faces, clearly hoping to see traces of the woman he'd loved.

Nayao looked to Lu-Jing, silently asking the question. *Do we go with him? Do we trust him?*

No and no! And yet, what other chance was there for them? Nayao would not become a nun. It had been foolish to pretend otherwise. She was too wild and free to be content inside the temple walls. So she would take the risk with this Lord Wenshire.

Did Lu-Jing?

'We go two,' she said in her rough English. 'Or no go.'

The man smiled. 'Together then. My daughters.'

Chapter Two

Lu-Jing was not terrified.

Fear wasn't the worst feeling. Indeed, she was so used to it that it barely penetrated her thoughts until the sensations lessened.

This morning, she noticed her belly did not clench painfully. She took a breath that expanded her chest. And when she looked around her, she did not see dangers lurking in every corner. Every other corner, perhaps, but not each one.

What a difference a month at sea made. A month where she wasn't constantly hiding in the temple from the dangers in Canton. A month where she, Nayao and their adoptive father got to know one another aboard a merchant vessel. A month where she expanded her ability with English and tried not to be afraid of what lay ahead.

And so far, the only cost had been their names. Nayao was now called Grace in a rough translation of her name. Lu-Jing became Lucy because of the similar sound. All in all, it was an easy trade. After all, no matter what they called her, she would not forget where she came from. Much though she might wish to.

They had five more months of travel to their father's homeland. Today's stop was in Bombay, a foreign city that produced a cacophony of noise heard even here on the safety of their boat. It was the noise of a thriving city and Lucy need only close her eyes to imagine the living beat of the marketplace. That was the place she felt most at home, at least in Canton. But they were in India now, and as much as she longed to go ashore, the rest of her was tense with renewed fear.

Marketplaces teemed with danger.

'But you have to come with us,' Grace said. 'We need stores for the ship. And you can negotiate—'

'I don't speak the language.'

'Neither do we! And when has that ever bothered you?'

Never. The language of commerce worked in hand signals, grunts and sidelong glances. She understood the money here, knew the value of most goods and could do the math in her head. But…

Marketplaces were dangerous.

Her sister sighed and gently took Lucy's hands. 'It has been two years since you were attacked—'

'In the marketplace!'

'Two years,' Grace repeated. 'You have hidden away in the temple since then, only venturing out when you had to—'

'And when I left the temple, I brought monks with me.' No one attacked monks. It planted bad karma. Plus, they rarely had anything worth stealing. But there were no monks here to give her the feeling of safety. 'Grace, you know it's not safe to go anywhere strange as a woman!'

They both had hidden their sex as long as possible, binding their breasts and wearing boy's clothing. And even so, Lucy had nearly died the last time she ventured alone into a marketplace.

Back then she'd been bold. She'd imitated Grace's fearlessness and taken big risks, strutting into the marketplace as a boy to bargain for goods. She'd made herself valuable in the Thirteen Factories district. Most merchants didn't want to sully themselves by negotiating directly with the whites, but a half child was already cursed. She'd served as go-between whenever and wherever she could, making coin that could not be gotten legally. At least not by a girl.

But she had taken one risk too many, slipping into the district at night when the most lucrative deals were made. They were discovered by the officials, and she'd been hurt as she ran. Hurt badly enough that she nearly died. Bad enough that she'd never be able to run that fast again.

And that made her lose her nerve.

'Do you know what can happen to a woman in a strange city?'

Grace was undeterred. 'We took a big chance, you

and I. We met Father and are now going to a new life. That has worked out, yes?'

'So far.' Their father seemed honest. Their future together might include a good life. But it was too new for her to believe in yet. And she certainly didn't want to risk everything by going to a marketplace! 'I'll be there to protect you,' Grace promised. 'Father, too.'

'Father's going?' Damn it, what would happen to them if something happened to him? They were on this boat by his coin. They were going to a new future with him as their father. She couldn't risk being separated from him just as she hadn't been able to risk being separated from Grace. But still she trembled at the thought of going ashore. 'I knew what my job was in the temple. I knew what to do, who to talk to and where to hide. I know nothing about Bombay.'

'We won't be alone. The sailors will carry the goods—cook can manage the money—'

'No, he can't!' Lucy was a middling pickpocket, and even she could lift his purse.

'Then you carry it. I won't let you out of my sight. I swear!' Grace had spent years on a ship. She had travelled all around the China sea. She was a bold, confident woman, whereas Lucy had spent the last two years keeping herself small, quiet and completely overlooked.

'Why is Father going?'

'He's looking for medicine. For his cough.'

'They'll sell him dog's piss and claim it's a miracle.' In one month, she had come to adore her adoptive father, but she also thought him incredibly naive at times. His first instinct was to believe what he was told whereas she and Grace knew that most people lied.

'Help me protect him,' Grace pressed.

It was laughable to think that Lucy could protect anyone. She hadn't the fighting skills that Grace did. She had a slender build and couldn't intimidate a fly. Her greatest asset in bargaining was that she appeared too timid to argue. She stated what she would pay and then cringed away when someone thought to bargain with her. They would meet her price—gently—or she would buy from someone else.

It was pretense—mostly. She had strength in her, but the fear was real.

'We'll stay together,' Grace promised. 'We'll help Father.'

Lucy couldn't argue against that. So she agreed—reluctantly. She stayed close to Grace and their father. She didn't hide in the trees to watch the exciting bustle of the square. And she discovered that she could barter as easily in India as she had in China.

It was a good day.

But far from making her more relaxed, the success made her more suspicious. Thieves attacked when one was relaxed, when one's arms were full of goods, when one smiled and thought that today was a perfect day.

So she was wary as they turned back for the ship. She watched everywhere at once until her body ached from the anxiety.

Then she saw *him*.

An Englishman with a delicious laugh and the kind of broad-shouldered height to make him stand out in the crowd of stooped natives. In truth, he wasn't head and shoulders taller than the rest. He just didn't hunch over his purchases or curl protectively around a purse, so he stood tall. He had no weapons that she could see, and when a child snatched his purse, he laughed even as he caught the boy.

His companion possessed a thicker body and an angry growl. He was going to cuff the boy, but the tall one stopped him. She knew enough English now to hear their conversation.

'Leave off, Graham. He's just hungry.'

'You cannot allow even one. We'll be mobbed within a second.'

The tall one should listen to the growly one named Graham. Lucy could see street children creeping forwards, waiting to see what he would do with the squirming thief.

He bought the child a meat pie.

'Cedric! What the bloody hell are you doing?' his companion cried as the boy grabbed the food and dashed away. 'That's your last coin, you oaf.'

She liked the sound of his name. *Cedric.*

'It is,' Cedric admitted as he cheerfully waved the beggars back. 'I'm done here. All let out.' He turned his pockets inside out to prove it.

'You'll have to pay for your food on the ship,' Graham moaned. 'How are you going to eat for the next five months?'

Cedric shrugged. 'I'll figure something out.'

'No, you won't,' the companion groused as he hunched his shoulders. 'You'll remind me of all the good times we had together in school and then call me a jolly good chum when I pay your way.'

'What?' he said with a charming twinkle in his eyes. 'I hadn't thought of that, but you are a jolly good—'

'Oh, stuff it. It'll be worth it to send your arse back home.'

'Don't be like that,' Cedric said. 'We've had a wondrous time together, haven't we? I've learned a lot.'

'You have. We have.' Then he grabbed Cedric's wrist and pulled him around. 'Stay in India with me. We'll find a job for you, I swear.'

'I would if only to watch you sweat in this heat.'

Graham pulled out a handkerchief to wipe his face. 'It's beastly, simply beastly.'

'But you know I can't. Besides all the nonsense at home, I won't browbeat a bunch of peasants all day. I'd much rather go drinking with them.'

His companion shook his head. 'That's your problem then. You'll drink with anybody.'

'I will. And have a right jolly time of it.'

Graham snorted and tugged his companion along. It was fortunate that Lucy was headed in the same direction. It allowed her to follow their conversation. And when her sister noticed what she was doing, Lucy whispered, 'I'm practicing English.'

It was a lie. The pair of Englishman intrigued her. Or more accurately, Cedric did. He was good-natured in the way of the best kind of wealthy men, and yet it appeared he hadn't a coin for his meals. She didn't know what the word *browbeat* meant, but she could guess. She'd received her own share of beatings. It was common for a half white, half Chinese girl like her, even in the temple where she was raised.

That he disdained such a thing reinforced her belief that he was a kind man very much like her adoptive father.

Were all Englishmen like that? If so, then England must be a land of generous plenty.

She wanted to linger, to hear more of the two gentlemen's conversation, but she didn't dare lose her party. And since her adoptive father had been pulled into a conversation with a so-called medicine man, she hurried to protect him.

She needn't have bothered. To her surprise, he was more knowledgeable than most about medicines. Even though his cough was a new development, he'd travelled throughout the world and knew a charlatan when he met one.

So they left the medicine seller and returned to *The Integrity*, only to pull up short when she saw their captain in discussion with none other than Cedric and Graham. They were standing at the base of the gangplank, talking in the formal way of wealthy Englishmen.

Mindful that she wasn't safe until she was aboard ship, Lucy hurried up the gangplank. But then she lingered up top, standing as close to the conversation as she dared without appearing obvious.

She couldn't hear anything that was said. She contented herself with watching the way Cedric's body stayed relaxed despite the dangers that she constantly feared. His English face was animated, and she liked his high cheekbones and bright blue-green eyes. But what she really wanted to hear was his laughter. When it rang out, it was as sweet as a bell.

How free he sounded!

And then, to her absolute delight, Graham handed over passage money to the captain and Cedric climbed aboard.

Cedric saw the pretty girl watching him from the main mast. He'd seen her in the marketplace as well, trailing behind them as they headed for the ship. He was well used to girls making eyes at him. It had nothing to do with him personally. The attention came because he was Cedric, Lord Domac, future Earl of Hillburn. And because he wasn't hideously ugly. But that didn't stop him from playing to his audience in the hopes of stealing a kiss or three. That was, after all, how he'd spent much of his adolescence, and he saw no reason to change that now that he was travelling.

Unfortunately, his title meant less outside of England than inside it. So he had to rely on his charm, of which he had plenty. As he boarded the ship home, he made pains to smile winningly at the girl and then stopped long enough to look at her more closely.

Such a face she had! Golden skin, dark brown hair, and eyes that lowered demurely when he looked. Not a bold miss then, despite her obvious fascination with him. He appreciated subtlety in his women, though in truth, one lady was much the same as another to him. If they made him smile, they were worth his attention, provided they required no coin whatsoever.

And if *he* made *them* smile… Well, that's how things became fun. Even the most awful day faded if there was a woman willing to ease his pain—and hers— that night.

He saw the Asian cast to her features, knew she was of mixed race, and was intrigued by the way two vastly different cultures combined to make a glorious whole. He noted with surprise that she was dressed in the English style, buttoned up despite the heat, and carrying a parasol which she'd obviously forgotten nearby.

He crossed the deck quickly, eager to learn more about her without once giving thought to who had care of her. That was probably because the girls he noticed rarely had a protector. Not so with this girl. He had no more than picked up her parasol when an older Englishman with a weathered face stepped up beside her.

'Hullo, hullo!' the older man called. 'I'd heard we had a handsome young buck coming aboard.'

'I don't know whether to feel the compliment at being called handsome or insulted that I could be shot by an eager huntsman.' He grinned as he shook the man's extended hand. 'I'm Lord Domac, and I'm pleased that I shall have interesting company on the long journey home.' As he spoke, he winked at the girl whose eyes widened in shock.

Well, that was a new reaction. She wasn't exactly frightened by him. She had not run away. But she clearly wasn't used to interacting with a flirt. He needed to soften his approach until she grew used to him. Then he intended to flirt outrageously with her for the next five months.

'I'm Lord Wenshire and this is my daughter Lucy Richards. Her sister is here somewhere, too. But don't expect too much conversation from them. They're still learning English. Though I'm constantly impressed by how much they do understand.'

Hmm. The girl didn't have the vacant look of someone who couldn't follow the language. If anything, she appeared bright and engaged, though obviously silent. 'I shall be sure to speak properly then, so she won't learn the wrong things from me.'

'I'm sure you will,' the father said with a note of steel in his voice.

A protective father. He could work with that, especially since the man followed up the hard stare with a fond one for his daughter. He was a kind man, then. That made everything easier. So he smiled and addressed the father in a respectful manner.

'I am sure you have a tale or three about how you and your lovely daughters came to be here. I hope you will share them with me.' He sent a warm look towards Lucy. 'I am most anxious to hear more.'

The girl pinked at his look but did not turn away. He held out his hand in a courtly gesture. She glanced uncertainly at her father, but at his nod, she held out her hand to be kissed.

Neither of them wore gloves. He had lost his ages ago and from the golden brown of her skin, she had never worn them. They touched skin to skin, and he felt a strange current of delight flow through him. It was nothing so striking as a shock. More like a recognition that went soul to soul in an odd hum.

He saw her eyes widen again and wondered if she felt the same thing. He drew her hand up to his mouth. He knew how to stroke a girl's palm to set her heart aflutter. But in this moment, he forgot to do it. He looked into her eyes and wondered what she felt, what she thought, and if perhaps the two of them might share something special.

It was nothing more than the magic of first meeting. He was well acquainted with the flutter of arousal that accompanied any new woman in his life. It meant nothing beyond his usual joy at something novel. Or rather *someone* novel.

And yet this moment felt unusual. The press of his lips against her skin felt unique. And the way their eyes met held extra delight.

He straightened slowly, wondering at his own clumsy confusion. Probably the heat and the distraught letter he'd received from his sister this morning. That was what had occasioned his return to England. A desperate plea for him to return and set the estate to rights.

As if that were possible. It would never happen unless his father was set to rights, and no one could do that but the man himself. Nevertheless, he had to return home. And now he had the intriguing Miss Lucy Richards to distract his depressing thoughts during the long journey.

'All right then,' came the hearty bellow from the captain. 'I'll show you to your berth. Won't be long until we set sail.'

'Of course,' Cedric answered, his tone warm though his gaze remained on Miss Richards. His fingers opened reluctantly, and hers slipped out of his grasp.

'Welcome, Lord Domac,' she said. That was it. One word plus his name, but her odd accent seemed to strengthen the connection between them. Or maybe he simply liked the sound of his name on her lips.

Either way, he was forced below decks, his mind on the girl rather than on what he was doing. She was clearly curious despite her shyness, and he thought her a kindred spirit. He imagined her a sweet flower, buoyed by life's precarious whims. If the winds blew them together for a time, he should be happy. If the winds changed, however, he would move on without a second's thought.

That was what he told himself, emphasizing the temporary nature of his connection to her. He would not dwell on that strange frisson that still hummed her name quietly inside him. She was a shipboard pleasure, and she would be gone the moment they landed in England.

To make sure he understood his purpose, he pulled out his sister's letter. It had taken months to find him in India, but he had it now and it said everything he needed to remember.

Dearest Cedric,
I do not know if this letter will find you. We have penned so many letters to no avail. Pleading letters to father and mother. Desperate letters to the banker in London. And now to you in your far-off travels as you search for gold.

Cedric, the money is gone.

The roof collapsed. Spring storms are the worst, and this one took half the ceiling as it passed through. All your allowance has gone to keep the rest of the house standing.

We had scrimped and saved, investing in the crops. You recall that I took over old Samson's farm when he passed two years ago? It's hard work, but I have help and my choices were good ones. We made a nice sum last fall, and I hoped to do the same this year. But with the roof gone, all of our spare money is, too. We exist on soup and hard bread.

You must come home, Cedric. You are the only one who ever could control father. You must convince him to leave us some coin, if only to keep us from starvation.

Plus, Lilianna has begun to flirt with men. I suppose we are all looking. None of us wants to be an old maid. The best of the lot is an engineer with interesting ideas about the canal. He's a good man, unlike the others. You must find out if there is any dowry money, if only to attract a wider variety of men. I know you had hope of it on your last visit. The bankers will not tell us anything, but you know how to get them to talk.

Please, Cedric, I beseech you to come home. I care not if you have found your pot of gold. We need your help at home. Father continues to bleed us dry, and you are our only hope of stopping him.
In desperate straits,
Your loving sister, Cora

There was no dowry. His hope had been that he could provide one. And there was no way to stop his father. God knew he'd tried every way he could think of to manage the man. That was why he'd gone to the East India Company to see if he could earn money that way.

But there hadn't been enough time. What little money he'd earned was already sent home.

Which left him one option for his future. One choice to help his sisters and repair the estate. He needed to marry an heiress. And so he would as soon as he landed in London. But at least he had these last few months of freedom as the ship wended its way to back to England.

Five months to flirt with the pretty girl on board before he chained himself to whatever heiress would have him. At least he had his own berth, thanks to Graham who had paid for it. He even had a porthole through which he could see the colourful shores of India shrinking when they set sail. It would take him a bit to adjust to the waves and the endless wet, but at least they would be out of the heat.

He smiled as his eyes drifted shut for a quick nap, thinking of the girl with the dark eyes and the sun-drenched blush. Asian skin didn't freckle like English skin did. She would be golden brown all over, with straight dark hair to hide the tantalizing curves of her body. Or better yet, she would part it to let him see the wonders beneath.

Ah, this was to be a sexual dream, he realised as he floated in a half sleep. That boded well for the journey. Even if she denied him in person, he could indulge in her charms every time he closed his eyes.

Chapter Three

It didn't take long for Cedric to get Lord Wenshire's tale. Sailing was a tedious process and it would take months to make port in England. The days and nights were long, and Cedric had with him a bottle of Graham's very fine Aarack. Which, it turned out, was a particular favourite of Lord Wenshire.

'Come now,' Cedric chided after the bottle was nearly empty. 'You must know everyone will ask.'

'About my girls? Of course they will talk, but only the boldest will ask me.' The man was rosy-cheeked with twinkling eyes as he spoke. But his words weren't slurred, and so Cedric knew he was playing, not drunk.

'Then I am bold, sir. How did you find them? I was told Canton is blocked off to westerners.'

'It is, except for a very small area. Just a quarter mile long. And women are not allowed there at all. It is a place for men.'

'But then, how—'

'Illegally, of course.'

He gestured for more Aarack, and while Cedric gave him the last of it, the man told a tale too fanciful to be believed and yet the emotions were real. And, obviously, the girls were real.

'You have my full attention,' Cedric said as he set down the flask. He'd waited until it was just him and Lord Wenshire in the mess to encourage confidences.

'There is competition among the Chinese merchants to get our silver. First, they must get approval from the emperor to bargain in the Thirteen Factory area, but then how does one Chinese merchant stand out from the next? Us poor westerners cannot effectively choose.'

'I assumed you pick by the quality of the goods and the price.'

'And when that is all the same?'

Cedric could guess. There were several sordid ways, including threats, bribery and women.

Lord Wenshire nodded, even though Cedric hadn't spoken his thoughts out loud. 'There were parties. Quiet dinner parties, loud, raucous fetes and everything in between, though none of it was legal. At least not if there were Chinese women there.'

'But they came as bribes and temptations?'

'Yes. And I was a young man very far from home.' He sighed as he drained the last of his glass. 'She was the seventh concubine to one of the merchants, which is a lucky number for westerners but not so lucky for the Chinese.'

Cedric said nothing. He had no understanding of numerology, though he had heard that many Asians put great faith in such things.

'So beautiful,' Lord Wenshire said, his eyes closing in memory. 'She was flawless in every way, but because her feet were not bound, she was unattractive to many Chinese.'

'But she was married.'

'She was a concubine. That means she had food, clothing and a kind of status. But her husband was not a kind man. I found out later that he married poor girls—he had a dozen or more concubines—just so he could use them this way.'

Cedric winced. 'For parties. With westerners.' It wasn't a question.

'Yes. But she was beautiful, could manage a smattering of English and I liked her immediately.' He shrugged. 'I made him a very rich man because I gave him my business. Because of her.'

Mr. Richards's gaze was soft, his focus off in some distant past. Cedric was no expert on love, but he could see when a man thought of a woman with tenderness. And when it was more than that.

'You loved her,' he said.

'I did.' He looked down at his empty cup. 'Young men fall in love so easily.'

Really? He'd never thought so. Lust, yes. Infatuation, certainly. But the kind of love that made a man search out and adopt his foreign daughter? That was rare.

'You never married?'

'I couldn't. She was already married.'

He'd meant to an English girl, but it was clear that Lord Wenshire thought of this Chinese concubine as his one true love. 'What happened?'

'She became pregnant. I didn't care. I loved her and the child. I didn't even care if it was his and not mine.' He shoved his cup away from him, the disgust plain in his face. 'He made me pay though. More and more demands. Bad product, high prices.' He shook his head. 'I was working for the East India Company. I had superiors.' His voice grew tight. 'It wasn't a situation they would tolerate.'

'They recalled you?'

He nodded. 'I was replaced. I tried to talk to her one last time. Hell, I even tried to buy her freedom. Nothing worked.'

'That's awful.'

'It took me two years to get back to China. Then, when I finally made it, I had to bribe his seventeenth concubine for answers. I had been told that mother and child died in childbirth. I didn't believe it at first. There were so many lies and no way to find out the truth.' His voice trailed away. 'Seventeenth concubine said that the babe had survived, but she did not. Another concubine said she had killed herself and the babe.' He shrugged. 'I didn't know what was true, but they all said the child was a girl.'

Cedric frowned, trying to put the pieces together in

his mind. 'But you found your daughter a few months ago. Grace is your daughter. You found her.'

'Not then. I had to leave, and I was too disheartened to keep pressing. I thought I would forget her, but I never did. I managed to return every five years or so to look again. Five trips in all, and I only heard about the temple this year.'

Cedric couldn't imagine a love that strong. To last for twenty-five years and still burn bright? That was the kind of love that changed a man completely.

'Where is this temple? If there are women there, it cannot be in the Thirteen Factories district?'

'No. It's in Canton proper, but it's where the unwanted children go. Assuming they're not killed at birth.'

Cedric shuddered at the very idea.

'I knew if my daughter was alive,' Lord Wenshire continued, 'she would be there.'

'But how did you get there? If the temple is inside the city?'

The man shrugged. 'I couldn't. But I got a message to the monks. I explained about my daughter. I knew her probable age. I promised to take care of her, if they had her.'

'And they did? She had survived?'

'They arranged a meeting. And when they arrived, I met both Grace and Lucy. I knew the minute I saw Grace what had happened.'

'They just brought them? And handed them over to you?'

'Do you know what kind of life a half child has in China? Of course, I took them. I offered them a future in England with me. I didn't force them.'

'I never thought you did. But it's such a big change for them.' He couldn't imagine it. To have the monks who had reared you take you one evening to meet a white man. And then to blithely go with the foreigner, not knowing what the future held.

'They're both smart. You see that, don't you?'

He did.

'They knew what their future would be in China. Best to roll the dice on me.' He smiled. 'And they both refused to leave without the other.' He leaned back in his chair. 'They wanted out of China. I offered to take them. The rest…' He shook his head. 'We're figuring it out. I have no other children, you know. Nothing but the memory of a seventh concubine from two decades ago.'

'What was her name?'

'Yue E. It means Moon Beauty.'

'And now you are adopting two daughters from China.'

'I am. Yue E would want me to.'

And that was it, apparently, because the man stretched his arms over his head before slowly straightening to his feet. 'I'm for bed. Thank you for the Aarack.' Then he paused. 'I mean to dower them, you know. I mean them to have good lives in England.'

And on that note, he departed, his last words ringing in Cedric's head.

Cedric had tried all the different ways to earn money. He'd gambled like his father with very mixed results. He'd tried working for it with the East India Company, but their methods turned his stomach, and the income wouldn't come fast enough. It took money to make money in that company, not to mention a ruthless disposition. That left one traditional route which he had disdained so far.

He could marry it.

Indeed, that had been his intention the moment he'd stepped aboard this ship headed for England. He was determined to charm whichever spoiled heiress his mother paraded before him this Season. But the very idea sickened him.

Until he met Lord Wenshire and his daughters. Clearly, the man was wealthy. Exactly how wealthy was a mystery, but he had enough to adopt two half-Chinese daughters because of an old love affair. More importantly, the man had spent most of his life working for the East India Company. That could easily make Lord Wenshire a nabob, and his daughters heiresses.

Cedric spent a very pleasant few minutes imaging how one dowry could set his family back on their financial feet. First, he would repair the farms that were falling apart, then he might invest in pigs, and the canal needed significant repair. All the marvelous things his father was supposed to be doing but wasn't. It was like the man had a sickness for gambling and nothing stopped him. Not three daughters who needed dowries, not a home that was falling apart and not several very blunt talks between him and Cedric.

Which left any hope for his family in Cedric's hands.

He would have to investigate further. Not the pigs, but the girls. After all, he had no competition on the boat. How hard could it be to charm one of the two Chinese girls when the only other men were rough sailors or men as old as their father? The idea of choosing his bride in such a mercenary way horrified him. But he would rather make the choice himself than leave it up to his mother's dubious selection.

He knew as well that he would give whichever girl he selected a good life as his countess. He would honour his marriage vows and treat her with the respect every woman deserved. It was not a bad bargain, and so he applied himself to the task of choosing between the two sisters. He watched their movements, lived in constant awareness of their locations, and he found his preference becoming stronger with every passing second.

The older Miss Richards—Grace—was an equal to the crew. She ran the sails, manned the crow's nest and worked as long and as hard as any of them. She had the backing of the captain and worked as the ship's navigator when the regular man grew tired. If any sailor dared disparage her, she got even in the way of all boys. She tripped the man or saddled him with a hated chore. Once she surprised someone with a bloody rat in his hammock. It was a quiet game of one-upmanship, which she always won because Captain Banakos allowed it from her and not anyone else.

In short, the elder Miss Richards met challenges head-on and dared anyone deny her. She had the skill and the canny to defend herself. It impressed him, and he should have found her fascinating.

He did not. It was the younger one who snared his attention.

Miss Lucy Richards always stood in the shadows, watching the coming and going of the crew. She seemed to be charting in her mind where everyone went and why. She watched, she followed and if she saw anything amiss, she whispered it to her sister who met the challenge in typical bold fashion. But the elder would not be nearly as capable without the younger one's sharp eyes.

He thought that interesting. A nice sign of cooperation between sisters. But then he discovered that Miss Lucy Richards was a great deal more.

Several weeks after he'd boarded, he sat at dinner in the captain's mess. Her father, the captain, indeed, all the men at the table, were in good spirits. The weather was fine and the breeze perfect for their travel. And since her sister was in the crow's nest, Miss Lucy Richards was the lone female in the room, sitting silent as everyone else conversed.

As often happened, the conversation turned to the food. 'I have never had meals such as this,' Cedric said.

'It is chicken, and yet the taste is beyond anything I'd ever imagined.'

'It's the Indian spices, my lord,' responded Captain Banakos. 'I'm surprised you like them. Usually, it is too spicy for Englishmen.'

'No, no, this is different,' Cedric pressed. 'I've been eating Indian food for months, but this... Your cook makes it better. Just the right amount of spice. Or in the right combination.' He leaned forwards. 'Have you ever tried selling it in England?'

The captain chuckled. 'The Dutch control the spice. Can't buy or sell it without tripping over one of them. And they're protective of it. No, our best bet is tea and that's what we've got in the hold.'

'Of course, of course,' Cedric said, thinking hard. There had to be a way to turn this to his advantage. 'But a little bit of the right spice could make a killing, don't you think? If I could make it fashionable.'

'You still have to deal with the Dutch,' said the captain.

'And make it fashionable,' added Lord Wenshire.

Making something popular with the *ton* was easy. He had all the connections for that. In truth, it was the only thing he had—childhood friends, many from school, who owed him a favour or three.

'I can buy spices.' Miss Richards's quiet voice brought the entire conversation to a halt. 'I managed all the food for the temple. It was my job for two years.'

The captain cleared his throat. 'Managing a kitchen is different from the buying and selling—'

'I bought and sold. And my first apprenticeship was with a spice merchant. I know how to buy it.' She flushed when everyone stared at her, but she didn't back down. 'I cannot fill your hold, but I can get you a fair price at the next port.'

'There isn't room in the hold for that. Or coin.' Captain Banakos's tone was dismissive, but she persevered.

'There is if you sell one crate of tea,' she pressed. 'I can buy an equal weight in spice. And if you allow me to look at the account books, I can see if there are other ways to save.'

If the table had been quiet before, it was nothing compared to the shock at her statement. A woman who had heretofore been silent now asked to see the account books. Cedric couldn't credit his own ears, and yet, her father seemed amused rather than shocked.

'You think you can make sense of the captain's handwriting? It's in English, you know. Numbers, not characters.'

She lifted her chin. Quiet confidence radiated out of her. 'I can make sense of it,' she said. Then she arched her brows. 'I can make a good profit.'

Cedric stared at her. Never had he seen a woman so sure about money. And at that moment, he realised the younger girl was the powerhouse, not the older. If what she claimed was true.

Meanwhile, the captain was not nearly as impressed.

'You want to look at my account books?' he scoffed. 'That is not a plaything for a girl.'

Her father focused on her. 'You believe you can manage the accounts better than the captain?' His tone was amused rather than insulting, and the girl took it as encouragement.

'Every man makes mistakes. He has no one checking his work.'

The captain stiffened in outrage. 'Sir, I have served you honestly and loyally since—'

'No one questions that, Captain Banakos. You are honest and thorough.'

'Yes—'

'But I should like to see what my adoptive daughter can do.' He shrugged. 'It is only one crate of tea and another of spice. If it is a complete loss, then I can afford it.'

That gave Cedric a shock. He had thought *The Integrity* under the sole control of the East India Company. That connection was how Graham had gotten him such a nice berth on the ship. It was a surprise to realise that the ship was privately owned and not by the captain, but by Lord Wenshire.

'I should like to accompany her, if I may,' Cedric said, speaking impulsively. 'I want to see how she negotiates.'

The girl arched her brows at him. 'Do you mean to look over my shoulder when I check the account books too?'

'Thank you!' he said, even though she had meant the words sarcastically. 'I'd love that.' He looked at the father. 'If you don't mind.'

Lord Wenshire frowned at him. 'Why would you want to?'

'You have told me about her temple. Hundreds of souls, several buildings, similar to a cathedral at home.'

'Larger,' Lord Wenshire answered.

'My mother complained about managing a staff of twelve. Imagine being in charge of a kitchen for hundreds.'

'I did not cook,' she said quickly.

'No. But you kept track of the food, yes? The shopping?'

She nodded.

'And I have seen her bargain.' They had made a supply run since he'd climbed aboard. He had gone on it mostly to get off the boat for a time. But watching her bargain was like watching a maestro at work. 'I should like to see how she managed all that.'

Captain Banakos didn't like it. No man liked being questioned by a girl, but he had no say when the owner of the boat agreed.

And so began Cedric's education in accounting. From a girl.

Chapter Four

Lucy loved the click-clack of abacus beads. As soon as she showed a talent with numbers, she'd been apprenticed to a spice merchant. Originally, the master hadn't believed a girl could calculate numbers accurately. He'd set her to watch for thieves and pickpockets, but she eventually proved her worth. Just as she was going to do now.

And so she click-clacked the beads in a rhythm that usually kept people away. It said, 'I am working.'

It did not stop Lord Domac.

He reminded her of Grace, unable to sit still, always looking, always thinking. That might endear him to her except that Grace found a use for her energy. Cedric used his energy on her.

'What does that mark mean? Is that in rupees, silver or pounds? How can you keep track of where something is in the hold? What does that column mean again?'

It was maddening! And it also flushed her body with heat.

She was a girl who'd had to fight for every skill she possessed. Every master, every monk who controlled the purse had doubted her ability with money. She'd constantly had to prove her understanding, and even then, they discounted her. Captain Banakos glowered at her as if she had poisoned his food.

But not Lord Domac. He begged her to explain, to teach, to share. And though his constant interruptions made her want to scream, she felt such joy when he blithely accepted her greater skills. He acted as if it were the most normal thing in the world for a man to learn from a woman, and that made her giddy with pleasure.

He knew exactly what he was doing to her, too. He would touch her arm, and her skin would tingle. She didn't gasp—not after the first few times—but her body tightened in reaction. Then he would give her a bashful look.

'I'm being a terrible bother, aren't I?'

What could she say to that? 'No, my lord—'

'No, no. Don't lie to me. I can see it in your eyes. You love this work.' He gestured to the account books and her abacus. There was something jarring in his tone. Admiration, yes, but envy, too.

'It is a pleasure to do something well, yes?'

He nodded. 'Yes, yes, of course.'

She turned to look at him. She could add up ten numbers in her head, she could see a storage hold and rearrange it mentally to fit everything well, but she could not read his face. People often confused her, but him most of all.

'You are not happy? With this work?' she asked. But if that were true, then why did he work so hard to learn it?

'What? Of course I'm happy. I'm amazed.'

Was he? She watched as he rocked back on his heels.

'If you were to pick a cargo,' he said. 'One to sell in England, what would it be?'

'I do not know your country.'

'Right. Of course. But from what you see here. *The Integrity* has sold different cargos. Not just tea—'

'Tea is the most consistent profit.'

'Yes, but the East India Company controls that. And the Dutch lock down the spices.' He exhaled. 'What cargo, do you think, would be best?'

She shook her head. 'I do not know. I can only show you the profit or loss from what has been sold.' She pointed at the account book. 'Those answers are in here.'

He smiled at her. 'Not a fortune-teller. I understand. But this...' He pointed to her neat columns of numbers. 'This is important.' It was a statement, not a question, and yet she responded as if he doubted what she said.

'It is,' she said, her chin lifted. And what she meant by that was, *Yes, I am important, too.*

'So teach me how you do it.'

That was like teaching him how to breathe. She knew how to do it. She could explain the mechanics. But there was so much more to how, where and when she worked. And yet, she didn't mind starting again at the beginning and waiting for him to get frustrated. After all, he was not the first person to learn her tasks. And none of them could do it as well or as quickly as she.

He was no exception.

He tired by mid-afternoon on the first day. He barely made it to midday on the second. But he kept coming back. At least three hours a day. And as they worked, she learned the rhythm of his breathing. She knew when he was growing frustrated with his inability to use the abacus quickly. She knew when he succeeded on the first try by his quiet 'hup' of satisfaction. And she knew when he was impressed when he released a low chuckle of amazement. If there was envy in him, she no longer felt it. And now when he touched her, it was all she could do to keep from melting.

'I like it when you laugh,' he said the day before they were to make the next port in India. 'I know something has gone right.'

'Nothing has gone right,' she countered. 'Nothing has gone wrong. I am merely finished.' She pointed to the large ledger book, now satisfactorily closed.

'And what are your conclusions?'

She smiled. 'That the captain is honest.'

'Your father said as much.'

'But he also makes mistakes.' She pointed to a sheet of foolscap. 'There should be enough now to buy spices without selling the tea.'

His eyes widened. 'Show me!' he commanded. And then he flushed. 'Or, I suppose, we should bring in your father and the captain.'

Familiar panic shot through her belly. 'No, no,' she said in a rush. 'I will show my father this paper. I can explain it to him.'

'I'm sure you can, but that's not very fair to the captain, is it? You're exposing his mistakes, aren't you?'

'They were normal mistakes, and it is not so much money. I will not embarrass the captain that way.' Nor would she expose herself to an angry man of the captain's size. By all appearances, he was a fair man, but she had been wrong in such assessments before. The worst mistake she'd ever made was when she trusted that a seemingly fair man had bribed the Chinese officials to stay away. In fact, he had tipped them off to the illegal trades she'd been facilitating.

She'd nearly died that night, and she'd learned not to trust others so blithely. 'I will show my father, and he will decide what to do.'

He studied her face, his expression shifting from confusion to surprise. 'You are afraid. But why? Captain Banakos is a good man.'

Maybe, maybe not. But she was not a woman who took blind risks. She stood up, taking her paper with her. 'I will see my father now.'

He nodded. 'But the account books are here. He will want to see what you have discovered.' He matched her stance. That was an English custom, she knew. To stand whenever a female of status stood. That he did so with her was yet another reason she liked him. 'You needn't be afraid,' he continued. 'I will keep you safe.'

Such confidence. Didn't he understand that safety happened one moment at a time, and they had months left on the boat. A cruel man could act deferentially one moment but then catch her unawares later.

'Come now,' he chided. 'You are the one who began this. You asked to see the books.'

Yes, she had. Looking back, she still wondered what had made her so bold that night. Boredom was a large part of it. She was used to being busy. But also the desire to prove herself in her own way, just as her sister did in the sails. But now she couldn't bring herself…

'You can't turn coward now,' he chided. His smile was genuine. 'I'll be right here.' Then before she could argue, he stepped into the hallway. It wasn't long before a sailor passed by. There was nowhere on the ship that was truly private for long. 'Fetch Lord Wenshire and the captain, please.'

She wanted to run. Indeed, she would have if he weren't standing there grinning at her as if he were giving her some great gift. The two men arrived a few minutes later, then everyone stood there looking at her with expressions she couldn't read. And if she couldn't read their expressions, she couldn't guess what would happen.

That wasn't safe. But there was nowhere to hide.

Damn it, she was confident in her numbers. Why couldn't she stand tall and face them?

'Er, hello gentlemen,' Lord Domac began. 'Miss Richards has discovered something marvelous, haven't you? All her hard work these days is finished. She's got notations on what cargo was profitable and by how much. Quite fascinating for me, but I'll let her show you the figures.'

Mutely, she held up her sheet of foolscap. She wanted to speak. She tried to, but the English words were locked tight in her throat.

Her father took the paper, frowned as he inspected it. 'This looks very close to what I was told. Very close indeed.'

'Well then,' the captain said with a hearty laugh. 'I'd say she did a fine job there. This is a complicated thing. No one can get it right on the first try. Close is excellent work.'

Her head shot up. Her figures were accurate. It was he who had made the errors. But her protest was strangled in the middle. Try as she might, she couldn't get the words out.

'Miss Richards,' said Lord Domac. 'How many times did you check your work?'

She tried twice before the words came out. 'Three times.'

'Three times. That's a lot. Did you find errors?'

She nodded.

'Where?'

She knew the captain expected her to indicate errors in her own work, but she had made marks on the account entries. Tiny dots on the relevant pages. Mutely, she pointed to the first error.

The captain was quick to look, frowning as she quietly stepped back.

'But that's...well, that's... Very well. A simple error in calculation. And it's in my favour, Lord Wenshire.'

Mutely, she turned the page to another one, pointing. That one was in her father's favour.

'Ah. Yes. I see,' her father said. 'But they nearly cancel each other out.' He looked at her. 'How many of these errors did you find?'

She hated pointing out other's errors. No one appreciated it, even those it benefited. But she glanced at Lord Domac's reassuring nod and found her voice.

'Thirty-seven in all,' she finally said. 'All small.' She flushed. 'The captain is honest—'

'Of course I am!'

'You are!' she emphasised. 'But everyone makes mistakes.'

Lord Domac stepped forwards. 'You didn't tell them the best part. There's money,' he said, pointing to the total. 'Errors end up in your favour, Lord Wenshire. Enough to buy a small amount of spice without selling any of the tea.'

'Now hold on here,' the captain grumbled. 'Just because I owe you coin, doesn't mean there's room in the hold or silver on hand to buy anything.'

'There's silver,' her father said, his expression delighted. 'And room on the boat somewhere. I should like to watch my daughter buy.'

She smiled. It wasn't quite a grin, but she was pleased. So pleased that she looked to Lord Domac who was beaming at her as if she'd just won a prize. She felt her cheeks flush and quickly looked away, but the warmth stayed inside her for a long, long time.

There was no logical reason for him to be proud of her. Indeed, it made no sense that he had championed her at all, but the fact that he did stayed with her. It buoyed her that night, and it strengthened her spine the next morning when the real test began.

Chapter Five

She woke him well before dawn. Cedric did not have a sore head from drink, though he'd toasted Lucy's success several times. He'd been drinking water because that was all he could afford. And all his toasts had been made silently as he watched her remain rosy-cheeked throughout dinner.

She was proud of herself, and that pleased him. He liked it when ladies were happy, especially the shy ones. But if he expected her delight to continue into the morning, he discovered his error when she roused him while it was still full dark.

'Good God, what time is it? And what are you wearing?' And why were her shoulders tight and her mouth pinched?

'The first customer of the day cannot be denied otherwise the entire day will go sour. You're the customer. I'm the servant.' She spoke while stuffing her hair into a sailor's cap. In fact, everything she wore was a rough sailor's outfit, probably taken from her sister.

'You still look like a girl,' he said. Damn, he was being surly. He needed to wake up.

'Not with my face dirty. And if you treat me like a boy, they'll think I'm a boy.'

Right. 'Let me get some clothes on.'

'Rich ones,' she said. Her father appeared over her shoulder. He wore his usual attire that set him somewhere between a sailor who wasn't foolish with his money and a ship's owner who didn't dress fancy. Which meant no one could tell exactly who he was.

'You don't need to come with us,' her father said. 'I can keep an eye on things.'

'Oh no, sir. I wouldn't miss this for the world.' That was the truth. Unfortunately, he punctuated it with a yawn.

Five minutes later he was on deck and ready to disembark. She came up behind him, speaking in a low voice. 'You understand what you're doing?'

'I've no idea.' He turned to her. Even in shadow, he could see that she was nervous. She resembled her sister as she continued to fidget with everything. Her clothes, her feet, and mostly her gaze as she looked everywhere.

'I told you. You're the customer.' She gestured at the eastern horizon. 'I only know of one merchant here, and I'm not sure of his address. We have to find him first.'

'First before what?'

'Before anyone else. We have to be the first customer. They will do anything—even accept a low price—to make sure the first customer buys something.'

'Because if they don't, it will be a bad sales day?'

She nodded. 'At least that is the way in China. Among the...the...' She frowned, clearly not knowing the English word.

'The superstitious? People who believe in curses, magic and the like.'

She nodded. 'Yes. That's it. But not so strong. It is the custom among business people. And the merchants I know are very...very...'

'Superstitious.'

'Yes. That.'

She tugged at her clothing. For a woman normally so composed, this was unsettling. 'Relax,' he said. 'You've done this before.' At least he assumed she had.

'No. Yes.' She shrugged. 'But not for many years. And usually as the seller. They would bring me out for the customers who tried to take advantage like this.' She shrugged. 'It makes no difference if a cursed child has a bad day.'

'You are not a cursed child,' he grumbled. He'd learned that in Asia, mixed-race children were often considered cursed or a half person. He had only to spend five minutes with her to know she was nothing so simple as that. She was a full, fascinating person, and he would not allow anyone—including herself— to speak of her like that.

'And you must pay attention to my knees.'

Clearly, he was not awake yet. He could not have heard her correctly.

At his blank look, she pointed to her knees under her rough pants. 'My knees.'

He liked looking there. She had beautiful calves and very trim ankles, though it looked like she had dirtied them.

'My knees!' she said again, as she twisted her leg such that her left knee turned in or out.

'Happy to,' he drawled. 'Why?'

'People look for signals with the hands. Or they watch the face. No one looks down except you,' she said, as she poked him beneath his chin. It lifted his face up. 'You are haughty. You stare at me as if I were a bug.'

'And I'm to look at your knees?'

'Yes. If my knees are tight together, pressing inwards, then you do not like the price.'

'But if you turn them open, then that's a good deal?'

'Yes.' She glanced nervously at the skyline. It was still dark as pitch. 'Come on. There is little time.'

They disembarked quickly, then moved through the streets. They were four people in total, with him in the centre acting as the wealthy one. Her father and a muscular sailor trailed behind. She went ahead. And though he itched to put her behind him, she was the one who knew where to go.

She'd said she wasn't sure of their destination, but then he'd see her whispering with a child curled up in a shadow. Another hiding in the branches of a tree. And a third tucked into a pile of rubbish. He wouldn't have seen them if she hadn't found them. She would whisper and gesture, then hold up a small coin.

Getting directions, he thought, and soon they came to a shop closed up for the night with a second story that likely housed the family. She went up to the door, hesitated and looked back at him.

'You remember where to look?'

He grinned, his chin lifting as his gaze went slowly and obviously down her body.

She rolled her eyes and hissed, 'I'm a boy!' But her lips were curled in a soft smile as she turned back and banged on the front door. 'Master Mukhtar! Master Mukhtar!'

Sounds came from upstairs and somewhere a lamp was lit because he could see its flickering light in the window. And there were responses from shops on the opposite side of the alleyway. People slept in those upstairs floors, and Lucy had just woken them all.

Finally, a girl poked her head out of the window upstairs, calling something in Hindi that Cedric couldn't understand. And neither could Lucy, as far as he was aware. And yet, she still communicated what she wanted to say.

Lucy pointed straight at Cedric. 'Englishman!' she cried. 'Buy spice!' She mimed a fat purse of money.

'Spice?' the girl asked.

'Cinnamon.'

The girl shook her head. 'No cinnamon.'

'Black pepper.'

'No. No pepper.'

'Salt.'

'No salt!' There was fear in the girl's eyes about that and he already knew why. The East India Company viciously controlled that. Indeed, it was even more tightly controlled than the tea from China.

This was getting them nowhere. He sighed loudly, as if he was incredibly impatient. 'Enough, boy. I will buy *silk* instead.' Then he turned to leave, but an adolescent stuck his head out of the window.

'Silk? Come! Talk!' Then both boy and girl disappeared from the window.

Cedric shifted uncomfortably, making a show of his displeasure. He wasn't exactly sure if that was what she wanted, but then she turned and started rambling in a fawning tone. 'You see? Good sale here. Good sale.'

What he saw was the spark in her eye and the way her knees were turned open. This was what she wanted. Very well, he could play along.

'Make it quick.' He made a show of consulting his pocket watch. He couldn't see the time in the dark, but he made a show of it anyway.

The door opened, and they were gestured inside. Cedric's back prickled at walking into a darkened room like this. He'd learned to be cautious entering foreign places without protection. There could be armed thugs on the other side of the wall. Her father and the sailor were equally cautious as they entered, scanning the room, then quickly shutting the door behind them. They were under strict orders from Lucy to remain silent sentries, watching for problems but not speaking or interfering in the negotiations.

Fortunately, their fears seemed unfounded. It was the adolescent boy who faced them. The girl hid in the shadows in the back, and perhaps he saw a woman hovering behind her. But it was the boy who strutted before them.

'You buy silk!' he said, pointing to a pile of cheap muslin. Even Cedric could see that it was in terrible condition.

Cedric curled his lip. 'No.' Then he turned as if to leave.

'Yes, yes!' said the boy loudly as he gestured for them to go further into the back storeroom.

'No—'

'Lord, Lord, please,' Miss Richards begged. 'Come.'

'Not safe,' he said in an undertone.

She tugged on his arm. 'Safe.'

He relented, though every part of him felt on high alert. Anything could happen here. In general, he was casual about personal risks, but he hated taking chances with her. If she got injured, the guilt would eat him alive.

But he had come along to see how she bargained, so he could hardly hamstring her now. He reluctantly walked beside her into a back storeroom filled with bags of spice.

Spice! Everything the boy had declared was impossible laid out before him. Cinnamon, pepper, salt, not to mention other more exotic fare. He frowned as he moved forwards, inhaling deeply as he tried to sort through the scents.

Meanwhile, the boy walked straight to a bag of cinnamon. 'Silk!' he said pointing. Then he held up fingers to indicate a price. Ah. So this was a fiction about what he was selling so he could claim that he never sold spices to an English foreigner.

Immediately, Miss Richards stood differently. Her legs straightened and her knees twisted inwards. She began making gestures that dismissed the quality and price. Back and forth they bartered. He could barely follow it except in the shifting position of her knees.

And though the price steadily dropped—as far as he could tell—she didn't relax her stance. It was all, no, no, no.

What caught him instead was the way she acted. She was supposed to be a boy so her body language was stronger, broader and more aggressive. He'd imagined that he would be repulsed by such a thing. He appreciated her sister's skill in the sails, but he preferred feminine attributes in a female.

And yet here was Miss Lucy Richards posturing as any pre-teen male might. Her stance was bold, her words rapid and her tone arrogantly dismissive. So impressive! Damn if he didn't like the extra power in her voice or the way her gestures took on force.

He glanced back at her father who was watching

with what appeared to be bored disinterest. But then he caught the man's eyes and saw a small lift in his cheeks. He was pleased with what he saw. And so was Cedric.

Then things changed.

Miss Richards turned to Cedric, her manner pleading. 'Good price,' she wheedled as she held up her hand. 'Good price.'

He frowned at the barrel of cinnamon then he looked at her. Her knees were decidedly tight together. This was not a sale she wanted, and yet her manner made him double think for a moment.

But only a moment.

'How much?' he asked as he lifted his purse.

The adolescent answered, then added in English, 'Good price.'

'Nah,' he drawled as he pocketed the coins again. Then he curled his lip as he looked around. 'I think we can go elsewhere.'

He started to turn with Miss Richards quickly tugging on his elbow. 'Please, lord. Please. Good price.'

'No. Not this trip.' He looked towards the door. 'Maybe across the street.'

'No!' the boy called. 'Good price here.' Then he offered a slightly lower price.

Cedric paused looking down his nose at Lucy. Her feet were slightly spread. So it was a decent price. But then he thought about what she had said. How it was a curse to lose the first sale of the day, and so they'd give difficult buyers to Lucy because she could have a cursed day.

But what if she had a good day?

He pointed to the girl still hiding in shadows. Her eyes widened in surprise, and she shrank back. But he gestured her forwards, and she stood slowly.

'What deal will she give me?' he asked.

Abruptly, the boy stood between him and the girl. 'No! Not for sale!'

It took him a moment to understand the boy's meaning. And then he was the one crying, 'No! No!' He had no interest in buying the girl in any capacity. Instead, he gestured to the same pile of cinnamon and offered a price. A good ten percent less than what the boy had offered.

The boy shook his head. 'No! No!'

The same was echoed by the girl as she shook her head.

He nodded. 'Very well.' He smiled and bowed to her. Personally, he hated it when girls were shoved into the corner like a sack of meal. At least he could give her some respect. Then he headed for the door. 'Come along. Maybe someone across the street.'

That was when panic flashed across the boy's face. Clearly, Lucy had been right. Losing the first sale of the day was a bad thing for him. Suddenly, he shoved the girl forwards.

'Sir! Sir!' he cried. 'We talk! We talk!' But what he

meant was, negotiate with her. Walk out on her. Then the girl would have a bad day, not him.

Cedric rocked back on his heels. He looked at the girl and at Miss Richards, and he pointed at them both. 'You two. Talk.'

Both girls stared at him, shock in their expressions. He didn't care. He folded his arms and waited, and then the two females squared off. Now the true bargaining began and both of them enjoyed every second of it. Indeed, it was a glorious thing to watch as the boy was sidelined, and the two girls began an animated discussion.

And though both made a show of being angry at times, he saw the sparkle in their eyes and the way their gestures took on more energy, more joy. Such a pleasure to see.

In the end, a bargain was struck. Several bargains for cinnamon, pepper and even a little salt. All of it was wrapped in the cheap muslin then packed in a pair of crates. They bought so much that everyone took a turn carrying as they made it back to the boat. And Cedric had the pleasure of seeing Miss Richards in her element.

She warned them as they left the shop to be wary. She even counseled him to act angry as they stomped out of the store, as if they were unhappy with what happened inside. And then they made their way quickly back to the boat.

Once safely aboard, he turned to see her face. Her

grin amused him. He'd expected her to be exhausted. He certainly felt drained, and all he'd done was watch her. She, on the other hand, was so happy she practically skipped.

And then, she turned to him, a smile stretched across her face. 'Thank you,' she said, her voice brimming with happiness. 'Thank you for a wonderful day.'

'Of cou—'

'She was happy. You made her so happy.'

'Who?'

'Priya. The girl. She never gets to bargain, and she's good at it.'

'Good?'

Miss Richards laughed. 'Not as good as me, but good. And you gave her that.' She squeezed his arm. 'Thank you.' Then she laughed as the sun topped the buildings to the east. Indeed, she laughed with such giddiness that his heart tumbled straight into love.

Chapter Six

Lucy was bursting with excitement and desperate for someone to share it with. But as much as she wanted to shout it to the skies, she'd had a lifetime of hiding herself away. Most half children did. She knew she couldn't go around making noise, but inside she was singing at the top of her lungs.

She'd forgotten how wonderful life could be.

Once upon a time, she'd lived this joy every day. She'd had to hide who she was, of course. She'd dressed as a boy and stood as translator for her master who bartered in the Thirteen Factories district. It was the only place where whites were allowed to bargain with Chinese for goods. And since she was a half person, she was allowed to taint herself by interacting with the English. She learned their language in halting gestures and grunting phrases. And the more she learned, the more capable she became.

That meant she got excellent deals for her master, and within a year, he followed her lead, not the other way around. Indeed, it went much like it had with Lord Domac, and how amazing it felt to be doing that again.

Her sister landed before her, jumping down from wherever she'd been in the sails. 'How did it go?' Grace asked. Then she held up her hand. 'Don't answer. I can see it on your face.'

'It was like being back in the factory district,' she said. 'Only better.'

'Better? How is that possible?'

Because of Lord Domac. Because he had watched her with respect instead of criticism, and he'd moved to protect her when he was worried. And because he had seen the girl in the shadows and let her shine, as well.

'It was so much fun. I got good prices, too.'

Her sister looked over her shoulder at where Lord Domac and a sailor were bringing on two crates. 'We don't have room in the hold for that,' she said.

'You can find someplace, can't you?' She leaned forwards and spoke the rest quietly because it was too wonderful to give full voice to. Good news was always whispered in secret, even though they spoke in Chinese that no one else would understand. 'Father has said the profits when we sell them will go into my dowry.' She squeezed her sister's fingers. 'I will have a dowry! Me!'

Her sister's eyes widened. To have money was the dream of all people, but especially the half children. 'Money,' she breathed. Then in a more moderate tone, she said, 'Husband?' In truth, the word came out more as a question. As if that wasn't also the dream of every young girl.

'Don't you want to be married?' Lucy asked. 'To have a home of your own?' Children all around. Nice clothing and food. These were things she dreamed about at night. Of being part of a family without fear of starvation or being beaten for whatever reason. She dreamed of a mother's love, if not from a woman to her, then from her to a child.

And she wished for a man who was kind and had a lightness to him. Just like Lord Domac.

'My home is aboard ship,' Grace said. 'I do not need a husband for that.'

No, but she needed a captain who supported her. And people who would protect her when they docked at whatever port. Life aboard ship was not as safe as a wealthy home on land. But Grace was not someone who could remain still. Lucy, on the other hand, looked for safety in the shadows in a place she could call home.

'I am building my dowry,' Lucy said, her happiness undimmed by her sister's skepticism.

'But where are you going to store that?' Grace pressed, looking at the two huge crates. 'There isn't room in the hold.'

'We could get one of the crates in our berth, couldn't we? And the other...' She looked around. 'You know this ship through and through. There has to be someplace.'

'That will keep it safe and dry?' She shook her head. 'There is no place except the captain's quarters. Maybe.'

'Then we will have to put it there.' She spoke with certainty, though inside she was fearful.

'Go to the hold first. Let's see what we can do.'

They couldn't do anything. Everything was tied down and bolstered. There wasn't even room for rats.

Her sister shook her head. 'Speak nicely to the captain.' Then she pressed a kiss to Lucy's cheek. 'I have to go back to work.'

'We could keep it in our room, yes? At least one chest?'

'And do we sleep on it then?'

There wasn't room in their tiny space. Not if both of them slept at the same time.

Grace patted her sister's shoulder. 'Speak to the captain. He may have an idea.'

The captain did not. And even she had to admit that there was precious little space in the captain's quarters. Which left her at a complete loss. Why hadn't she thought about storage before she'd purchased so much? But she'd gotten caught up in the negotiation.

Now what was she going to do?

'Can't find a storage place, can you?' Lord Domac asked when she came back up on deck. The two crates were sitting exactly where they'd set them down near the gangplank. They couldn't remain there. It was too wet, and the crates would slide.

'I don't know what to do. I wasn't thinking.'

'There is a place. At least I think they will fit.'

'Where?'

'My berth.'

His room was tinier than the one she shared with her sister. 'I don't think they will fit in the door.'

'They'll fit. One atop the other.'

'But you won't.'

He shrugged. 'I can sleep with the crew. It's what I'd been planning anyway.'

'But why? Why would you give up your bed?' He didn't have a stake in the bargain. He put up no money and would not make any profit. And yet, he would give up his berth for it? It made no sense.

His smile was slow as it spread over his face. A sweet curve of the lips that lit his eyes and warmed her heart. 'I'd do it for a price.'

Ice slid into her veins, and she took a step back. She'd thought he was different. And while she was still reeling from that, his eyes widened with horror.

'No, no!' He held his hands up as if in surrender. 'Nothing like that.'

'Then what?'

He gave a charming shrug. 'A percentage of the profit when you sell. Do you think your father will agree?'

She nodded. 'He will, but I won't.'

'Why not? Where else would you store them?'

'I'll pay you a set fee. Same as if it were in the hold.'

He leaned back against the side of the ship. 'But it's not in the hold. It'll be in my bed.'

'Maybe it will fit beside your bed.'

'Maybe it won't.'

They set about bargaining. And though the stakes were tiny, the pleasure was the same as it had been that morning. He was a strong opponent in this, happy to negotiate, but secure in the knowledge that he had the upper hand. After all, she had no other options. But he didn't exploit her, and he was going to be very uncomfortable for several months.

Once they agreed upon a price, she ended up feeling very grateful to him. And because of that gratitude, she helped him move the crates to his cabin. The ship was not busy, but most of the crew had gone into port on their own business. Her father had retired to rest and even her sister was nowhere around.

Fortunately, Lucy didn't mind. She had done manual labour before. And though she wasn't nearly as strong as he was, she wasn't useless either. Together, they got the first crate shoved through his door. And, after a few resting minutes, they shoved in the second.

She had to squeeze in first and pull. He was the stronger, lifting the second crate atop the first and putting all his weight into it. The result was a room that had two badly stacked crates taking up all the space while his narrow cot was shoved against the side and currently held all his belongings on it. The only way in or out now was by walking on the bed and squeezing out the door in the few inches there.

'Not too bad,' he said as he climbed in, effectively

trapping her in the tiny space. She was on her knees, leaning against the second crate.

'If the top crate slides, it will crush you.' She frowned.

'I'll tie it down. There are ropes that will make it secure. And my things can go underneath.' As he spoke, he grabbed his bag and awkwardly shoved it underneath his bed. Then he didn't say anything as he faced her. His gaze roved over her and his expression intensified. 'You were amazing this morning.'

She smiled, feeling a rush of heat throughout her body. 'I'd forgotten how much I love bargaining.'

'Tell me what you did. Tell me how you learned.'

She chuckled. 'The way everybody learns. I was apprenticed to a spice merchant when I was very young. We all start in the temple as babies. But as soon as possible, we are apprenticed. Because I was good with numbers, I went to a merchant. At first, he only let me watch his children, but I watched the sales instead. I learned how to bargain from my master and his wife. And when he started offering his spices in the Thirteen Factory district, he brought me along as translator. His sons were terrible at it, and I...' She grinned. 'I was good.'

'You loved it.'

She nodded. 'I did. I do.'

'So why did you leave China?'

She flushed as she looked down. 'I'm a girl. Girls aren't allowed in the Thirteen Factory area, much less inside the bargaining halls. There came a time when I couldn't hide who I am anymore.'

'But you did today.'

'I think they knew. But since the girl does it, too...' She shrugged.

'So you know spices. Any other cargo?'

'It's all buying and selling. There are things one has to learn, but I can barter with anyone.'

He nodded. 'I think I could study for a thousand years and not have the talent you possess.' He leaned forwards. 'But I still want you to teach me.'

Her breath caught. He was so close, and no one could see them past the crates even if they opened the door. She knew she shouldn't be here, alone and trapped behind crates with him. But for the first time in her life, she didn't feel fear. She knew she ought to. She didn't truly know him that well. But he had protected her and had shown her respect.

How dangerous could he be?

She lifted her head. His fingers felt wonderful as he stroked her cheek. Her breath caught, her lips tingled and she wanted such things. Dangerous things for a girl like her, and yet, she couldn't stop herself.

So when he leaned down to take her mouth with his, she welcomed his kiss. She stretched up to him and let his tongue tease against her lips and teeth.

She knew what to do. She knew he would press his tongue into her mouth, and they would dance that way.

But he took his time. He nipped at her lips while his fingers caressed down her jaw and neck.

She gasped at the feel of his fingers on her flesh. She was not in restrictive English clothing but rough sailor's garb. Her breasts were bound, but the shirt over her bindings was loose. His fingers found the ridge of her collarbone and teased the skin just above her bindings.

Her head dropped back as she gasped for air. She had to steady herself with one hand on the wall, and all through that, he was stroking her neck and the opening above her breasts. His caress was gentle. Tantalizing, even. And when she opened her eyes, she saw such hunger in his.

'What do you know about kissing?' he asked as his fingers toyed with the top of her binding. She didn't even remember her shirt falling open, but she realised that the tie at the top had come undone. And since the shirt was so much larger than her, it gaped above her breasts.

'I have been kissed,' she said.

His gaze shot to hers. 'Willingly?'

She nodded.

'Anything else?' he asked.

She didn't know how to answer, so he showed her. His hand brushed down over the cloth binding, rubbing her breast and her tight nipple. She gasped as she swayed on her knees. He caught her around the waist, then angled her such that his fingers kept brushing across her breast.

'Have you ever felt that before?'

Not like that before. Not with her body pulsing with every stroke. Oh, the feelings he gave her.

'Lucy, has anyone touched you like this before?'

She swallowed, her mind dizzy with want. 'Yes.' Then she looked into his eyes. 'But then I made him stop. I know this is wrong, but I was so lonely. Grace was sailing, and...' How could she explain that the boy had helped her, and she'd been lost. But even then, she knew she could not continue. Pregnancy would be a disaster.

'You stopped him?'

She forced herself to grab hold of his wrist and push his hand away. Pregnancy now would be a worse disaster. 'We cannot do more,' she said, though the words had to be forced out.

He nodded as if he approved. Then that sparkle entered his gaze. 'But we can share a kiss, yes? That is not so bad a thing?'

It was a wonderful thing. And they had already touched lips, but he meant more. He meant...

Oh! His hands returned to her face, brushing the hair from her cheek. She let go of the wall and wrapped her hands around his upper arms, feeling the muscles there. He didn't need to angle her face. She lifted up for him. And when he pressed his mouth to hers, she opened for him. She wanted to give him everything.

His tongue invaded with a thrust, and she met him, matched him, and surrendered to him.

They kissed for a very long time. She learned from him the joy of quick domination and slow surrender. She let him lean her back against the wall as he showered her face with kisses. And she thrilled to the way he gave her one last kiss and then couldn't stop himself from giving her another and another.

It was magical. And when he asked her to release the bindings around her breasts, he respected her answer when she said no.

'I am weak for you,' she confessed. 'But I will not risk everything for you. I will not be that foolish.'

He dropped his forehead to hers, breathing deeply as he held her. And then he whispered words she never thought to hear.

'I will speak to your father tonight.'

'About what?'

'About marriage.' Then he pressed a kiss to her hands. It was slow and reverent, thrilling her to the bone before he raised his head and regarded her with serious eyes. There was a question there, but she did not understand what it meant.

'Why do you look at me like that?'

'Do you know what a dowry is?' he asked.

She nodded. 'Coin that goes with a woman to her husband. It makes her more valuable.'

'I need coin, Lucy. A great deal. Do you know how much is in your dowry?'

She shook her head. 'Some, I think. Sale of these spices will fill it.'

He nodded. 'You showed me the money you hope will come from that sale.'

She nodded. 'This ship has carried spices before. From that, I guessed—'

'It is not enough,' he said quickly. 'I need there to be more money in your dowry. It is for my sisters and my family.' His expression sobered. 'Do you know what I am saying?'

That she was not valuable enough alone. It made sense. She was a half child and he was an important person in his country. He needed more to balance the scales when they married.

'I can make you coin. Show you where to put your money so that it returns a good profit.'

His expression was mocking, but she did not think he was laughing at her. 'It takes money to make more money, and I have nothing.' He stroked his thumb across her cheek and the caress sent sweet tingles throughout her body.

She swayed forwards then, wanting his kiss, wanting everything she'd denied him not five minutes before. He stopped her, holding her away from him.

'I will speak with your father tonight,' he said, then he maneuvered out of his bed. He was careful with the door, opening it slowly before winking at her. 'Come to dinner in a nice dress.' Then he was gone.

Chapter Seven

If Cedric were in London, he would meet with his banker and have detailed information regarding his accounts. He would also discover the particulars of Lord Wenshire and his daughters. Dowries were flexible things, but general details were always available if one knew who to ask.

Additionally, he would have talked to his many female friends about Miss Richards, learning if she were shrewish or had a gambling habit. And best of all, he would have danced the waltz with her several times. Enough to indicate his interest in her such that gossip one way or another would find its way to his ears.

But he was not in London. There was no way to subtly find out what he wanted to know or to communicate his desire. No way except in the crudest manner possible. And he didn't even have another bottle of Aarack to help ease the awkwardness of the discussion.

Nevertheless, he did his best.

There were few people at the captain's table that

night. Indeed, even the captain had gone into town which left three crew aboard ship. Miss Grace Richards came to the table in her sailor's clothing. She ate quickly, smiled at him and then rushed back up into the sails to do whatever she did up there. He got the distinct impression that staying below bothered her.

Miss Lucy Richards dressed wonderfully, though the gown was of poor quality. No doubt it was the best available to her when she'd departed China. Still, she looked beautiful to him. Her cheeks were pink, her eyes seemed to sparkle at him, and yet she remained poised at the table, eating sparingly. She reminded him of a fawn, filled with life but still skittish. Unless she was negotiating spices, of course. Then she became a tigress.

He loved the variety of that and looked forward to seeing what she would become when she was a lady of the *ton* as his bride.

Her father sat beside her, listening to tales of India from the sailors who joined them. He was not a talkative man. He listened, chuckled, and smiled fondly at his daughters. Then the meal ended, the sailors departed, and Cedric knew it was time.

'If you wouldn't mind, sir,' he said as Lord Wenshire set down his napkin. 'I should like to converse with you. Over cigars, perhaps?' He didn't have any on him, but most gentlemen puffed when they could.

'Bah,' Mr. Richards said. 'I stopped that habit when

I started coughing.' He smiled at Lucy. 'My daughters made me.'

Cedric grinned. 'Did you smoke your last one?'

Lord Wenshire stifled a cough. 'Last week.' Then he narrowed his eyes to look first at Cedric, then at Lucy. 'Dearest,' he said as he took her hand. 'You should take a walk on deck. Watch the port. There's always something interesting going on out there.'

Lucy looked at her father and then at Cedric. She understood the man's meaning, but it was clear she was reluctant to leave. 'Perhaps I could stay—'

'That is not how the English do it, my dear. The hour after the meal is reserved for men speaking to men.'

She grimaced then gave in. She lowered her head and clasped her hands in front of her, though she still managed to look at him. He gave her a reassuring smile as she left the room. And then he did something unusual for him.

He waited. He looked at her father and knew that revealing himself immediately would be a mistake. He had to let her father guide the conversation. Except for one thing. He was the one who asked for the time alone with him. Still, he waited, feeling anxiety build in his belly until Lord Wenshire began to muse aloud.

'I knew your father. Went to school with him, though I was several years ahead.' He shifted to stare hard at Cedric. 'What do you think of him?'

As little as possible. 'He is the Earl of Hillburn, I am his heir. In that way, he deserves my respect.'

'Does he?' the man challenged. 'Do you respect your father?'

This was not a topic he wanted to confront, but it was a legitimate question from Lucy's father. And damn the man for getting right to the heart of it. Cedric looked down at his dirty plate and wished he had some very strong brandy at hand.

He did not. Neither did he want to lie, even though polite society generally expected him to.

'My father is a gambler. Over the years, he's sworn to stop, but he never has. I remember one Christmas when he was flush. He burst in like Father Christmas, dropped packages for everyone, and talked of all the wonderful things he wanted to do with us that winter. I remember being so happy.'

'How long did it last?'

'Not even a day. To be fair, we were the ones asking him to go riding in the snow with us, to listen to my sister sing, to praise me for my marks at school.'

'He wasn't one to praise?'

'Oh, he was. Deep in his cups he had praise a plenty for everything and everyone. My father is a joyous drunk whom everybody loves.'

'And what happens when he has no more money to gamble?'

'He comes home and waits until quarter day when he can again return to London to lose it at the tables.'

'So your title is hollow and you came to India to make your fortune.' He leaned back in his chair to study

Cedric. It was not a comfortable moment, but Cedric had experience in enduring uncomfortable moments. He sat still and tried to explain his situation in positive terms.

That was a near impossible task.

'I wanted to learn what the East India Company did, to see if there was a place there for me.'

'And is there?'

'There might have been,' he admitted. If he hadn't seen some of the techniques used by the company. If he hadn't talked with farmers. If he hadn't learned how the company forced them to grow poppies, then paid them pennies for the crop. If he hadn't stood in the factory that processed the opium and witnessed the conditions there. And if he hadn't befriended the daughter of one of the natives and learned from her all the quiet, untidy things that Englishmen did in India.

He said none of that out loud.

'I received a letter from my sister begging me to return home. I have three, and they are of an age to marry.' He shook his head. 'She needs me to sort through things for them.'

Mr. Richards's brow lifted. 'Sort through things?'

Might as well tell it all. 'Their dowries, sir. My father won't give them any details.' He sighed. 'I don't know what's become of the funds.'

'Yes, you do. Your father gambled it all away.'

'Most likely.'

'So what are you going to do?' The question was

posed casually as if it were the same as choosing a cravat for the evening or a new style of haircut. It wasn't that simple, and even though he was his father's heir, there was precious little he could do to control the man. Which meant he didn't have an answer.

Abruptly, Lord Wenshire leaned forwards. His posture, which had been lazy, was suddenly taut as he stared hard at Cedric.

'What are you going to do?'

Cedric felt his temper flare. He did not like being questioned by anyone, much less a man who had all the advantages of the rich. Lord Wenshire might not be in line for an earldom, but he came from the aristocracy. The second son of a second son. He'd been educated with the elite and had travelled the world making money. He did not know what it was like to have disasters for parents. And to be constantly crippled beneath the weight of his father's addiction.

'Lord Domac!' the man said, his voice harsher than before.

Cedric matched it, his words coming out hard and angry. 'I tried gambling as a teen. I was clever and understood the games.' He shook his head. 'But I could not sustain the profit.' Not without resorting to trickery, and that was something he could not stomach. 'I tried businesses in England, learning about mills and factories at home.' He shook his head. 'I could not buy my way into any of the profitable ventures. And I haven't the stomach needed for coal mining.'

Lord Wenshire grunted as he fell back against his chair. 'I've been in a coal mine. Filthy, awful work. And what it does to the children.' He shook his head.

Cedric shuddered. He'd seen that, as well. Even if he had the money to invest, he couldn't do it. 'So I followed Graham to India. There are ways to make money with the company here.'

Lord Wenshire nodded. 'I worked for them for a decade. It's the basis of my wealth.'

'Only a decade? I thought it was longer.'

'Well, maybe fifteen years.' The man shook his head. 'Once I was transferred out of China, I began searching for something different. India worked, for a time, but I wanted something...' He shrugged. 'Wholesome.'

Cedric nodded. He understood the desire. 'Did you find it?'

Lord Wenshire snorted. 'In lots of different ways. But mostly, I was searching for the right cargo. The right product to take back to England.'

Now this was something he needed to know. 'What is it? What did you find?'

'Chinese tea.' He shook his head. 'I spent years searching the globe, and in the end...' He pushed his plate away from him on the table. 'I came back to the East India Company and tea.'

'I want to be in shipping,' Cedric blurted out. It was a shock because he'd never said that aloud before. 'I am not a farmer. I can manage whatever estate remains from my father, but there is little money there. I will not process opium. It is not...'

'Wholesome?'

That was as good a word as any. There was medical value in the drug, but also a great deal of abuse. Plus the Chinese government had made it illegal to import, so only black market deals were available.

'Cargo is the way to go,' he said. 'Shipping it from one place to the other, as you do.' He leaned forwards. 'I want to learn from you, sir. I want to understand how you have made your fortune—'

'So you can imitate it?'

'Yes.'

'You need money to start. Do you have any?'

No sense in denying it. 'None.'

'Then how—'

'I must do it as my father did it and my grandfather.' Not to mention a large portion of the world. He looked down at his hands. He had not wanted it to come to this. Indeed, he had spent most of his life looking for another way to find coin. How bitter it was to admit that he had failed.

'You are going to marry it.' There was no condemnation in Lord Wenshire's tone. It was how most of his peers and compatriots made their coin. The process was as old as the aristocracy.

As his bride, a wealthy girl would eventually become his countess, and he would have the funds to make something substantial for himself, his sisters and his children. That was the plan. All it needed was a moneyed wife.

'You look to my daughter.'

'Yes.'

'I have money in cargo,' Lord Wenshire said. 'And money in a bank in London. But my real asset is this ship.' He leaned back and fondly stroked the wall. 'She's beautiful, isn't she?'

'Absolutely.'

'And she will go into my daughter's dowry. This boat plus whatever I make from the cargo below. It will all be hers.'

His breath caught and his heart soared. That would be a great start for him. Especially if he could learn from Lord Wenshire. He could figure out a cargo that wasn't controlled by the East India Company. Or maybe he could find a lucrative arrangement with the company. That was, after all, what Lord Wenshire had done.

It was possible. There was hope!

'I will honour my vows to your daughter. I am not a man who cheats at cards or any other venture. And I will learn from you and work hard. This I swear to you.'

Lord Wenshire held up his hand. 'You misunderstand me.'

'What? I am asking for Lucy's hand in marriage. I am asking for her dowry of a ship and its cargo. And I swear I will care for her and our children. I can give them a good life and she will be a countess one day!

Surely that is far beyond what you had imagined possible for her.'

The man's brows went up and his tone darkened. 'Why? Because she is Chinese?'

And a bastard, but he would not say that aloud. They both knew that the English aristocracy would not easily accept one such as her. But it was possible. If she came in as a future countess.

'I will support her,' he vowed.

'But she does not have the dowry you want.'

It took a moment for his words to reach Cedric's brain. 'What?'

'Grace's dowry is this ship and the money from the cargo below. I haven't dowered Lucy yet beyond whatever she gets from the spices.'

His thoughts had been on Lucy, never Grace. He needed a woman who could become a countess, not a wild girl who ran the sails like a sailor. 'But you have adopted Lucy, as well. You said as much.'

'Yes, I have. But Grace and this ship go together. She is the one who knows how to sail it. She is the one who can navigate better than any man. She is—'

'But Lucy understands the buying and selling of cargo. That is where the profit is.'

'And Lucy looks at you as if you hung the moon and the stars.'

Cedric frowned. He was to be punished because his choice of bride liked him?

Lord Wenshire scoffed at Cedric's confounded expression. 'I am not a fool. I have seen women destroyed by a bad husband.'

'But I'm not a bad husband!'

'Maybe, maybe not. Grace is a woman who knows her own mind. She has worked and fought toe to toe with men since she began sailing. She is a woman who forces a man to live up to her expectations. And believe me, she expects a great deal.'

'I am offering a title. I am offering to work as hard as any man would.'

'And Grace will make sure you do it well. Gain her respect, and you will gain my trust. She will have this boat and the cargo. It is her dowry because she knows what to do with it.'

'And Lucy?'

'Lucy is too young to marry.'

'They are nearly the same age!'

'She will give herself to you and hold nothing back.'

'As a wife should.'

'A wife, yes. But to become your wife, you must prove worthy of being her husband.'

Cedric threw up his hands. 'I am willing to work!'

'Maybe, maybe not.' His gaze hardened. 'I return to England every so often, and I hear things. I know you are called The Inconsistent One.'

His cheeks burned. 'That came from my aunt.'

'The Duchess of Byrning. Yes, I know.' Lord Wenshire's brows arched. 'A worthy woman. She is a leader in society.'

And a shrew who tarred Cedric and his father with the same brush. 'She does not know me.'

'Neither do I. At least not well enough to hand you either one of my daughters.'

Cedric ground his teeth, knowing that any father of an heiress would say the same thing. Still, it burned that he was being denied his choice of bride. It had made little difference to him before when one heiress was the same as another. But he had a preference now. He wanted Lucy.

'What can I do to earn your respect? What can I—'

'Earn Grace's respect.' The man folded his arms across his chest. 'My decision is made.'

Cedric stared at Lord Wenshire. He saw the hard jut of the man's jaw and the calm challenge in the man's eyes. 'But Grace has no interest in me.' And the feeling was mutual.

'Then learn to be consistent as you wait for Lucy.'

It was a test then, to see if he could be patient. If he could wait for what he wanted. If it were his life alone, then he could. He would! But his sisters did not have that kind of time. And neither did the tenants who had buildings falling down on their ears or the canal that was already rotting.

And yet he still considered it.

'How long?' he whispered. 'Until you believe Lucy is of age?'

The man shook his head. 'I cannot say. She has not found her strength yet.'

Cedric shook his head. 'Did you see her this morning? Did you see how she negotiated—'

'She was brilliant.'

'Too right!'

'And she did it to impress you.'

Cedric shook his head. 'She loved it. And, I think, she wanted to impress you.'

Lord Wenshire snorted. 'I have adopted her. She has no need to impress me.'

'Clearly she does if you give a dowry to her sister and not her!'

Lord Wenshire's slammed his hand down on the table, his first show of violence that Cedric had ever seen. 'She is too young. If you want this boat and its cargo, then impress Grace. Bring Grace into your heart. She will make sure you are worthy of it.'

'And what of love? What of the feelings between me and Lucy?'

'They are the feelings of children. I thought you were a man.'

It wasn't true. Neither he nor Lucy were children playing games, but he could see that Lord Wenshire would not budge on this. And Cedric had no other options.

Damn it, he couldn't marry a dowerless girl! He needed coin, and the only way to get it was with a wealthy bride. Tender feelings could not come into it. And yet, his chest hurt as if he had been stabbed.

'I will change your mind,' he said quietly.

'No, you will not.'

Cedric was used to wild emotional swings from his father. He'd been screamed at, doted upon and completely ignored by his father. If he wanted to persuade his father of something, he merely needed to wait for a congenial mood.

But Lord Wenshire was of a different sort. He was a man of commerce, and he could not be easily swayed.

'I am a fortune-hunter,' he finally said, the words more for himself than for Lord Wenshire. 'I have no other choice.'

'I know.'

'But you are forcing me to go against my heart. Against her heart!'

'I am forcing you to be a man who thinks things through logically. And I am protecting my daughters. Grace will keep you in line. Lucy will not. She is too young.'

Cedric closed his eyes, all his dreams for the future refusing to realign around Grace. They didn't work without Lucy.

Except, of course, they did. He needed the ship. He needed the money from the cargo. The wife was simply the means to these things.

'I told Lucy I would speak with you tonight.'

'And so you have.'

'But...' He swallowed. 'How do I tell her that...' He couldn't say the words aloud. How could he tell a woman that he must put her aside for money? That the man she had chosen—himself—was nothing but a crass fortune-hunter? He couldn't speak that aloud to her because he couldn't bear to see the light die in her eyes.

'Don't say a thing,' Lord Wenshire said.

'What?'

'Lucy!' he called. 'Step around the door. I know you are there.'

Cedric's head snapped up, his gaze trained on the galley room door. And sure enough, a moment later he saw her step around the wall. She'd been standing just out of sight, no doubt listening to every word.

'See?' Lord Wenshire said with a sigh. 'Eavesdropping is a childish thing. She could have demanded to stay or demanded an accounting afterwards. Instead, she hid around the corner.' He looked to her and his gaze softened. 'You are too young to marry, Lucy. I'm sorry.'

And with that, he stood up and headed for the door. She met him a step inside the door, and he pulled her into a hug.

'You will see,' he said to his daughter. 'You will see how little feelings matter in this world.'

'That's not true!' Cedric said as he shot to his feet. 'You are the one forcing this. You are the one ignoring what we feel.'

'If they are so important to you, then you can wait.' He looked down at Lucy. 'I am not forbidding this marriage if you both want it. But it will have to wait several years.'

Cedric did not have several years to wait. And Lucy did not have a ship or cargo. 'You are forcing me to become something I do not want.' To court Grace he would have to go against his nature. He would have to woo her in as calculated a way as any general waging a war. It would be coldhearted and demeaning.

'Life often forces us to change. It is the mark of a man to adapt.' Then he squeezed his daughter's shoulder and directed her out of the galley. 'Come along, my dear. It's time for us both to rest. We were awake much too early this morning.'

And so the man took his daughter away, leaving Cedric to stand in the empty galley and fume.

A man adapted? Damn him!

Cedric had refused to adapt his gambling to win all the time. He would not become a cheat.

He had refused to adapt to torturing peasants for opium, and so he had left the East India Company.

And now his only hope—his sisters' only hope for dowries—was if he adapted to court a woman he did not want. Marry an heiress for her coin. That had been his plan, after all, once he landed in London. So why not begin it here?

Could he make that adaptation? Could he give up Lucy forever?

He had to. And the truth of that cut deep.

He dwelled in that pain as long as he could. He dropped down into his chair and stared numbly at the floor. But in time, he had to move. He had to make a choice. If he could not have Lucy, then he would court her sister because she was the one with the boat and the cargo. That was what a man did to provide for his family.

How he despised himself for it.

But he did it anyway.

Chapter Eight

Lucy was a girl who hid. The only time she'd ever been bold was when she was pretending to be a boy. But there was no pretense here and little room to negotiate. Her life was completely under her adoptive father's control. If he refused to give her a dowry, what could she do?

Exactly what she did when she negotiated. She began with flattery and servitude. That usually worked.

She brought him tea the next day as the ship was preparing to leave port. Everyone was busy, including her sister. Her father stood on deck in a tiny, quiet corner and watched. Lucy offered him the drink.

'I made it very hot,' she said as she offered him the drink. 'Do not let it burn you.'

'Thank you, Lucy. You are looking very lovely this morning.'

She had dressed with care. She knew he appreciated it when she looked as English as possible.

'I am constantly impressed with Captain Banakos,' he said as he watched the organised chaos around them.

'His bookkeeping is not so good.' She said it under her breath, but not so quiet that he couldn't hear. And at his arch look, she shrugged. 'It is not so bad either.'

'But you found errors.'

She nodded. 'I can always find errors because everyone makes mistakes.' She cast him a coy look. 'Every man makes mistakes because no man is perfect. It is therefore honourable, at times, to change your mind.'

'To correct an error?'

'Yes.'

'Like refusing to dower you?'

She lowered her eyes and kept her body position contrite. 'You are a wise and kind father. I would not question your decisions.'

'Then you are not a wise daughter.'

Her gaze jumped up to his face. He was watching her closely, but his expression remained unreadable. 'I do not understand.'

'It is a good thing for people to ask questions, especially when they listen to the answers. Men as well as women.' He leaned back against the railing as he sipped his tea. 'What do you want to ask me?'

Many questions pushed forwards, none of them strategic in getting what she wanted. So it was a shock when the most important one slipped from her lips.

'What do you want with me?'

His brows lifted. 'You are my daughter. I want you to be happy—'

'I am not your daughter. I came with Grace when the monks presented her to you. She is your daughter.'

He nodded. 'But you are her sister, yes? I don't mean by blood. She refused to leave China without you. And you her.'

'We were two girl half children in the temple.' Even among orphans, the boys were more valued. 'From my earliest memory, we held on to each other.' Grace had been older, so she was the one who first comforted Lucy. But as they grew, they loved one another.

But that didn't explain why Lord Wenshire had taken two girls, not one. Was she nothing to him? Just an extra piece of Grace's baggage, like an extra pair of shoes or a hat?

'I can be valuable to you. I can earn money.' She lifted her chin. 'I found errors in the account books. You have other ships. I can look at all those account books. And I am very honest.'

He smiled at her. 'If that would give you pleasure, I would be happy to let you check all the account books for all my ships.'

'It is not pleasure,' she returned. 'It is for money. So that your accounts are correct.'

He nodded. 'But I can hire other people to check the accounts. I don't need you to do it. But if that would give you pleasure—'

'It is not pleasure!' she repeated. 'It is work. Good work. Done to please you.'

'But I don't need you to work for me.'

Damn it. She had meant to exchange her work for his boat, the dowry that Lord Domac wanted.

She squared her shoulders. 'I can do many things. I am a good learner. What other work do you need someone to do?'

'I don't need a worker.' He glanced up as the sails were unfurled. 'I have plenty of those. What I need,' he said as he looked back to her, 'is a daughter.'

'And what does a daughter do?'

'She lives a good life and shares it with me.'

Ah. He wanted a maid and companion in his old age. 'Perhaps you want a wife. I could help you find one. Someone who will make you happy. Who will grace your bed and—'

He chuckled. 'I have no need for a wife. The woman I loved is gone.'

'But I could find you another one. Many women want someone to care for. It need not be me. I am no good at cleaning and serving. Not like men want.' She sighed. 'I can make hot tea. I cannot ease your old age.'

Her belly trembled as she spoke these words. This was a risky gambit. If she wasn't what he needed, would he leave her behind in a foreign country? What would she do then? But she didn't want to spend the rest of her days playing nursemaid to this man. Not when Lord Domac wanted her, and she wanted him.

'I will find you a good wife,' she pressed.

'I don't want a wife,' he repeated.

'But you want me. Why?'

He sighed as he looked out at the ocean. 'When I was young, I met a woman with a terrible life. We found happiness together despite that. At least for a time.'

'Grace's mother.'

He nodded, though his gaze was abstract. 'I could not save her. I tried, but...' He lifted up his cup and tipped it over. Two drops of tea splatted on the deck. 'I did not have enough money to save her.' He looked at her. 'I have enough money now. So I went back to China. I paid the monks silver. Lots and lots of silver.' He leaned forwards. 'And so I saved you and Grace.'

'But why? We are not her.'

He smiled. 'Why? Because you came. Because I could. Why did the monks take care of you as a baby?'

'So we would grow up to serve the temple.' And they had. She'd even seen the silver that Lord Wenshire had given the monks. Thanks, he'd said, for bringing him his daughter.

'And now you wonder what you owe me.' He tilted his head. 'Why has it taken you so long to ask me these questions?'

Because her command of English was not as good back then. And because she was afraid of being left behind. She was afraid of what he truly wanted, and she'd had no real desire of her own except to stay with Grace. But now she wanted Lord Domac. And to bargain for him required her to know what Lord Wenshire wanted so she could provide it. That's how transactions were done.

'Lucy, I could not save the woman I loved, but I could save you and Grace.'

'To what end?'

He stroked his knuckles along her jaw. She allowed it because there was no lust in his eyes when he did it. It was a simple gesture of tenderness.

'So that when I die and go to meet my maker, I can point to something good that I have done with my life. I can look at you and at Grace and know that I made a difference in your lives.'

As if to emphasise the point, the cough that often plagued him came back. It was a dry rattle, barely heard above the surrounding noise. He needed more tea. Something with healing leaves, but she did not have medical knowledge. That had been someone else at the temple. The most she had done was get him the right ingredients.

'You have helped me,' she said, her words earnest. 'I shall always love you,' she said, wondering if she lied. 'But if I am to be a good daughter to you, then I should marry and give you grandchildren. Boys to play at your feet and girls to make you smile and bring you—'

'Tea?' he rasped.

She wasn't sure if he was finishing her sentence or asking for her to fetch him more. 'Would you like another drink?' she asked.

'Let's go down below and make it together,' he answered. 'And get out of this beastly sun.'

She readily agreed. It seemed as if he were softening, pleased with her affection. With a little more daughterly attention, he might agree to give her what she wanted. So they went together to the galley. She helped him sit when another coughing fit gripped him. And she heated more water for tea. The tea leaves weren't even as good as what was served at the temple, but it was all she found. And she served it to him as if he were the emperor himself.

He patted her hand and drank, his fit easing the longer she sat with him. But eventually she grew impatient.

'I want to honour you,' she said, 'for the kindness you have shown me. What do you need from me—'

'Nothing, Lucy. You don't have to serve me or pay me anything. That is not why I brought you out of China.'

'But you want me to be happy, yes? And you want to be remembered and honoured. Grandchildren will do that for you. They are the greatest legacy of all.' She took his hand and squeezed it. 'That is what you want, isn't it? A good legacy?'

He nodded slowly, his expression wary. 'It is,' he slowly acknowledged. 'But I do not think you understand what that means.'

Maybe not, but she had a good guess. 'I will give you grandchildren,' she vowed. 'Little boys who praise your name. Girls who will bring you honour. I can give you what you want—'

'But only if I let you marry Lord Domac?'

She smiled. 'He is who I want.'

'And you mean to bargain with me for him. Give you the dowry he wants, and you shall marry him and live happily ever after. Yes?'

'Yes.'

'No.'

The finality of the word hit her heart. There was such firmness in it that she knew he hadn't softened at all. Had she pushed too hard? Did he need something else?

'Lucy, you think that you need a dowry to be valuable. You are enough of a treasure.'

'But he needs the boat! He will not marry me without it.' That much she'd already understood. He was a fortune-hunter, and so she needed a fortune.

'Then he does not see that you are the treasure.' Her father sighed. 'And neither do you, apparently. Don't you want to be loved?'

Fancy words, idealistic words. Words that she thought only children believed. And yet here was this aging Englishman who adopted foreign girls and spoke in such ignorance of the world.

'I want a man who will not beat me. I want a man who lets me help him earn coin. And I want his children to love. Lord Domac will do that.'

'Or any of a hundred others. Wait until you are in London. You will meet other good men there.'

'Let Grace meet all the other men. Give me her dowry so I may have the man I choose.'

He shook his head. 'Even his own family calls him inconsistent. He may truly love you now, but it will not last. I will not make it easy for him to marry either of you.'

'But you have given Grace the dowry he wants.'

'She knows her worth. If he earns her respect, then perhaps I will allow the marriage. But you still think you have to buy your future from everyone else.'

'But he doesn't want her! He wants me.'

'I'm sorry, Lucy. You don't know your own value yet, and until you do, no husband will make you happy.'

She rocked back on her heels, angry and frustrated to the point of clenching her hands into fists. She would not hit him. That would risk everything she had to no point. But she was angry and had no way to express it.

'You don't understand!' she cried. 'How can I find value when you give me nothing!' It was a ridiculous statement. He had given her a way out of a country that reviled her. He had given her food and clothing. Even now he promised to care for her in his home country. That was a safe life. It was a good life.

But it was not a life with Lord Domac. And that was what she wanted.

'Grace does not want him!' she cried.

'Then maybe he will wait for you.'

Maybe. But she did not trust in maybes. And she knew that men had short attention spans.

'How long?' she finally rasped. 'How long must I wait? How long before you dower me?' Assuming he dowered her at all.

Her father sighed and looked away from her. She recognised the look. He was calculating things in his head, and she had to wait while he weighed her worth like pebbles on a scale. In that moment, she hated him for doing this to her. But she had no other option.

Finally, he decided. 'One year,' he said. 'We will arrive in London in time for a Season. Grace will come out first, of course. That will be her time. Yours will be the next year. That is the way things are done in England. The eldest goes first.'

It was the same in China, but it didn't make sense. 'Grace does not want a husband. I do.'

'Grace may change her mind. She cannot run the riggings forever. She must grow up, as well.'

'But she doesn't want—'

'One year, Lucy. If he loves you, he will wait.'

Chapter Nine

Cedric groaned as he climbed up to the main deck of the ship. It was late and he ached from head to toe. Never in his life had he worked as hard as he had in the last couple weeks.

He'd done everything he could to impress Grace. He didn't want to climb the riggings to earn her respect. He didn't want to sit frozen in terror in the crow's nest. And he sure as hell didn't want to scrub, haul or tie off any of the millions of things sailors had to do on a routine basis.

But it was the only way to gain the woman's respect and—hopefully—her dowry. Which would give him and his sisters a lifeline. Or so he hoped. And so he worked until his hands were bloody and his back ached.

And yet when he climbed into his narrow space between the spice cargo and the wall, all he could think about was the woman he'd kissed in this tiny space. How she'd felt in his arms and what he'd promised her only to have to take it back a few hours later.

It made him sick of himself. And so he left his berth to go up top. He needed to get some fresh air and maybe a fresh perspective. Because what he was doing now was hell.

He saw her immediately. Of course he did. And maybe, deep in his heart, he'd known she'd be there staring into the inky black water. Maybe she was wondering why he had abandoned her. He'd tried to explain, but how could she understand that his family faced starvation?

He stepped onto the deck, and she turned at the sound. Would she come to him? Talk to him? God, he hoped so. But she didn't. A moment later, she turned her gaze back towards the water.

He tried to resist joining her, but it was a futile effort. Lucy drew him even when she did nothing to call him forwards. Or maybe that was why. She was a quiet soul who noticed everything, and he had long since learned that those were the souls who knew things that no one else did. Whereas he spent much of his time entertaining those around him with noise and a quick wit, the quiet ones watched and learned things that could only be seen over time and at a distance.

And because he could never bear to be ignored by anyone, he found himself drawn to quiet souls. He wanted to draw them out, he wanted them to share a laugh with him, and he desperately wanted their love. Such was his nature.

At least that was what he told himself. It was the only

explanation he had for why he ached for her so desperately when all logic told him to leave her alone. He had chosen her sister, after all.

'If you are looking for a mermaid,' he said, 'I promise they are none so lovely as you.'

She jolted, clearly startled by his words. He suppressed a pang. He had not been subtle in his approach.

'My apologies,' he said. 'I did not mean to startle you.'

'You did not startle me. I did not expect compliments from you.'

His brows went up. 'Did you think I would insult you?'

She turned to face him. 'I don't know if you still care for me.'

'Of course I care for you.' She would likely be his sister-in-law. 'And I would never lie to you. Certainly not about your beauty.' He gave her a wistful sigh. 'You will have men tripping over themselves for you in London.'

'I don't want men tripping on me.'

She didn't understand the expression, and the comedy of the image gave him a surprising jolt of humour. But rather than focus on that, he leaned back against the railing. 'What were you thinking about, just then?'

'That I cannot change my father's mind. I have tried every way I can think of, but he will not give me this boat.'

He nodded. 'I know.'

She touched his arm, the gesture bold for her. 'But I

can earn us money. I have worked with merchants all my life. I am a good saleswoman. And with the books, I can show you where to make money. There will be a good profit from the spices. Father says I can have that, at least. In my dowry.'

'I know. You should make a nice sum.' Enough to pay for a few dresses. Outfits for her Season, if she economised well. 'But it is not enough. I must marry a fortune.'

'You do not believe I can do it.' Her voice was low. Almost a growl.

'I do believe it,' he said honestly. 'You find it fun. I think you would balance accounts for free.'

She shrugged. 'I did do it for free at the monastery. I could make you an excellent profit.'

He didn't doubt that, but he didn't have the time. He had an idea how bad things were at home. His sister's letter had taken five months to find him. God only knew how much worse it might be now.

He needed this boat. He couldn't take the time that Lucy needed to build enough equity for him to save his family.

'Back when I was in school,' he said. 'I ran around with boys who gambled, boys who had a great deal more than I did.'

She didn't ask what happened. It was in her expression as she matched his pose, leaning against the railing and angling her head to his.

'Flush with coin one day, completely let out the next.'

He shook his head as he remembered. 'Do you know what happened?'

He had her attention. He did not need to ask, but he found he wanted to hear her voice. And so he held back until she spoke.

'Tell me,' she said. 'Please.'

How sweet that word was on her lips.

'Every waking moment, I thought of nothing but money. How could I get more, when could I gamble with it. You would think that when I was flush, I would be a generous, carefree man.' He shook his head. 'I wasn't, though sometimes I pretended to be. I counted every penny, I measured every man by his coin and how I could get some of it.'

She nodded. 'I know many such people.'

'I was miserable. As was everyone I gambled with. We drank, we had a jolly good time while doing it, but eventually, it consumed us.'

'The gambling?'

'The money. Everything was money. Win or lose, everything was money, and I hated it. I'd lost the ability to laugh purely because something was funny, to sing because it was joyful.' He looked to her mouth, a soft bud hidden in shadow. 'To kiss a girl because she is beautiful.'

It was too dark to see if her cheeks flushed, but he thought they did. He imagined she was remembering. That her body was heating, and her thoughts were on something a great deal more intimate than their conversation.

'Did you quit gambling?'

'For the most part. Penny stakes sometimes, but the temptation is always there. I need more money, you see. A lot more money.'

'Why?'

'For my sisters' dowries. To repair the estate. To keep all of us—my family and our retainers—in food and good cheer. None of that can happen without coin.' He stretched an arm out towards India. They'd been on the ship together for more than a month and had only recently left that coastline on their way to Egypt. 'It's why I came to India. I wanted to learn how to make more coin.'

'But you left without any,' she said. 'I heard you in the marketplace. You gave your last rupee to that boy.'

He nodded. 'I didn't like how they made their money. Graham is the best of fellows, and even he was turning mean. Squeezing work out of peasants. Insulting artists to steal their work for pennies, then sell it for thousands back home.' He sighed. 'If such a thing turned Graham mean, I would become a monster within a month.' He looked down at his hands. 'I must find another way.'

'You think you are too kind to do it?' she asked.

'I think their way of making money will turn me cruel. Just as gambling did.'

'Then I will do it,' she said. 'I will make the money, and you can help your family.'

She didn't understand. 'You cannot make it fast enough for what I need.' He twisted so that he looked at her more directly. 'What I need to know from you is something else.' He touched her chin so that she met his gaze. 'How do you make money fun?'

'What?'

He winced, struggling to express his words. 'You love it. You bargain like a native even when you don't know the language. And when you are done, everyone seems happy, you included. You do not doubt yourself and you don't hoard. How is this possible? When you are so sweet?'

She didn't answer. Her expression was open, but her brows were tight as she probably tried to sort through his foreign words. He sighed. He was being foolish to imagine anyone had the answers he sought. If Graham had no answer for him, then what could a half-Chinese woman know?

He heard nothing for a long while. Just the beating of his own heart to the steady drumbeat of despair. And then her touch. Fingertips skating across the back of his hand in a stroke so gentle, he had to close his eyes to be sure the sensation was real.

'I learned,' she finally said. 'From a boy named Ah-Lan. He is the one who saved me when I was dying.'

Chapter Ten

'There was a boy at the temple,' Lucy said, trying to put her thoughts into foreign words. 'He was older than me. If he had been of normal parents, he would have studied with a doctor. It was his joy to tend to hurts and to make the sick more comfortable. But because he was a half person like me—'

'You are a whole person,' Cedric interrupted.

'Yes,' she said quickly. 'Yes, I know.' But she had grown up thinking of herself as a half. It was hard to adjust her words.

'Good,' he said, his tone gentler. 'Now tell me more about this boy.'

'I was older then. No longer watching children and catching thieves.'

'How old?'

Old enough to have breasts and hips. Old enough to know how men would have looked at her if she dressed provocatively, which she did not. And yet some people still saw. And since her status as a half person was stamped upon her face, many thought that gave them permission to do as they willed with her.

'Old enough to know better,' she said. 'We do not go out at night,' she said, meaning all the half people like her. It was too dangerous. 'But I was making money for the silk merchant. I was bargaining between him and a ship's captain outside of the official halls.'

She saw his face tighten down. He understood that all commerce occurred in specified halls in the Thirteen Factories district. And every transaction was overseen by the emperor's men. They watched every exchange with foreigners, and naturally, they took their cut from every bargain.

So it was that greedy merchants and whites alike wanted to make secret deals without the interference of the overseers. And if she were willing to help, then she too could make a lot of money. But it was against the law, and the emperor's men protected themselves.

Black market sales were profitable, but they were also very, very dangerous.

'You were caught?' he asked.

She nodded. 'I trusted the wrong person. He said the officials would not be there that night, but he lied.'

'What did they—' He cut off his question, then rephrased it. 'How badly were you hurt?'

'Not as bad as you fear. The monks taught all of us half—' She caught herself at his arched look. 'All of us children to fight. It is not normal to teach anyone but the monks, but one of them believed we needed to know. Especially the girls. We needed to defend ourselves.'

'He sounds like a good man.'

'Yes.'

His expression softened. 'So you were able to fight them off?'

'Not all. My arm was twisted, but I ran.' She demonstrated how her shoulder had been wrenched in her escape. 'I stumbled because...' She swallowed. She'd never forget the stunned shock of having a knife sink hilt deep into her thigh. At first the pain hadn't even registered. She only knew she couldn't scramble to her feet as usual.

But she had to run. She was dressed as a boy. If they discovered she was a girl, then that would be the end of her. In the most hideous way.

'How bad?' asked Lord Cedric, his voice a harsh rasp.

She looked up to see a sick fear on his face and she was quick to reassure him. 'A knife in my leg. The scar is there still, and I can no longer run fast. I might have died from the loss of blood, but I still ran. And ran. And ran.'

'You escaped?'

'Yes. But I could not go back to work in the morning. They would know who I was because I could not walk. They would know what I had tried to do.' She looked back out at the dark water. 'I worked so hard to become a trusted worker in the halls. I had found a place. I made money. I had respect despite my face.'

'They would never fully respect you,' he said. 'Not as a woman.'

'They thought me a boy.' A half boy, but still one of them. 'In one night, I lost everything because I wanted money.'

'But you needed the money. You needed to survive somehow.'

'All the more reason to follow the rules.' But she had been greedy.

He sighed as he joined her in staring down at the water. 'What did this boy tell you?'

'That I should not have pulled out the knife.' At his startled look, she explained. 'I didn't bleed much until I pulled it out.'

'Oh.'

'But I was close enough to the temple by then.'

'He took care of your wound?'

She winced at the memory. 'It was painful.'

'I imagine so.'

'There was a fever, too. That began the next day.'

'Infection.'

'Infection,' she said, testing out the English word. 'Illness.'

'Yes,' he confirmed.

And when he remained silent, she moved on to the reason she had shared this painful memory with him.

'He told me to love what I love but remember that it will not love me back.'

He frowned. 'I do not understand.'

'I loved the buying and selling. A day in the factories district was exciting. Always something new to bargain over. I loved that they needed me to speak. To say yes or no, and that sometimes I would be given extra coin for a difficult negotiation.' She grimaced. 'I had that every day, but still I wanted more.'

'More money?'

'I thought so, but I was wrong.' She turned to him. She had never said this out loud. Worse, she had no carefully constructed words to hide the truth. And so she gave it to him baldly. 'I wanted to be loved. I loved the bargaining, and I thought with more money, I could make more bargains.'

'That's how it works.'

'But that is not love. More bargains did not love me back.' She grimaced as she thought of what happened afterwards. 'Ah-Lan got me work with the monks to manage their business. It was work I had done before, counting and recording things in the storeroom. He told them as a woman, I could not work in the district anymore. So they set me to work in the temple for no coin at all.'

It had been a bitter pill to swallow, but the only way she could survive. And since she worked daily in the temple again, she saw Ah-Lan daily, as well.

'In time,' she admitted, 'I was allowed to bargain for

the temple. It was not for the same amount of money. It was not fast like in the halls. But I still had my love for it even though I received no coin at all.' Did he understand what she was saying? 'I love the barter of a thing for coin and a coin for a thing. If I make money, if I do not, it does not matter. It is fun. I love it, but it does not give me love.' That was a hole that had to be filled in a different way.

'I see,' he said slowly, and she wondered if he really did. 'Did this boy, this Ah-Lan give you love?'

She flushed, embarrassment heating her cheeks.

She'd thought so, yes. She believed that what she and Ah-Lan shared was true love, but in the end, what he loved was more important to him. Despite all the time they'd spent together, he left her and the temple behind. He had a chance to learn medicine in the mountains far from Canton. He'd met someone who would teach even a half person. And so he'd left Lucy behind.

Which was why, when Lord Wenshire came, she joined Grace and left China behind.

'I can see from your face that he did.'

'For a time. I thought so.'

'Was he the only one?'

'What?'

'Was he the only boy to give you love? The only soul who showed you tenderness?'

'The monks were kind to us. They raised us, taught us. There was love there.'

'The love of a parent to a child.'

She nodded.

'But this boy—'

'Yes,' she finally admitted. 'Yes, he was the only man to show me that kind of...' Her throat closed down. She could not say the word *love* out loud. Not when it was gone.

'There will be others, you know,' he said, his voice gentle.

She shrugged. She had known Ah-Lan all her life, but they'd become close in the last year before he left. When she was a young woman and he a young man, for all that Lord Domac called him a boy. They'd been teenagers together, and she'd thought Ah-Lan would be everything.

She hadn't even realised she was looking down until she felt his hand on her cheek. His thumb stroked across her jaw, and his fingers gently pressed her chin up until she looked into his eyes.

'There will be others,' he repeated firmly. 'People who will make you feel as he did.'

'You did,' she said. 'You do.' He looked anguished, but no more than she felt. So she took his hand and pressed it against her cheek. She held him there and she looked into his eyes. 'I am worth it,' she said, though she wasn't even sure what 'it' was.

'Yes, you are.'

She knew that he was going to kiss her long before his mouth descended towards hers. She knew from the heat in his gaze and the way he leaned closer to her.

He tilted her head for a better angle, and she gave no resistance. Indeed, she helped him as she stretched up towards him.

Neither of them spoke as he stroked his thumb across her lips, but oh, how she wanted to give voice to the feelings inside. How could she give sound to the way she desperately wanted to be touched? How could she express the swelling, the hunger and the aching please, please, please?

He pressed his mouth to hers. He did not rush her, nor did he need to force anything. She was more than willing to let his lips brush back and forth across hers, then again with firmer pressure. And when she pressed closer to him, he deepened the contact.

He slipped his tongue between her lips, darting inside and pulling back. Inside harder, before slipping away. Each time she opened wider for him, and she tried to capture his tongue with hers. Twisting and turning, she tried to bind him, but he always slipped back and away.

By the fifth time he pulled back, she gave a mew of distress. She liked the way he thrust inside her mouth. She wanted him to keep touching her teeth, the roof of her mouth, and the deepest places that he could reach. Which was to say nothing of the way his hands slid to her bottom and pulled her tighter against him.

By the eighth time he wrenched apart from her, he pressed himself against the railing. 'I am playing with fire,' he gasped.

She felt like a living flame. From the tips of her curled toes through the aching heat in her belly to the way her heart pounded a steady refrain of more, more, more, she felt alive with need.

And it felt *wonderful*!

He turned to her then, his gaze roving over her face and lower. Did he know that her breasts had swelled, that her nipples were tight and aching? Did he see that she ached lower and deeper? Apparently so, because his eyes widened, but then he shook his head.

'I cannot have you,' he said. 'And I cannot give you what you want.'

'But I can give you what you want!'

'God,' he said in a groan, 'how I wish that were true.'

Then he backed away. After a very stiff bow, he turned and went below.

Chapter Eleven

The last months on board were torture. Cedric spent every moment trying to gain Grace's favour. Never in his life did he think he would have to work so hard to charm his future countess. Unfortunately, Grace was from China. She had no understanding of the consequence of his title or that she should feel honoured by his attention. Instead, she made him work for every ounce of attention she gave to him.

And work he did. Captain Banakos put her in charge of his education. He'd made the mistake of saying how he wanted to become a competent sailor. He meant that he'd like to stand next to the captain and listen to his commands, learning from him. Instead, the man gave him to Grace who made him perform every filthy, difficult task on board.

It was humiliating, mostly because he was rubbish at everything. But he learned. And he didn't complain. And eventually, he gained everyone else's respect, if not Grace's.

Nevertheless, that was a new and welcome experience for him. He was respected not because of his title but because of the things he knew how to do. And he knew them all. By the end of the month, he knew every rivet, cask and bolt hole on *The Integrity*. And Grace had begun to smile at him.

Progress.

Or so he told himself because truthfully, after every day spent sweating under Grace's watchful eye, he crawled back into his cramped bed between the bulkhead and boxes of spices, and he dreamed of Lucy. He told himself that he'd had many women over his short lifetime, and she was simply the latest infatuation. Nothing more. And yet, he couldn't stop dreaming about her kiss. Or the way she looked when she'd been negotiating for the spices.

And wasn't that odd? Usually, he'd dwell on the sweet worship in her eyes whenever she looked at him. But no, when he closed his eyes, he saw her come alive as she dickered about prices.

Obviously, the heat and the exertion were affecting his mind. He needed to return to England where he was a respected aristocrat, where his hands ached from writing, not hauling on ropes. And women did not threaten to whip him if he didn't swab the deck to their satisfaction.

But since England was still in the far distance, he decided to bring a bit of the aristocracy to the boat. He suggested it that evening at the captain's table.

'Lord Wenshire, is it your intention that your daughters will have Seasons when we get to London?'

'Indeed, it is. I look forward to seeing them decked out in the finest English fashion.'

'Then you should look to France for the designs,' he drawled. 'The *ton* forever follows Paris in that regard. Even with the mad Corsican interrupting things.'

Lord Wenshire had no comment. Given his attire, he was not a man who cared overmuch about clothing.

'And...' he said, 'they will need to learn to dance. Can't attend a ball without knowing the basics.'

'Yes, yes,' the man said. 'I intend to engage a dancing instructor as soon as we land.'

'But why wait? I learned my paces in the nursery. I stood partner to each of my sisters as they grew.' Not that his sisters had had a Season or even attended a London ball, but that was why he was courting Grace. So that he could change all that.

Meanwhile Lord Wenshire appeared to like the idea. 'That's an excellent suggestion. I'm too old to prance about now,' he said, 'but I can hum a tune for you. If my cough isn't acting up.'

Cedric grinned. 'Then I say there is no time like the present. Captain Banakos, will you stand as our fourth for the quadrille?'

The captain was game, as were several of his mates. The only one not thrilled was Grace.

'Dancing has never been one of my loves,' she

groused. 'I'd rather be in the crow's nest watching for—'

'Of course you would,' her father interrupted. 'But there'll be no need to watch the horizon in London. And you will be required to dance.'

'Come on, Grace,' Lucy said, her tone coaxing. 'It will be fun.'

'What it will be,' Grace returned dryly, 'is a chance for Lord Domac to get even with me for trussing him up like a fat duck when he climbed the rigging.'

His eyes widened in surprise. Had Grace just made a joke? Perhaps she was finally thawing to his suit.

'I swear there will be no ropes for this,' he said with his most charming smile. Then he pushed back from the table and held out his hand to her. 'Miss Richards, would you honour me with this dance?'

Out of the corner of his eye, he saw Lucy's hand twitch. She wanted to be his partner, and indeed, she was the more delightful sister. But she did not have the dowry, and so his smile didn't falter when Grace slapped her palm down on his in the most unfashionable way.

'I am not a barrel of whisky to be tied down,' he chided. 'Remember, Miss Richards, you will be a London debutante. Pray smile and curtsy before me as if you were pleased with my company.'

She grimaced but did as she was told. Sadly, everyone could see that her heart wasn't in it. Not so for her sister. When Captain Banakos stood before her and bowed, Lucy accepted his invitation with a dimpled smile. And when she curtsied, her skirt flowed about her ankles in a tantalizing display.

Grace, on the other hand, was wearing sailor's breeches, and so looked ridiculous pretending her loose shirt and trousers were a ball gown.

Nevertheless, he persevered. And honestly, she danced well. Her natural athleticism meant she mastered the steps quickly, though her memory faltered. She wasn't interested in learning the intricacies of the dances, only the rote steps and for that, she lacked style.

Her sister, on the other hand, started as a shy dancer. She bit her lip as she concentrated, which was adorable. But once she memorised the steps, she began to enjoy herself. She grinned, her happiness obvious. And when Cedric clasped her hand in the quadrille, she squeezed him in a way that called to mind their many kisses. She was a woman who held on, and he liked the idea of that.

Grace was too independent, and he was tired of wooing a disinterested woman. But that was the cost of being an adult. He'd tried all the other ways to make coin. Marriage to money was the only path left to him, and so he refocused his thoughts on Grace.

'Perhaps a waltz,' he suggested when it was clear Grace was thinking of other things.

Her father frowned. 'Isn't that a scandalous dance?'

'Goodness no,' he lied. 'At least not by most of society. The sticklers will always find something to criticise.' He held his hand out to Grace. 'It is an easy dance on a three beat.' He demonstrated the steps. 'Da, dum, dum, da, dum dum.' Then he pulled her into his arms.

She went stiff and though neither of them wore gloves, she felt as far removed from him as if she wore thick furs. She was rigid, if not awkward, and when her father took up the tune, Cedric tried to cajole her into a better frame of mind.

'When you are in London, you will be dancing every night. It is the lifeblood of the *ton* and every girl's delight.'

She frowned at him. 'Every night? But why? I thought my father said I would be with the people who lead the country. Who make decisions about laws and such.'

'Well, yes. That is what the men do. The women dance. And they talk and make decisions about…well, about what is proper behaviour.' At least he thought so. He wasn't clear on what women discussed.

She frowned as she mulled over his words, then she shook her head. 'It is hard to talk when dancing.' Then she flashed him a polite smile. 'But you are kind to teach me. Especially if I must learn it.'

A dismissal if ever he'd heard one. And damn, if that wasn't the most aristocratic thing she'd ever done. He'd been dismissed in the politest way possible. But at least disinterest was better than disdain, which was where they'd started. So that was progress, right?

He would count this as a win. And so he smiled warmly down at her only to stop as her father began to cough. The man did not sound well and everyone in the room heard it. Grace turned to her father, concern etched in her face. Same for the captain and Lucy, who had been waltzing beside them.

'No, no,' Lord Wenshire gasped. 'Keep dancing. I'll be fine. In a minute.' And indeed, his voice grew stronger as he spoke.

Nevertheless, Grace stepped away from Cedric, going to her father to put a gentle hand under his elbow.

'I'm tired, Father. Perhaps we could talk as I head to my bed.'

A lie if there ever was one, but a polite one nonetheless. Her father smiled warmly at her. 'Don't be afraid. I shall live long enough to settle my affairs in London. I won't die and leave you both stranded.'

Cedric winced. He had no idea if either girl had thought about their future if Lord Wenshire passed unexpectedly. But Cedric had, and he'd brought up the possibility in private with the man. He'd done so honestly, to offer his aid in case the unthinkable happened. Though what he could do to help was as limited as his funds.

Lord Wenshire had not taken it well. He'd dismissed Cedric's offer with an annoyed wave, but then he'd baldly stated his intentions in front of the girls. Cedric tensed, watching both women closely. If they were shaken by the idea of their father's death, neither showed it. Grace continued to guide her father to his bed while Lucy promised to search the kitchen stores in hopes of a soothing tea.

As if discussing one's demise was a natural thing.

Meanwhile, the captain bowed out, claiming he had work to do and the other officers disappeared. That left Cedric alone in the galley while Lucy headed for the kitchen stores.

'I'll help you,' he said because he couldn't keep himself away from her. He'd been secretly looking forward to waltzing with her even when he knew he shouldn't.

He followed her to the galley stores. They searched through everything but knew there wasn't anything there. He had no understanding of herbs so he couldn't even identify what was there. Her knowledge was equally sparse and so they ended up staring at each other in confusion.

And there he saw her true reaction to Lord Wenshire's statement. Fear etched hard lines on her face, and so rather than fruitlessly looking through jars he couldn't identify, he sought to comfort her instead.

'Humming likely strained his throat. He'll be fine after a good night's rest.'

She looked at him, her eyes hard. 'Do the ladies in England accept lies so easily?'

He sighed. Polite lies were the stock and trade of the *ton*, but she had a point. Burying her head in the sand would not help her. It was possible that her father would die sooner rather than later, and then she would be alone in a very big world.

'I swear I will help you if he cannot.'

She dropped her hands on her hips. 'And how can you help me if all your plans are for my sister?'

It was a peevish statement, but he understood its cause. 'She will go nowhere without you. You know that.'

Frustration built in her face until he thought she might hit him. Instead, tears filled her eyes as her fists balled on her hips.

'I hate this! Why does she get the dowry? You don't want her!'

He had thought the same thing a thousand times, but he had come to terms with the statement.

'She is his blood kin,' he said gently. 'It's only natural that he give his coin to her.'

'But she's not!' she exclaimed. 'We are the same! Two half children. She is a little too old to be his child, and I am a little too young. Neither of us—' She cut off her words at his shocked face. And then her eyes widened as she pressed a hand to her mouth.

'I didn't mean to say that,' she whispered. Then she squared her shoulders. 'You are right, of course. Grace is his daughter. She's the right age. I am just an extra piece of baggage hanging around her neck.'

Another lie, though the emotions were the same. 'You are not baggage,' he said, his words careful. 'And she is not his child.'

'Of course she is—'

'The monks lied,' he realised as he made the logical

conclusion. 'They heard a white man would take an orphan off their hands and offered up you and her. They likely never even looked for his true child.'

'If the child survived, it would have gone to the temple like the rest of us. There is no other place for us.'

He nodded. 'There is now. You are here. You have a father who cares for you.'

She dashed away tears that seeped from her eyes. 'I shouldn't have come. I should have stayed at the temple and waited for Ah-Lan to return.'

He hated the sound of another man's name on her lips but consoled himself that this horrible Ah-Lan was far, far away.

'You are here now. You have a new life ahead of you. And your father has a simple cough—'

'That has plagued him for months.'

He nodded. 'That happens. You know it does. His lungs are weak, but he will get better once he is on English soil.'

'You don't know that,' she said, her voice tight as she fought tears. 'And when he is gone, what will happen to me?'

The anguish in her voice destroyed him. It didn't matter that the danger was far-fetched. She was a woman used to being cast aside. And so he did the one thing he knew would help her.

He took her into his arms.

He pulled her tight against him as she cried against

his chest. He stroked her back and set his cheek against the top of her head.

'It's not so bad a gamble that you have taken,' he said. 'A frightening one, to be sure, but that just shows how brave you are.'

Her tears had slowed, but she wasn't able to speak yet. So he kept talking, keeping his voice soothing as he gave her his truth.

'Your father is a wealthy man who generously took you in. You need only trust him for a time. He has offered to care for you as a father, and you honour him as a daughter would.'

'I don't need a father,' she murmured against his chest.

'In this world, you do. At least until you have a husband. But never fear. Lord Wenshire has a great deal of life left in him. You'll see. And that gives you time to pick the perfect husband.'

It was the truth, but the knowledge ate at him. If only he had the time to wait for her. If only her father thought to give even half the dowry to Lucy, Cedric could find a way to make it work. If only his own father wasn't such a wastrel as to put Cedric in this position.

If onlys didn't help anyone.

He held her there, his thoughts turning darker by the moment. He was in an impossible situation. She was equally stuck. And they had no choice but to endure because that was what one did.

But there was some comfort to be found. Something

that would not damage her chances of a husband and perhaps would ease his own hunger for her. Something forbidden, and yet impossible to refuse.

She had stopped crying. She lay her head on his chest and fitted her body to his. How his body hungered for her.

'Lucy,' he whispered. 'We cannot wed. This only causes pain.'

She looked into his eyes. 'Kiss me,' she said.

He tried to be honourable. He knew his thoughts were going into a very dangerous place. But another part of him liked the idea.

If he ruined her, if they were caught together, would Lord Wenshire insist they marry? And would he dower her? Would that be a way to force her father's hand?

'Kiss me!' her words were a command, but still he resisted. He counted himself an honourable person. He did not want a wife by trickery, even one who fired his blood so fiercely.

He stroked his thumb across her cheek. He looked into her eyes and hungered. And he resisted.

'No,' he said.

'Yes,' she said.

Then she dragged his head down to hers and kissed him. More shocking still, she thrust her tongue into his mouth. It was like taking a knife to all his restraint. His basest desires broke free.

Chapter Twelve

Lucy knew the moment Cedric gave in. He'd been trying to spare her, believing that he knew better than she did what she wanted.

He didn't.

She knew she wanted his hands on her body, his tongue challenging hers and all the storm of feeling he created inside her. Nothing had ever felt as explosive as what he did to her now. And she never wanted it to end.

His tongue pushed against hers while her body tightened with the invasion. Heat burst across her skin and her head dropped back. She loved the way he dominated all her senses. He kissed across her jaw and down her throat. And when his hands found her breasts, she cried out in welcome.

Yes, yes, yes. Touch me there!

He squeezed her nipples and lightning pierced her womb, even through the dampening feel of her clothing. Always she had been afraid when someone touched her. She knew the dangers of such madness, but she knew him now. He would not hurt her.

And so she was the one who pulled open the buttons across her bodice. She unraveled the tie of her shift, and she shrugged her shoulders until dress and shift slipped down to bare her breasts.

He pulled back, his breath coming as fast as hers. His eyes were wild, but no more than hers. And while her heart beat fast in her ears, she could see the rapid pulse in his neck as he gazed down at her.

'Perfect,' he whispered. 'You're so damn perfect.'

His words sank into her heart. She felt perfect with the way he looked at her. And she needed to be perfect if she were to keep him. Her hand trembled as she caught his fingers and pulled them up to her breast. She wanted to feel his hands on her flesh with nothing between them.

He cupped her breasts. First one, then the other. She felt the new callouses on his fingers as he sweetly abraded her nipples.

'You don't understand,' he murmured. 'You think this is love.'

She barely heard him. She was so absorbed in the way he squeezed her breast, in the exquisite bite when he twisted her nipples. She wanted it to continue forever. And she wanted more. Her belly trembled and her knees softened. If she weren't leaning against the wall of the galley, she would collapse.

And still he tormented her. His left hand slid to her

waist, resting atop the bunch of fabric there. It took only a slight amount of pressure for him to tug her hips forwards, her back arching as she lifted her breasts to him. And to her delight, his mouth soon descended upon her flesh.

He flicked her nipple with his tongue, and when she gasped in shock, he sucked it into his mouth.

Such skill he had, sucking and flicking. Did he bite her? She didn't know. She was lost in a whirlwind of sensation that obliterated all thought.

She clutched at his shoulders, holding herself to him or him to her. Either way, she quickly began to want more. Soon she framed his head with her hands and brought his face up to hers.

'Make me yours,' she said.

Did she speak in Chinese? The shocked look he gave her made her frantic with frustration.

'I want to be yours,' she repeated.

He dropped his forehead to hers. 'You don't understand.'

'I do.'

'You don't know how powerful lust is.'

She didn't know that English word, neither did she care. She wasn't a child. But before she could say more, he abruptly stepped back. She would have cried out, but he pressed two fingers to her mouth.

'I'll show you,' he rasped. 'But not here.' He quickly pulled her gown up, but he didn't tie or button the clothing. Glancing through the galley door, he whispered, 'Come to my room when it is safe.'

She nodded, though she thought it safe now. Still, she would make sure her father and sister slept.

'I will show you,' he said one last time. 'If you can promise to be quiet.'

She flashed him a smile. 'I have always been quiet.'

'Not to me, you haven't. To me, you are a siren song. I cannot be rid of it.'

She grinned. 'Good.'

But it wasn't good to wait. He checked the hallway again. It was clear. So he gestured her on before he headed to his own cabin. She checked on her father. He was sleeping as was Grace on the floor beside him.

She woke her sister and sent her to bed. 'He will sleep soundly now,' she said. 'You don't need to lie here on the floor like a dog.'

Grace flashed her a sleepy smile. 'I have slept in worse places.'

They both had, but there was no need to do it now. 'Go on,' she said, gently pushing her sister out the door. 'I'll stay with him a while. Maybe even take a walk up top.'

'Can't sleep?' Grace asked after a huge yawn. 'You should run the sails with me. That will make you too tired to think.'

'No, thank you,' she said. 'My leg won't work well up there.' Then she pushed her sister towards their berth.

She waited for a time. Long enough that she was sure

that her father slept deeply. Long enough that Grace would be sound asleep. And long enough for her mind to question her choices.

Did she truly want to give her virginity to Lord Domac? It was a rarity that one such as her would still have such a prized thing. But she had been quick and careful for most of her life. And she'd also pretended to be a boy.

She truly ought to wait, but she wanted it to be her choice. She wanted the man to be her choice. She knew nothing was assured in her future. Why not give in to what she wanted now? And if it bound Cedric to her, then so much the better.

When she judged it time, she crept the two steps to his cabin and slipped inside the darkened interior. There was little room between the spice crates and his cot. Just the narrow crack as she crawled into his bed.

'Shut the door,' she heard him whisper.

She did, startled to realise that she was so distracted that she'd forgotten so elemental a thing.

'Take off your clothes,' he commanded.

There was barely room to kneel on his bed, much less strip. But he had been living in such a state for months now. She could hardly complain. And besides, it made her pulse race to hear commands through the dark. She imagined such things, and it was all the more thrilling—terrifying—exciting to unbutton her gown and push it aside. Her shift came next, her nipples tightening painfully in the cooler air. And then, awkwardly, her slippers. It was too hot to wear stockings, and so very soon, she knelt on his bed completely naked.

'I wish I dared light a candle,' he murmured.

'I can't see you,' she said.

'I am here, backed into my little corner.'

'Are you...' She didn't know the word *naked* in English. 'Are you like me?'

His snort was filled with derision. 'I am nothing like you, my dear. I am as corrupt as they come.'

She knew that wasn't true. She knew corruption, had seen the men who took and destroyed. He was not such a man.

'You know very little of ugly men,' she whispered.

'I do. And I have chosen you.'

He was silent for a long moment. And then she felt his fingers stroking across her arm. 'Thank you for that,' he whispered. 'No matter what happens between us, I will cherish your gift until my dying day.'

'I do not give it lightly,' she said.

'I know.'

He drew her forwards into the dark alcove. She could see nothing, but that only made the sensations all the more overwhelming. She felt the tug of his arm as she maneuvered her way in. She felt him twist her shoulders and struggled to move where he wanted.

'What do you want?' she asked, confused as he faced her back towards the door.

'You,' he answered. 'And your sister's dowry.'

She winced at the mention of money. That was not why she was here.

He stroked a hand up her back and she shivered at the caress. 'I must have that, Lucy. I cannot marry you.'

'We will find a way. I can make you a lot of money.'

This was old ground between them. Indeed, she was speaking by rote as she felt his lips kiss a trail across her shoulders.

'I can give you this,' he said as his teeth scraped across her neck. Then his hands slid around her ribs to cup her breasts. 'I can show you lust.'

She still did not know that word, but it hardly mattered. His hands were shaping her breasts, tweaking her nipples, and pulling her back against his front. He was as naked as she. She felt the heat of his chest, and the rough brush of his hair against her back. And she felt his thick, hot organ throbbing against her spine.

Her mind focused on that place. On the way his cock pressed against her bottom. On the pulse and slight wetness she felt there. And she worried for a moment if it would fit inside her.

Then he chased those thoughts away. He kissed along her shoulder, and he pulled at her nipples. And then he let one hand slide down. Down across her belly, which quivered against his large hand.

He surrounded her now, completely capturing her against him. She could not run if she wanted to, and her breath caught a moment in fear.

'Lucy?' he whispered against her.

'Yes,' she said, answering a completely different question. Yes, she wanted this. Yes, this was frightening but also thrilling. Yes, please keep going.

'Tell me to stop,' he said as his hand moved lower. His smallest finger teased the top of her curls. 'Tell me no.'

In answer, she widened her knees. She dropped her head back against his shoulder. She opened herself up to him for whatever he willed.

'So be it,' he said against her neck. And then his finger slid lower.

She bucked when his finger slid between her folds, but she kept her cry inside. Never had anything touched her there except a cloth held by her own hand. His finger was so alive as it pressed there. Moving and teasing while her body strained forwards and back, away and closer. She didn't know what she wanted. It was too much and too little.

'Shhh,' he said against her ear. 'You must be quiet.'

She knew that. But how could she contain her voice when every part of her was focused between her thighs? Even as he spoke, his finger pushed and explored.

She bit her lip. She felt him spread her wetness everywhere. And as her knees slid further apart, she felt his fingers press deep inside her.

She couldn't catch her breath. She tried to press her face against her shoulder to muffle her sounds, but there was no way to reach.

And so he withdrew.

She mewed in dismay, but then his hands slid down her arms to her wrists. He tugged her forwards so that she bent at the waist.

'Put your palms on the wall. Press your mouth against your arm.'

She did as he bid. And now she was effectively on all fours before him. He could touch her everywhere and she trembled as she stayed there, her mouth pressed against her arm.

Such things she felt. He touched her everywhere. He kissed her back, he kneaded her breasts, and he put his fingers between her thighs. He opened her petals there. He stroked her up and down. And he thrust his fingers inside.

And every time she thought she would lose control, every time the sensations became too much, he pulled away. He went back to her breasts, he pushed his fingers in and out of her, but he did not touch her at that spot—that incredible place—where he'd first begun to probe between her thighs.

Such wonder to have him surround her. His chest was pressed to her back. His hands were everywhere on her body. And low at her bottom was his shaft. So hot against the base of her spine.

Once, when he pressed his fingers deep inside her, she arched her back and he hissed. It wasn't pain. It was the same hunger she felt, and so she did it again. Soon, she heard him growl against her ear, and she knew she tortured him as much as he did her.

Until he abruptly shifted his position.

He didn't move her. He straightened up, setting his feet beside her lower legs where she knelt upon his bed.

'Keep quiet now,' he warned, his voice a low gravelly sound. 'We are going to do this, you and I.'

How big he was as he surrounded her. There was nowhere for her to move as his arms came around her, pinning her in place. His finger—so thick and calloused—rubbed up and down her folds.

Yes. Oh yes! She arched, reacting to the feel. She wanted more of that. She needed more!

She felt him thrust along her bottom, but he didn't go inside. His organ lay upwards along her spine, hot as he rubbed against her.

Faster, he went. Faster for them both. His finger on that spot. His organ against her back.

So much. She arched.

Yes.

Yes!

She cried out, muffling the sound against her arm. She went wild as pleasure burst through her body. Wave after wave. She drowned in wonder.

And while she was still pulsing, he grabbed hold of her hips. He held her back against him as he thrust against her spine.

Once, twice, while his breath rasped against her ear.

And then he shuddered and released his seed against her back.

Against her back.

It took a while for her to understand what he had done. They had shared what happened between man and wife, but he had not taken her virginity. He had not tied her to himself.

He had shown her pleasure while still holding himself apart.

She was still dazed. Her legs were weak, her body sagging as she pressed her hands against the wall. And he still lay atop her, his breath ragged in her ear.

But… But they hadn't done…

He hadn't taken her.

'You aren't mine,' she said, her voice soft.

'Because you can't be mine,' he whispered. 'But now you know.'

What did she know? She tried to twist to look at him, but he held her still.

'You know how to do this yourself,' he said as he pulled himself off her. A moment later, she felt a cloth gently brushing her back clean.

She waited, her thoughts slowly coming to order. 'I don't understand,' she whispered.

He pressed a kiss to her back. Then another and another. Little presses of his mouth before she heard him dispose of the cloth.

'I am teaching you lust,' he said. 'This…' He cupped her right breast. He fondled it, squeezing it and twisting the nipple. She wanted to pull away, but there was no room. And a moment later, she began to like it.

How quickly he built the need inside her.

'Touch yourself this way.'

When she didn't respond, he pulled one of her arms off the wall. He angled her hand until she cupped herself.

'Do what I did,' he said. 'Touch yourself how you like.'

She didn't move, but he guided her. He set his large hand around hers.

'Do it,' he commanded. And then she felt him grin. 'I want to feel you do it to yourself. I want you to come apart in my arms. I want to be the man who opens your body to lust.'

So that was what the word meant. This driving hunger. This excitement in body and mind. She had labeled it love. She had to love someone before she allowed such a thing between them.

But perhaps, not for him. Perhaps he could do this to her and not feel love.

Either way, it didn't matter. She would take what she could get. And this felt too good to stop.

He guided her to caress her breasts. He kissed her shoulders as her hands learned the way she wanted her nipples pulled. And then he pushed her hand down her belly and into her curls.

It was wet there and so sensitive. She wanted his fingers there, but he refused. He guided her to explore. He held her open and told her to stroke herself. And when the positioning became too awkward, he pulled her backwards.

He settled her on top of him, her head on his shoulder, her breasts open to the ceiling. He set her legs on either side of his and he spread her wide.

'Do whatever feels good,' he said. 'I will hold you safe.'

'But you—'

'I am in heaven, Lucy. Show me what you like.'

And so she did. At his urging, she touched herself. She pushed inside her own body as she had never done before. And she stroked herself until she writhed.

'If I cover your mouth with a pillow, will you scream?' he asked.

She would do anything he wanted. 'Yes.'

'Scream my name,' he said.

Easy. She had been crying it out in her thoughts for weeks now.

He still would not stroke her. He still insisted she do it to herself. So she spread her legs and pleasured herself while a small pillow lay over her mouth.

'Cedric,' she said as her belly began to tighten.

'Cedric!' she gasped as her legs tensed around his.

'Cedric!' she repeated as she pulsed upwards into her hand.

'Yes,' she gasped. 'Yes. Yes!'

I love you.

Chapter Thirteen

Cedric did not touch her again, not even to kiss her hand. Not before she crept silently back to her berth. Not in the morning when she looked at him with eyes so full of wonder. And not again for the rest of the journey.

He was too afraid of betraying what he had done with her. Someone would see that he couldn't look at her without wanting her. Someone would know that when he climbed into his berth at night, he still smelled her there even after her scent was long gone. Someone would know that the sound of her name made him weak in the knees.

He had called it lust. Indeed, he still believed that for her it was true. She was too innocent to know the pounding demands of the body. One handsome, considerate man was as good as another. It was only that he was the first man to ever give her attention as a woman deserved.

But he, on the other hand, knew the power of lust. He had indulged it too many times. And if this infatuation was built upon lust, indulging it—as they had done—should dissipate its power.

It had not. He nightly relived how she had come apart in his arms. How she had discovered her body under his guidance.

And since he could not think of touching her again without revealing all, he resolved to stay far away from her. Strict absence, he reasoned, would cool the fire.

In fact, it made it worse. He left whenever she entered a room. He took his meals with the sailors or on deck rather than sit at the captain's table with her. And so he longed for the briefest glimpse of her as he fled. And he turned over the sight of her wan face, examining it in his memory as if it held the secret to a pot of gold.

This was not like any lust he had ever experienced, but he refused to give it any other name. If he did, then he would never be able to court and marry her sister. If he felt anything more lasting than lust, then the idea of seeing her every holiday or family gathering would destroy him.

So he labeled it lust. He avoided her as if his future depended upon it. And he courted Grace with the kind of determination he'd never felt for anything else in his life.

Her father noticed the change. Indeed, everyone probably did, but it was Lord Wenshire who asked him point blank for an explanation.

His answer was equally blunt, if not the full truth.

'I mean to marry Grace. It does no good to encourage her sister's interest.'

Lord Wenshire approved of the statement, but he was clearly skeptical. 'You think Grace will have you?'

'She has shown me favour,' he said. It wasn't exactly a lie. Grace no longer tortured him. Indeed, she had recently begun complimenting his work and smiling when they spoke.

Her father, too, now looked at him with approval. 'I have been impressed with you these last months. I think your aunt did you a disservice with your Inconsistent One nickname.'

'I am no longer a child. If I was inconsistent before,' he said, 'it is not who I am now.' No truer words could be spoken. Months at sea had brought out a new strength in him. He appreciated the honest work on a boat. No peasants were beaten here. No overseer exploited the ignorant poor. They all worked together to move the ship from one place to the next.

'You like this work.' There was surprise in the man's tone.

'I do. And I will be a good steward of the ship and your daughter.' He meant Lucy, but of course her father thought he referred to Grace.

'If Grace wants you, I will allow it,' he said. Indeed, he went so far as to explain the details of Grace's dowry—the ship and the proceeds of this cargo. It was an extraordinary sum. One that would attract every fortune-hunter in England. Which meant he had to finalise his arrangement with Grace as soon as possible.

He thought for a moment about pressing again for Lucy. Perhaps an arrangement could be made. He opened his mouth to broach the possibility, but Lord Wenshire was there ahead of him. 'I knew that your infatuation with Lucy was a passing thing. And now she has seen it, too. But Grace knows her own mind. If you can secure her, then I will wish you both happy.'

Is that what Lucy thought? That he had been toying with her? He had been honest from the start. He had told her they could not wed. And though his chest squeezed tight at the thought of her hating him, he knew it was for the best. She was out of his reach. No point in belabouring that, no matter how much it hurt him.

And so he redoubled his efforts with Grace. Except Grace would not be finalised. Indeed, though she was never impolite, she was also never fully warm. And that, perhaps, would be how their marriage would stand. There were worse things, he supposed. Indeed, he knew of several love matches that fared much worse than polite disinterest.

So he contented himself with trying to woo her while remaining distant from her sister.

They continued in this manner until the very last day when she agreed to join him at the captain's table for dinner. No doubt her father had helped in that regard. Especially since everyone was aware of the timing. They were to dock in London tonight. If he wished to capture her hand before she was beset by every fortune-hunter in London, then he had to secure her promise now.

He knew, of course, that Lucy would be there, too. That would make things awkward, but eventually, they would become brother- and sister-in-law. They would have to find a way to get along. Might as well start that now. The dinner was very good, and that gave the evening a congenial air. And though he was excruciatingly aware of Lucy throughout the meal, Cedric gave her no more attention than he gave the moon outside the porthole. The conversation was pleasant as everyone discussed their plans once they arrived in London. Everyone, that is, except Cedric. His plans would depend on Grace.

Then, once the meal was done, Cedric escorted Grace to the deck to gaze at the moonlight. Well, he looked at the moonlight. She kept scanning the sails.

Best make his case quickly before he lost her attention. Catching her hand between his, he began to reiterate the things she already knew. He explained that upon his father's death, he would become an earl, which was a title that was respected throughout England. His wife, of course, would be a countess with equal consequence.

He was honest about his financial prospects, but reassured her that with her dowry, they would have an excellent life. Especially since he would honour his vows to her and treat her and their children well. That was his vow to her as he began to sink down on one knee before her.

She stopped him, using his grip on her hand to keep him standing. 'What about my sister?'

He froze, his mind blanking. 'Uh...'

'She will have a dowry, too. A large one.'

He flinched. Was it possible? Could he wait for Lucy to come of age? His heart lurched in his chest. 'You have been gone from England a long time, my lord. Neither of us knows what awaits us when we land.'

His sister's letter ran through his thoughts. He'd read it so many times, it was committed to memory. Of course, he'd imagined that he'd arrive home to find that everything had miraculously changed for the better. Just as he'd imagined the damaged roof coming down on their heads, killing everyone.

Unfortunately, Cedric was well versed in playing the odds. He knew his father would not change. Which meant that his sisters were in a miserable situation. Worse, the moment the word was out about Grace's dowry, every fortune-hunter in England would appear at her door. He couldn't risk the competition much as he might want to.

'I have made my choice,' he said through the constriction in his throat. 'Miss Richards,' he began, but he couldn't force the next words out. And his knees appeared to be locked. Why wouldn't they bend?

'I need more time,' she said, her words rushed. 'I need to learn your customs.'

'I can teach you whatever you need to know. And if not me, then my mother.' He nearly choked on that last bit. His mother would not treat a half-Chinese bastard well, but that was tomorrow's problem.

Time to drop to one knee. Time to propose. But his legs would not bend, and he kept thinking, what if he waited? Could he hold off disaster another year? Could he wait for Lucy?

And in his hesitation, he lost Grace. 'This is a very great honour,' she said, her words stiff. 'But I need more time.' Then, despite the fact that she wore a dress, she escaped his grip and scampered up the sails. She had to hike her dress up an indecent amount, but she did it anyway, no doubt to hide in the crow's nest.

Thank God it was dark, though he knew several people had watched the scene unfold. They did not see her bare legs. Nor could they mark his red face.

He had been denied. His last hope for his family snatched away.

He had tried gambling for coin, but that was a miserable, hateful existence. He had tried to work for it, but the East India Company was not the place for a moral man. And so he had done what generations of gentlemen did. He had tried to marry the coin. And even that had been refused.

The weight of his failure turned to acid in his gut. Why had he hesitated? He knew Lucy was lost to him.

He abruptly spun around and headed to his cabin. The captain tried to catch his eye, his expression sympathetic. He wanted none of it. He would not accept sympathy from a lowly captain. He was a future earl! And he should not have to beg for his bride!

He spoke to no one after that moment. He paused briefly to think of Lucy, but even her company was not welcome. Nothing could soothe the fury building in his heart. Nothing would stop the coming explosion.

Only one choice then. He had to leave as soon as they made port in a couple hours. He burst into his room, slowing just enough not to brain himself on the spice crates. Damn it, he was going to have to drop to his knees to grab his meager belongings from beneath his bed. He did so, cursing the delay. And when he had finally prepared everything so that he could leave as soon as they made port, he climbed back onto his berth, scooting backwards for his pillow, and lay down with his satchel on his lap.

Or rather, he landed in the lap of the one person he couldn't bear to think about much less see. Or touch. Or lie in her lap.

Chapter Fourteen

Lucy hid herself away in Cedric's berth. She knew he would come down here eventually. Knew too that this was the only way she could speak privately to him. Grace would spend the night in the crow's nest, trying to sort through her thoughts after that disaster of a proposal. Lucy had seen her father retire for the night. No one would know that Lucy hid herself in the pitch-black corner of Cedric's bed until he came in.

She waited in silence, feeling and hearing his foul mood. No man liked being refused. And the way he stormed into his room made her fear he'd wake her father.

His emotions blew through him quickly, his only violence done to himself when he banged his elbow against a crate. He cursed then, quickly and efficiently. But in time, he pulled himself together and maneuvered into his berth.

She had placed herself very specifically there, and

it was no surprise to her when he dropped backwards into her lap.

He, however, was shocked into sputtering. 'Wh-ahh!'

'Shhhh. You'll wake my father.'

'Lucy! You should not be here!'

'And where else should I be when you have worked so hard to avoid me? I have been waiting for a private word with you, but—'

'Damn it, Lucy, there is no point. This only tortures us both.'

There was a wealth of meaning in his words, but what Lucy focused on was that he felt as tortured as she. Which meant he had feelings for her. How deep those feelings were, she didn't know. But that was why she was here.

'I wouldn't have to resort to these things if you weren't such an idiot.'

He tried to sit up, but she held him down with both hands on his shoulders. This was a very small space, and she liked him exactly where he was. And he was too much of a gentleman to fight her. One of them would certainly get hurt.

'I'm not an idiot,' he huffed. 'I'm trying to do what's right. I can't marry you. My family—'

'Needs the money. Yes, I know. You've told me.'

'So why—'

'Hush,' she said as she pressed her fingers to his mouth. 'Listen to me.'

He quieted because he had no choice. And she took

a moment to relish the feel of his lips against her fingers and the weight of his head in her lap. It was a casual position despite the tension between them. And neither of them could distract themselves with each other's bodies. She would need to fold herself in half to effectively kiss him. And he would have to drag her down his body and twist her around somehow for anything that they both would enjoy.

That too was by design, though part of her regretted it. Especially since they had the time for an intimate encounter, and she missed his hands on her body.

She refocused her attention on what she wanted to say. Unfortunately, some of her irritation came out instead. 'I have had to sit for weeks, watching in misery while you courted my sister for her dowry. And now—finally—she has refused you—'

'It wasn't a refusal,' he groused. 'She said she needed more time.'

Lucy winced, though she'd known that would be her sister's response. She had spoken with Grace about it nearly every day and night since the man had begun courting her. She knew her sister felt no strong passion for Cedric. At least nothing like what Lucy felt, but that mattered little to either woman.

They had both been raised to expect little from life. They had been taught that passion was a danger that always ended in tragedy. And that the best any girl could hope for was a man who treated them kindly.

Cedric was a kind man. Even more than that, he was

honourable. If he were less honourable, Lucy would not be a virgin right now. Which meant he was a good husband candidate for them both.

The two women had dissected every one of Grace's encounters with him, from the way he climbed the sails to his grumbles when he didn't remember which kind of knot went where. They discussed his finances and their own. And they examined every minute detail of his character that they could discern.

Fortunately, Grace had spent hours every day with him, so there was plenty to discuss. Which allowed Lucy to keep silent about what she had done with him. Her experiences were too intimate, too intense for her to confess.

And so Grace was ignorant of Lucy's feelings, which was exactly how Lucy wanted it. If Grace chose him, then she would not stand in her sister's way. She loved Grace that much.

But her sister was undecided, and now they were out of time. The ship would make port in an hour, and Lucy wanted one last private discussion with him. So she needed to be brave and say exactly what was on her mind.

Still, it was hard, so damned hard to bare her heart.

'What I feel for you is powerful,' she whispered. 'It does not fade and…' She decided to use his word. 'It tortures me. Don't you feel that too?'

He sighed and the sound filled their tiny space with despair. 'It doesn't matter what I feel, Lucy. It cannot be.'

'But—'

'You are young in this.' He tried to sit up again, but she still held him down. And she kept holding him while he spoke words that hurt. The only reason she listened was because they were also true. 'You have never been free like you are now. You will go to London as the daughter of a wealthy, titled man. You will meet dozens of men. You might even fall in love with one of them.'

'I am in love with you.'

She felt his body react to her words. Shock. Pain. Not revulsion, as far as she could tell. But he didn't welcome it, and that was agony enough.

'You don't know what that is, Lucy,' he finally said. His voice was tight, his body even more so. 'You will have opportunities you've never had before. You cannot know what they are or how you will feel in a month or a year. Especially after you've had a Season.'

'I do not care about that. I know what I feel now. Don't you feel it, too?' A plaintive note had entered her voice, a desperate hope that he wanted her as much as she wanted him.

'I care. And I know.' His breath seemed ragged, but he kept speaking anyway, his words harsh with self-condemnation. 'I know that I have hurt you. I did not mean to, and I am so deeply sorry for that. I thought…' He exhaled. 'I was wrong. And this…this conversation does us no good.'

She swallowed, hurt making her voice brittle. 'I don't want you to be sorry. I want you to fix it.'

He snorted. 'Fix it? My God, what do you think I've been doing all my life? I'm trying to fix my family's problems! I'm trying to—'

'Listen!' she hissed as she squeezed his shoulders. 'Didn't you hear what Grace said? She needs more time.'

'Yes—'

'And so do you. You have been gone a long time. What if your sisters have found their own solution? What if things aren't as bad as you thought?'

'I don't know how that would be possible.'

Men! Sometimes they could be so stupid.

'Are they smart women?'

'Of course they are.'

'Then they know better than to wait for someone else to save them. They will have found a solution of their own.'

He was silent a long moment, clearly thinking. But in the end, he shook his head. 'I don't see how that is possible.'

'Did you see me sitting in your bed here?'

He jolted. 'Of course not!'

'Then perhaps you do not see everything you should.'

He snorted, amused despite the seriousness of the conversation.

'We will dock soon,' she said.

'I know.'

'Grace needs more time.'

'I know,' he said, irritation in the words.

'Use the time to go home. Go see your clever sisters and discover how they have solved their problem.'

He blew out a slow breath. 'I suppose it's possible.' Hope had entered his tone, and she smiled to hear it.

'Then afterwards,' she said as she stroked her fingers across his lips. 'Come find me and see what clever solution I have found.'

He caught her wrist and held it still as he pressed kisses to her fingers. They were slow, gentle presses of his mouth. And then his tongue stroked lazy circles around her flesh. Her body tightened in response. Her head swam as her heart accelerated.

Suddenly she was cursing this position they were in. How could she maneuver herself beside him? Underneath him?

But then he stopped. He pushed her hand away and spoke, his words a whisper in their dark alcove.

'Why do you love me?' he asked. 'Why do you think I am the only one for you?'

She thought of all the things she knew about him. His kindness to the street boy in India. The way he saw her skills and was willing to learn from her. She knew, too, that he was diligent in his work and a friend to every sailor on board. She had paid attention to everything he'd done since they'd met. She heard when he had broken up fights between sailors or done extra work when someone was ill.

She saw, too, that even though he had no official status on board, all the sailors deferred to him, even Captain Banakos when it was not critical to the ship. No one obeyed his orders because he gave none. But they took time to teach him, they praised him when he learned and they trusted him with their friendship. That was no small thing among men. And it was the mark of a good man.

She thought of all those things, but none of them were the full answer.

'Lucy?'

'I love you,' she said, 'because you see me. And you love me, too.'

It was a risk to say that. A risk and a fervent prayer. Her words might as well have been, *Please, say you love me, too.*

'No,' he said, the word sharp. Then he caught her arm and levered himself up, twisting so he could face her awkwardly. 'I will not say that, Lucy. I cannot!'

'But—'

'What kind of man would I be?' he rasped. 'What kind of man would say he loves a woman he cannot marry? That man would be the worst kind of cad. He would attach a woman when there is no hope. He would catch her when he could do nothing with her.' He scooted away from her until he put his feet on the floor. 'I am not so cruel nor so lost as to do that.'

She swallowed, hearing the anger in his tone. Seeing that he meant to leave right away.

'Don't go,' she pleaded. 'There is time still. We haven't yet reached port.'

'We have already done too much,' he said. 'You need to see London and meet more gentlemen. And I…' He put his satchel on his shoulder. 'I need to see my sisters.'

Then he was gone.

Chapter Fifteen

Cedric disembarked as soon as it was possible, then found some of his old friends. If nothing else, he was rich in old friends. Better yet, though it was barely three in the morning, they were awake and in their cups.

They fed him good English food that wasn't damp and had excellent meat. They plied him with brandy that went straight to his head. And as soon as it was light, he borrowed his friend's horse and headed to his family estate.

Maybe Lucy was right. Maybe his family's fortunes had recovered on their own. Maybe…

He stopped when the manor came into view. Of all the things he had imagined—both good and ill—none came close to what he saw now.

First and most disturbing, the roof was still in pieces. Fortunately, it was only one section of a very large house, so there was room for his sisters on the other side. But the damage was extensive, and he flinched every time he got past a tree and saw the whole of the mess again.

His second look showed him children, lots of children everywhere. Every urchin in the county was somewhere in front of the house. His mother had hated noisy children, so their home had been a silent tomb. But now it teemed with life. Noisy, arguing, giggling, singing and running about life!

Eventually, he spotted his two sisters. The youngest, Lilianna, sat under a tree, telling a story to several children while she painted in a book. Lilianna had always had a pencil at hand. Right now she seemed to be adding watercolour to the book while entertaining several little ones.

His middle sister, Rose, was standing at a large table sorting...vegetables? As he neared, he could see that she was giving a mathematics lesson using cabbages, watercress and peas. Several of the children had a slate and chalk, showing their answers to her in turn while she began to chop up the cabbage.

Good God, when had his frail sister developed muscles? He remembered her as an elfin child, but all of a sudden, she dropped the knife to lift up two fighting boys—one in each hand—as she gave them a stern talking to. Rose! The girl who spent most of her childhood with her head in the clouds as she sang to the fairies. She was scolding two boys while she held them aloft in her two fists.

That alone was shocking enough, but then he saw

his oldest sister, Cora. She was the most level-headed of all of them. Responsible and always calm in a crisis. He was just rounding the corner when she stepped out the front door. It wasn't so much the way she walked, but what she did when she stood still.

She looked fondly out at the sea of children and let her hand drift slowly over her belly. Over her rounded belly.

It was possible that she had simply gained weight from an abundance of food, but given the thin size of his other sisters, he doubted it. It was possible that some ailment had filled out her lower half, but again, she didn't look ill. What she looked like was a woman who was increasing.

Cora was pregnant.

He spurred his horse forwards, no longer content to watch from the road. He was tired and had a sore head, but this…this was not something he could take quietly. Had he missed a wedding announcement? Surely one of his friends would have mentioned it to him. A pang hit him hard that he had not been here for her nuptials.

He dismounted as soon as he got close, walking his horse forwards when he really wanted to run. With all these children around, someone might get trampled. So he took care while he tried to see his sister's hand. Was she wearing a wedding ring? Who could she have married?

He knew—or thought he knew—all the local gentlemen. Not a one was good enough for her. This is what came of not having a Season! Had she settled on someone who was unworthy of her? And who could blame her with no dowry and no relief in sight?

Thoughts spun uselessly in his head as his sisters finally noticed him. All three cried out in their particular ways. Lilianna looked up with a small start of surprise. Rose giggled in the way he remembered, the sound more like bells than laughter. But it was Cora who held his attention. She flushed red and slowly lifted her hand from her belly.

Dread settled deep in his gut. She looked guilty rather than happy. And while the children fell into chaos around him, he smiled grimly at her.

'I came as soon as I docked,' he said by way of greeting. 'And I can tell that there is a great deal that has happened while I was away.'

Cora shrugged. 'We had to do something, Cedric. We couldn't just sit around and starve.'

He looked at her face. She didn't look on the verge of starvation. None of them did. But none of them had the full blush of health either. Not the way the daughters of an earl should. He could already see that their hands were rough, their bodies unfashionably strong and of course, there was the pregnancy. He would be an uncle soon.

The thought wasn't displeasing. Just the circumstances which, truthfully, he didn't know yet. So he shouldn't judge. And he shouldn't be afraid.

And yet, as he greeted each of his sisters in turn, he

could see guilt written in their downcast faces and hear it echo in their overly loud greetings.

Good God, what had happened here?

It took a while to get everyone sorted. The children's lessons had to be finished, the vegetables collected and set to cooking and he had to groom his horse. There were no servants, not that he'd expected any. But it was still a shock to see that his sisters had no help whatsoever. His mother had always insisted on a full staff.

All of that took a couple hours. And though he tried to talk to his sisters along the way—when he came out of the stable, when he entered the kitchen to find some water to wash and on the way to and from the well with two heavy buckets—all three women pushed him off with one excuse or another.

'At dinner,' they said. 'We'll explain everything at dinner.'

So he took matters into his own hands and went to inspect the collapsed roof. He needed to know if the house was about to crumble into dust.

'It needs repair,' Cora said. 'Immediately.'

Cedric turned slowly, forcing his expression and his tone to be gentle when everything inside him teetered towards violence. 'Cora, what happened?'

She frowned. 'A storm blew the roof right off. Didn't you get my letters?'

He nodded. He had one, in fact, in his pocket. 'I'm referring to the baby.'

Her cheeks pinked and her gaze slid away. 'You're uncomfortably observant, brother.'

He swallowed, doing his best to keep calm. 'Were you forced?'

Her eyes widened as her gaze jumped to his. 'What? No!'

He exhaled slowly. One fear dissolved. But there were so many more concerns pushing forwards. 'Who was it? And where is he?'

'So you can call him out? So you can—'

'Cora,' he interrupted. 'I'm trying to help. And I'm sorry I wasn't here earlier.'

She sighed as she looked back at him. 'This is not your fault.'

No. It was his father's fault for impoverishing the estate, for continuing to disregard his own daughters, for not being here to protect his own children. And yet, guilt still ate Cedric.

'Who, Cora?' he demanded.

'Eric Wells,' she said.

He frowned. Did he know that name? He certainly hadn't gone to school with the man. Nor was he a local, as far as he could remember.

'He's the engineer I wrote to you about. The one I hired to look at the canal.'

Cedric thought back to the letter. 'I thought Lilianna was interested in him.'

His sister shrugged. 'Lilianna is interested in every eligible bachelor. But he liked me best.'

'And so you… You and he…' He couldn't even say the words.

'We're engaged,' she said, her expression lifting.

'And where is he?' Why wasn't there a ring on his sister's finger?

She sighed. 'He's in Yorkshire—'

'Yorkshire!'

'He got work there.' She sighed. 'He's fixing a canal up there, and when he's done, we'll have enough money to marry.'

'It doesn't take money to marry!' he snapped back.

She held up her hands to stop him. 'He doesn't know.'

'What?'

'He left before I realised. We were planning on marrying as soon as he got back, as soon as he was paid. We didn't know…' She dropped her hand onto her belly. 'It's not something I want to put in a letter.'

Cedric swallowed, panic clutching his throat. 'How far along are you?' He guessed maybe four or five months. But what did he know about pregnancies?

'Six months. You'll be an uncle this summer.'

The panic exploded in his brain, making his knees go weak. Good God, three months to get her a dowry. Three months to find this engineer and force him back here. Three months to fix the roof and get them a decent place to live.

Three months to prevent a bastard.

'We'll be fine, Cedric,' she said, her voice strong. 'I have it all worked out.'

'Really?' he said, sarcasm fighting hope in his voice. 'Please tell me.'

'He'll be back in time. His letters say he's nearly finished.'

God, he prayed that was true. 'Does he have family money? Any way to support you?'

She stiffened. 'He's an engineer. He's working!'

In other words, no.

'His grandfather is Viscount Copekett.'

Copekett, Copekett, Copekett. He wracked his brains for who that was. And when he finally placed it, he groaned out loud. The family had tons of children. There was no way this Eric would inherit the title. Worse, theirs was middling money, all reserved for the title. Nothing at all for the cousins and second cousins. At best, they could get a good education among the elite. At worst, they could end up no better than the average labour man.

Eric, apparently, split the difference. He was educated, but not flush.

'Do you have a place to live?' He couldn't imagine raising a child in a home with half the roof caved in. He hated it for his sisters!

Cora extended her hand to her brother. When Cedric touched it, she tugged him out of the damaged section of the house. 'We can talk over dinner.'

'I think I want the answer now. I get the feeling everyone's trying to hide things from me.'

She turned to him. 'We'll live on old Samson's farm.'

'What!' he exploded. His sister—the daughter of an earl—would live in a tenant's cottage? He imagined a vermin-infested hovel. He knew how badly his father had neglected those homes.

'Oh, don't get high-handed with me. Do you think this is better?' She gestured behind him at the damaged area of the house. 'Besides,' she said as she flushed pink. 'It's private.'

He did not want to think about that! Instead, he focused on the facts of the situation. 'You cannot want to live there,' he whispered.

'It's the best we could manage,' she said flatly.

'You cannot raise a child there!'

She shrugged. 'Then repair this house.'

'I sent you every penny I made!'

'I know,' she said, her tone softening. 'Thank you, Cedric. It's because of you that we have managed at all. But we are living people. Life must go on for us.' She set her hand on her belly. 'And it has.'

She was happy with her fiancé and her growing family. He could see that. But all Cedric could think was that the child was another mouth to feed. Another generation to raise. There would be more children who would grow. They would need a proper education with tutors and eventually school. All of that cost money.

He never realised how heavy that burden felt until the weight doubled at the thought of the next generation.

'He's a smart man, Cedric. There is not a waterway,

bridge or lock that he cannot improve. He'll get work all over the country. Yorkshire is just the beginning.'

'That'll take him away from you.' And the child. God, could this get any worse?

'I'm not the one you should be worrying about,' Cora said, her voice tart. 'Lilianna has met someone.' She sighed. 'Someone very unsuitable.'

Cedric groaned as he collapsed down into the nearest chair. He'd never felt more weighted by responsibilities.

He spent the next day and night inspecting Eric's work on their canal (impressive), Cora and Eric's future home on Samson's former plot (not as bad as he feared) and going over the family accounts which were every bit as disastrous as he'd imagined. He wouldn't have understood it before, but thanks to Lucy's tutelage he understood exactly how desperate the situation.

As for Lilianna's gentleman, the man was no gentleman at all. A little investigation turned up the man's other wife and children in a neighbouring county. Lilianna was crushed, but that only emphasised the need to get her to London for a Season. And that required coin.

Which left him with the only solution as the one he'd already been working on. He must marry an heiress. Nothing was more important or more urgent. Indeed, he wanted to have a woman's dowry in hand by the time Cora and Eric married, which had to be *before* she gave birth. He would not let that child spend his first years shivering in a tenant's hovel or a dilapidated manor home.

Which meant any dream of marrying Lucy was gone.

He accepted that fully now. What tiny portion of him had hoped was now smothered beneath the weight of the account books.

Despair hit him hard. Despair and fury and crushing responsibility.

That made him rash. And stupid. And completely, bull-headed.

Chapter Sixteen

London was not what Lucy expected. No, it was better! The Chinese believed that nothing outside of the middle kingdom could ever compare to what the emperor had built. And so despite everything her father had said, she had low expectations. And how surprised she'd been!

The sheer press of bodies was the equal to Canton. And the excitement that generated filled her with joy. London was alive as every big city was, and she adored it. Granted, she was coming to the city as the pampered daughter of a wealthy man, or so they pretended. Therefore, she should be accepted everywhere, right?

She was not.

Her mixed race was stamped upon her face and sidelong glances followed her wherever she went. But that was nothing! Compared to the beatings she'd endured in China, sniffs of disdain meant nothing. She was finally off the boat, finally in London, and now she could step into her future.

Because she had coin if she wanted it, plenty of food and a soft bed on which to sleep. Life had never been so good for Lucy. Especially now that she had a secret goal.

She meant to learn everything she could about English customs. If she married Cedric, then she would have to learn what was expected of a countess. She must live as he would need her to live.

That was task one. Task two, as always, was to find the coin that he needed. She would fill her dowry with as much money as she could manage. Her father had already promised her all the money from the sales of the spice. And so she worked with Captain Banakos to learn how that was accomplished in England.

Her father hired dancing instructors, paid for English clothing and found a woman to teach her and Grace how to act in England. It was hard, especially when the maid was a sour, angry woman who delighted in chastising them. But Lucy did the best she could given that she was not 'out' yet, as if any of the young English girls had done half the things she had in her life.

They hadn't, but she was English now, according to her father, so she had to sit in itchy dresses, practice pianoforte as if she wanted to master a musical instrument and wait interminably for Grace to choose a husband.

It was maddening, and she was feeling the strain every second that she sat and stared at a city she could not venture out into. Her only relief was when Captain

Banakos visited to explain what he'd done when selling her two boxes of spices.

Two weeks after docking in London, they received an invitation to return to the boat for a time. The message came from Cedric, along with coins for a hackney, and directions to the ship. Clearly, he did not mean to escort them. And equally clear was the fact that he was inviting Grace, not Lucy. But Lucy insisted she go along. After all, she was the savvy sister when it came to cities. Grace had spent most of her childhood hiding from the glorious places she'd visited. A boat was safety to her. Travelling through a busy city was intimidating.

And so Lucy got to go, as well as the nursemaid chaperone whose greatest joy seemed to be catching the foreigners in doing something un-English. Their father was occupied elsewhere and that was good. The fewer people who saw her reunion with Cedric, the better.

She couldn't wait to see him again.

She wanted to show him what she and Captain Banakos had done with the sales of the spice he had so generously allowed them to store in his cabin. That money would soon be in her dowry, and she wanted to see his face when he saw the exorbitant sum.

She needed to show him that she had found her solution. Unfortunately, when they arrived at the boat, Cedric was not there. Grace, naturally, did what she always did. She changed into sailor's clothes and lost herself among the sails. Which meant that Lucy could do exactly what she loved most.

She went below decks to the captain's quarters to run through the accounts. And she too lost herself in the click-clack of the abacus beads and the steadily growing numbers of profit reported there.

They had done well with the spice sales. She now possessed in her dowry more money than she had ever had in her life. Surely Cedric would see that total and drop down on one knee before her this time. And she would not dismiss him like her sister had. She would happily take him into her arms, her bed, her life. She didn't hear when he arrived on the ship. Captain Banakos was the one who told her after he finished giving a duke a tour. And what was a duke doing looking at *The Integrity*? She had no idea except that she wanted to go on deck to find out, but her chaperone glared her back into place.

'A lady does not seek out gentlemen. They come to her.'

Privately Lucy thought the woman was bitter because she couldn't control Grace and now took out all her distemper on Lucy. But there was little she could do. She needed to learn English customs and so far, this sour woman was her best source.

So she stayed put. She worked on the account book. She pictured Cedric down on one knee before her. And she waited.

'Who is this duke?' she asked the captain, who had started working at a central table studying maps.

'He's Lord Domac's cousin. I expect they've met your sister by now.'

Of course they had. And as always, Lucy was the afterthought, the one left to wait on someone else's pleasure. In China, she had expected it. In England, she was beginning to tire of it, especially when Grace seemed to be able to do whatever she wanted.

She knew she shouldn't be bitter. After all, it was thanks to Grace that she was here in the first place. If she'd stayed in China she would have no future at all. But it was so hard to be patient when Grace had every opportunity—every man—and Lucy had nothing but the account books.

What a child she was being, sulking when she was the luckiest girl alive. Or perhaps, the second luckiest after her sister. She returned to the safety of numbers. She scratched her sums in neat rows. And she waited.

Eventually, the captain went up to see what was happening. Lucy could hear men's voices filtering down to her, but she couldn't make out any words. Which meant she ended up sitting and waiting, which is all proper English girls seemed to do.

Thankfully—eventually—her patience was rewarded. She was making some final notations in the account book when Lord Domac finally, gloriously, knocked and entered.

'There you are,' he said, his voice so warm it sent tingles down her spine.

She turned immediately, her gaze eagerly scanning

him. He looked leaner, if that was even possible, but his clothes looked fine, at least to her. It was the wariness in his eyes that made her pause.

'What are you doing there?' he asked, a teasing note in his voice. 'Have you been counting all your money?'

'I'm told that it is not polite to talk about money.'

'Oh, it's not,' he said. He pulled out a chair and settled close enough to see what she was doing, but not near enough to touch her. 'But between us, it is the most magical discussion of all.'

She smiled, knowing that this was her moment. 'Well, as to that...' she said, drawing out the excitement. She opened up the account book to the appropriate page, her gesture expansive. 'Look at that,' she said, pointing. 'That is how much father is putting in my dowry. I have never had so much in my life! And I know I can make more. It is only a matter of the right cargo, you see. And finding the right merchants to sell to here and along the way.'

He craned his neck to see while she waited for the shock and pleasure to come across his face.

It didn't. If anything, his expression tightened down.

'Most impressive,' he said.

She stared at him. Those were the words she wanted to hear, but she could tell he was disappointed.

'Isn't that a large amount? In English money, I mean.'

'It's an extraordinary amount,' he agreed, his tone flat.

'But not enough for you.'

His expression turned rueful. 'This boat is worth nearly ten thousand pounds. And you know what the sale of this cargo is worth.'

She did. It was a fraction of the boat, but several times what she had.

'You need so much?'

'Not me. I can survive on nothing. Have for much of my life.' He exhaled slowly as if trying to control his emotions. 'I have been home,' he said. 'I have seen the state of things there. And I have been to see my father. I—' His voice choked off. 'This is not polite talk, even between us.'

'No,' she said, her spine straightening. 'But I am tired of being treated as a child. I will hear it all. Now.'

'I have never thought you a child,' he said. 'And I have never lied to you. I told you we could not marry.' He looked away, his expression infinitely sad. 'I went home. I need to marry now.'

Her heart lodged painfully in her throat, but she pushed out the words anyway. 'And this is not enough? What I have in my dowry—'

'No, Lucy.' Then he swallowed. 'No, Miss Richards. I'm afraid we do not... We cannot...' He sighed. 'No.'

The finality in his voice hit her hard. There was no hope there, and a darkness had entered his eyes. She reached out a hand to comfort him, but he pulled back from her.

'Never fear,' he said, and she could tell that he was making an effort to be lighthearted. 'You will meet all sorts of people now. And once you are out, every gentleman in London will clamor after you. But don't be too quick to choose. I shall be loath to lose you.'

He winked at her as he spoke, a painful echo of when he had first tried to flirt with her. But now there was so much between them that the shallowness of the expression irritated her.

'You cannot lose what you do not have.' What he would not marry.

Pain flashed across his expression, but he quickly suppressed it. Then he spoke quietly, in an undertone that was just for her. 'I had hoped to have your help,' he said. 'As my sister-in-law. I have looked at the estate books. Thanks to you, I understood much of it, but I am sure you can point out more. You will see more.'

'As your sister-in-law?' she squeaked. 'You still mean to marry Grace.'

He nodded. 'I will treat her and you honourably,' he said. 'You will both have a good life with me. I swear it. For as long as you choose to remain by her side.'

As an unwed sister. As baggage attached to Grace's side. As someone who laboured over his wealth while her sister grew fat with his children. Did he not see how demeaning that would be to her? To toil while hidden away? She had hoped for better outside of China. Indeed, he had been the one who gave her that dream because he saw her as a whole person.

'My father has three other ships,' she said, her voice

and tone low. 'He has already said I can look at their accounts, too.'

'Of course, of course,' Cedric said, nodding. 'And I would never take you away from your father. But if you would like it, it would be an enormous help to me. I would be so grateful—'

'If I helped with your affairs. To bring you some coin.'

'I'm sure your sister would be pleased, too. Eventually, it would go to her children, you know.'

Grace and Cedric's children.

'Do you truly want this for me?' she asked, stunned that he could say such a thing to her.

He looked into her eyes, and his expression fell. His eyes widened, and all his false cheer disappeared. Instead, she saw desperation and pain. Such awful pain that it verged on madness.

'I have no other solution,' he rasped.

'I offer you everything,' she said, her voice breaking on the words. 'I love you.'

He jolted upright, awkwardly scrambling out of his chair. 'Never say that again. Not to me. Not to yourself. Don't even think it.'

Tears clouded her vision, but she refused to let them fall. 'But you—'

'No!' He backed away, reaching behind him for the door.

Tears slipped down her cheeks. She couldn't stop them now, but such was the price of understanding. He was not the man for her. No matter what she wanted, no matter how her body still ached for him. He was not for her.

She turned away. 'I hope you and my sister will be very happy,' she said.

'Miss Richards,' he said. Then he touched her arm. 'Lucy, please. You knew from the beginning—'

'I did,' she said, interrupting him. 'And now I understand.' She turned to face him directly. 'There is no true feeling inside you. Only greed for coin.'

He reared back as if struck. 'That's not true!'

It wasn't true. She knew it wasn't, but she was in pain, too. She'd offered him everything she had, everything she was, and it wasn't enough. *She* wasn't enough.

So she twisted him in her mind. She changed what she believed about him so the future would not destroy her soul. He was a monster, she told herself. One lost to greed.

She straightened out of her chair, facing him as directly as she could. She did not offer him her hand. It was trembling too much.

'Good day, Lord Domac. I hope I never see you again.'

He stiffened as if she'd slapped him. And maybe she had. She saw the hurt in his eyes, but also saw a dawning understanding.

'I have hurt you,' he said.

She shook her head. 'You have shown me your true

colours. Money will always rule you.' Then she turned her back on him.

'Lucy,' he whispered, her name filled with anguish. She kept her back straight, refusing to look at him. If she did, she might break. She might run to him and beg him to reconsider.

She stood still, unwilling to move.

A moment later, she heard him sigh. There was a rustle of fabric as he probably bowed to her. A ridiculous nod to propriety, given the very improper things they had done together. She didn't turn to see. And a moment later, she heard him leave the room.

She waited longer, still fighting the tears. No matter what he felt, she knew that this was a true ending between them. And she was satisfied with that result.

For an hour. Maybe as much as two.

And then she changed her mind.

An hour later, she changed it again.

Indeed, she descended into a madness born of anger, loneliness and despair.

Cedric pursued her sister with intent. Lucy found ways to sabotage it.

She tortured him on a walk in Hyde Park. She disparaged him in whispered secrets at night with Grace. And she watched with excitement as Grace began to fall in love with someone else.

Grace wanted Declan, the man who was the Duke of Byrning. It was added spice that he was Cedric's cousin.

Chapter Seventeen

The Season began in earnest with Grace going to parties every night. Lucy was stuck waiting, learning, passing the time as best she could while her sister tried to decide on a husband.

Lucy didn't hear from Cedric. She didn't expect she would. She knew he was still pursuing Grace. He showed up at her coming out ball. He asked to escort her to balls and musicals. Lucy tried to stay upstairs, but always, at the last second, she would descend to the parlor to see if he noticed her.

He did. Their eyes would meet, and she would see the hollow-eyed look of a drowning man. And she would freeze.

She wanted to help him. She wanted to wrap him in her arms and fix whatever problem he had. But she did not know how to fix anyone. And her first instinct was always to hide, to protect herself. And so she stayed back from him and he turned back to her sister. He smiled too brightly and exuded such charm that everyone else seemed fooled.

But she saw through it, and she worried. Even as she ran back to her bedroom to hide. It was during these nights that she discovered a love of reading. Not the awful sermons her chaperone handed her, but journals about adventures by very strong-willed men.

She began with her father's. Indeed, he was the one who first offered it to her. And after she sorted through his cramped handwriting, she went on to read other stories that he procured for her. Some of them factual, at least so the writers claimed. Others that were complete fantasy. She loved them all. And they helped the hours pass as Grace went off to dance with handsome gentlemen.

Until the day Grace came home. She was white-faced but determined. She was done with England and the ridiculousness of the *ton*. But before she left for good, she wanted to do something for Lucy and her new friend Phoebe.

They were to go to Almack's for a night of dancing. It was the most hallowed place in English society where ladies met gentlemen interested in marriage. Lucy didn't care if it was the most wretched place in London. She was getting out of the house, and she couldn't be more excited.

Not to mention her dress was the most beautiful thing she'd ever worn. It was a soft butter yellow that matched a ribbon in her hair. And her father gifted her with a slender golden chain to hang about her neck. He declared her beautiful, and she felt it all the way down to her toes.

Phoebe was, too, with her bouncy blond hair and her bright blue eyes. As a cit, the girl would never have been able to get a voucher to Almack's, but Grace had arranged it. She wore pale blue, but nothing could match the sunny brightness of her optimism. She was sure all three of them would find their true love tonight.

And so they set off, with their father serving as their chaperone. And if her sister was exceedingly quiet, Lucy and Phoebe made up for it in sheer excitement.

When they disembarked from the carriage, Lucy was shocked to see the line of beautiful English girls in front. All of them were decked out in fine clothing, most with jewelry that put Lucy's slender chain to shame. And each one whispered and pointed at them.

She ought to be used to the startled looks. Whenever she'd gone anywhere in London, people had stared. But no one had beat her or spit at her, so it was an improvement from how she'd grown up. Or so she'd consoled herself.

But these ladies *did* want to hurt them. These ladies were angry enough to radiate hostility. Normally Lucy would run from such people. They were too dangerous. But Grace did not flinch. She lifted her chin and continued for the front door. Phoebe as well, with her bright smile and excited chatter.

It was an act. Lucy could see the fear in both girls'

eyes, but they covered it well. Which meant Lucy could do the same.

They made it to the front of the line, and Lucy finally got to meet Cedric's mother. The countess stood as one of the official greeters into the hallowed dance hall. She was dressed simply, but in exquisite fabric. Her hair was pulled upwards, as most every older woman's was, and she wore a single large emerald at her neck. It wasn't real. She knew that much from Cedric, but the illusion was good.

All in all, the countess appeared a handsome woman except for the pinched way she held her mouth and the fact that her smile never reached her eyes. Indeed, it never reached the fullness of a smile, falling far short of anything resembling a true emotion.

Nevertheless, the woman greeted them warmly, exclaimed loudly about their dresses and hair, and then gestured towards a line of gentlemen. That was the bargain Grace had struck, and the Countess was fulfilling her side of the bargain.

So the three of them went where they were bid, and suddenly Lucy was meeting gentleman after gentleman, all in a blur. Grace had memorised their names, knew how to curtsy and introduce them to Lucy, and generally acted as if she belonged exactly where they were.

It was shocking to see. Grace fit in whereas Lucy felt like a clumsy oaf. She didn't know exactly how to move, what to say or even where she should look. So many people and none of them matched anything that felt familiar. Indeed, as the men wrote their names one by one on her dance card, she suddenly lost the ability to read English. Such strange names in unsteady handwriting. Who were these men?

It got better when the dancing began. She had practiced the steps of the dances with Grace. And, of course, so long ago with Cedric. She remembered, for the most part, where to set her feet. It was rote memorization, not pleasure. Dancing was not her favourite pastime, but she managed it. And there were several men who were helpful in that.

So she relaxed, at least a little. And then he walked in.

She saw Cedric enter when she was changing partners between sets. His clothes might have been dashing, though they did not fit well, which told her it was borrowed attire. Or maybe not, since the man had lost weight.

His skin looked paler than she'd ever seen it, almost sallow. And his shoulders hunched beneath his dark brown jacket. But it was his eyes that shocked her. They glittered with desperation. His mother rose to greet him. She cut through the crowd quickly, but he gave her only the most cursory glance. She tried to force the issue. She was clearly not a woman who appreciated being ignored. But when she touched his arm, he rounded on her with a dark look.

Fortunately, he wasn't a violent man. His mother did not cringe away from him, but the two clearly had words. And though Lucy wanted to watch the exchange, her next partner was drawing her onto the dance floor.

The set began as usual. Lucy was distracted, trying to both smile at her partner and keep an eye on Cedric. That's why she didn't realise when another figure strode through the room.

The Duke! Striding straight through the dancers like a ship cutting through the ocean. People scattered before him. And when she looked up, she saw exactly what she'd expect from the man who was stiffly proper in all the English ways. Personally, she preferred Cedric's easy ways. Which was all to the good because the Duke was headed straight for Grace.

Chatter erupted immediately. Everyone seemed shocked to see the man. His mother, the Dowager Duchess, rushed to his side, trying to pull him away. The Duke didn't even spare her a glance.

He stopped directly in front of Grace, took hold of her hands, and spoke words that shocked everyone.

'Marry me.'

If there were startled chatter before, it was nothing compared to the shocked gasps at the Duke's command. Especially when he followed it up with the most romantic words Lucy had ever heard.

'I love you,' he said. 'I am the best that England has to offer. I am clever, educated and titled. I want more than the best of England at my side. I want the best of China.'

Grace stared at the Duke while Lucy silently willed

her sister to say yes. Take the man who so obviously loved her. Instead, her dazed sister shook her head.

'But I am not the best of anything.'

'You are beautiful and clever,' the Duke said. And then he sank down to one knee before her as he continued listing things about Grace that Lucy thought no one but her understood. But clearly, he did. And still her sister did not react. The woman was stunned into silence and Lucy was ready to shake the silly woman into saying yes!

But then a commotion caught her attention. It was Cedric, of course, pushing his mother aside as he burst into the conversation.

'Have you lost your mind?' Cedric roared. 'You can't marry her any more than I can!'

Lucy flinched at the roar. The awful thing was that she wasn't even surprised. She'd seen that Cedric was drowning. And she knew that he thought Grace was his last hope. But the Duke was taking Grace away, so Cedric had to fight. He had to clutch at her in any way possible.

But that didn't mean she was going to allow it. Cedric was not going to take away her sister's chance at happiness.

Fortunately, she didn't need to interfere. The Duke didn't even glance at his cousin. His attention was focused completely on Grace. 'Cousin, you are a boor.'

'She's a liar and a thief.'

That was too much for Lucy. Damn it, why had she

stood quiet these past weeks? She should have stopped him ages ago. She shoved past the onlookers, her blood hot. Of course, Grace was a liar and a thief. They were orphans who had done whatever they could to survive.

'Not here,' Lucy cried. 'Not in England,' but no one was listening to her. Certainly not Cedric who was saying everything and anything to end his cousin's proposal.

'She's not really Lord Wenshire's daughter. She is not his child!'

How dare he say that! He'd sworn to never reveal it and now he'd just bellowed it out to the world. The one secret that could destroy everything for her and Grace.

Lucy slapped him as hard as she could. She didn't even remember crossing the room to his side, but the pain in her hand and the bright red on his cheek told the tale.

'I didn't think you could stoop any lower,' she hissed. 'And to think I once thought you clever. Safe, clever and kind.' She shook her head. 'You have fooled me just as your father fooled your mother.' She saw it all so clearly now. Hadn't he said that his mother had the large dowry? That his father swept her off her feet only to squander away the money on gambling? Any woman who married Cedric would end up as bitter as the countess and living off the charity of the nearest relation. 'You are a villain!'

She didn't know which of her words broke him out of his bitterness. She saw his eyes widen as he pressed a hand to his cheek. And then—just like in Hyde Park—he looked around, saw the audience and realised the disaster he had created.

'Lucy,' he gasped. 'I didn't mean—'

The Duke didn't let him finish. 'Step away, Cedric. Or I swear to God I will put you into the ground!'

The two men squared off, exchanging words that echoed in the room. Lucy didn't care. Let him be beaten to a bloody pulp. Her gaze went to her sister, but Grace's eyes had shifted somewhere else. She was looking at her father, an apology in her eyes.

And what was their father doing? He was barrelling forwards, leading with his cane. Everyone jumped away or received a hard blow. And that included the two cousins. 'Stop it!' he bellowed. 'Good God, I am ashamed to be English!'

Lucy watched him, her heart in her throat. She knew he was taking his anger out on Cedric and the Duke, but what would he do with them? Would he still care for the daughters who were liars? Who weren't actually the blood kin they claimed to be?

Cedric and the Duke both fell back. And then, Mr. Richards turned to his daughters. Unable to wait for his reaction, Grace stepped forwards, her expression stricken.

'I'm so sorry,' she said.

Lucy was on her heels. 'We didn't mean to lie.'

'I didn't speak English. I didn't realise why you had

chosen me. I didn't know what you believed,' Grace continued with Lucy agreeing with every word.

'Hush...hush, child,' their father said as he set his cane on the floor. 'Girls, I knew the truth from the beginning. The woman I loved and our child died years before. I knew that long before I sent word to the temple.'

Lucy's hands clasped tight before her. 'You knew?' she whispered.

'I did.' He stroked her cheek. 'I could not save my child, but I could save you. I could bring you here and give you a life such as I would have given my own flesh and blood.' His gaze included both of them, and for the first time in a long time, Lucy did not feel like an afterthought. 'But I can see now that my own people are as ignorant and as cruel as yours.' He turned to Grace. 'If you wish, we can leave now for Italy, or Morocco or any other land.'

Lucy gasped, her head spinning. Could she do it again? Leave a place where she'd become comfortable, if not exactly happy? Go out in search of another home? It was too much to think about. And looking at her sister, she could see Grace thought the same.

But the Duke was not finished. He moved in front of Grace, drawing her attention as he sank back down on one knee. And while he spoke words from his heart, Lucy looked to Cedric. It burned that she wanted to hear such words from him. After everything he'd done, it hurt that she still ached for him.

He didn't speak; he didn't try to interrupt. If he had, she would have cut him down with her bare hands. But he didn't say a word to stop the love flowing between Grace and his cousin. And a moment later, Grace accepted the Duke's proposal.

They were in love. And Cedric's hope for a dowry worth a fortune was destroyed. She saw the bleak realization hit him. Saw, too, that he was a defeated man, and she feared for what that might lead him to next.

He caught her gaze, an apology burning there. She wanted none of it. He had betrayed her in every way. Or near enough. He had not whispered about what they had done together, but he had tried to destroy her relationship with her father. That was the one thing upon which she depended for everything.

And so she shook her head. And she deliberately turned her back on him. How many times could she cut him from her heart? How many times could she turn away from him and swear to never think of him again? How long would it take for the love she had for him to shrivel away to nothing?

Too many. And too long.

But she would find a way to do it anyway.

Chapter Eighteen

Cedric walked the London streets. He knew he was risking his life, moving through dark places where villains lurked. No one touched him. Perhaps because they recognised a fellow soul with nothing left. Or perhaps his feet knew better than him where he should go.

It was two days after the debacle in Almack's. But it was weeks since he'd left his sisters, filled with a desperation that became madness. Looking back, he could see all the mistakes in his courtship with Grace.

They stemmed from the moment he'd ceased thinking of her as a person. She'd been a prize to win, a chit atop a mountain of gold that he'd take by hook or crook. She was the means by which he'd repair the roof on his sisters' house and provide a decent home for the coming niece or nephew.

What a fool he was. Shame filled him, and he knew he needed to try to make recompense somehow. He needed to apologise. That wouldn't fix what he had done, but it was a beginning. And it was the only thing he could think of to do.

He wrote formal letters to Grace, Declan and Lord Wenshire, expressing deep remorse for what he had done. It had taken all of his strength to write out his shame, but once done, he felt cleaner somehow. He would have written to Lucy as well, but she was an unwed girl, not even officially 'out' yet. It was not proper for him to write to her. His only option was a face-to-face apology.

It took him three more days to work up the nerve, and even then it was not a conscious choice. His feet took him to her home, as they often did. But tonight, the house wasn't dark.

He stood there, unresolved as to what to do. It was too late for callers, and he wasn't dressed for a visit anyway. But if she were home, then this was his best chance to speak to her. He needed to beg for her forgiveness and to feel the well-deserved pain when she refused to give it.

He had just begun to approach when she opened the door. She wasn't surprised. Indeed, she quietly swung the door wide and stepped back, silently bidding him enter.

He meant to refuse, but once he'd seen her face, he knew he had to speak to her. He needed to make things right between them. He stepped inside, pulling off his hat and gloves. But there was no butler to take his things, and so he set them aside on the table designed for such things.

'Where are your servants?' he asked.

'The butler has been dismissed.' She shrugged. 'We have had trouble hiring good servants.'

He nodded. It took training to learn who to hire and who was a blighter. He could help her with that, but of course, she wouldn't want his help. 'What about your nurse or maid? One should stand as chaperone.'

'I sent them home for the night.'

'You—'

'I knew you would come, Cedric. Once I saw the apologies you wrote to my sister and father, I knew you would seek me out.'

She knew him better than anyone, it seemed. Even himself. 'Then get your father, please. He should stand as chaperone.'

'He and Grace are out for the night.' She faced him squarely. 'I *knew* you would come.'

'You waited for me.' It wasn't a question. And then he remembered how they would speak at night on the ship. Before he'd hatched his ridiculous plan to pursue Grace, he and Lucy would find each other in the darkness of the ship. They'd stare into the inky blackness of the water or up at the starlit sky and talk of so many things.

That's how he'd learned of her first love, Ah-Lan. And he'd told her of his gambling days at school and the misery of returning home during the summers. His home had never been happy until both his parents left to reside in London.

But this wasn't a ship in the middle of the Arabian Sea. They were in London now and proper apologies required proper behaviour.

'I came to apologise to you,' he said. 'But I cannot be here without your chaperone. It would only compound my crime.' He reached for his hat.

She stopped him by shutting the front door and putting herself between him and it. 'I would speak with you.'

'I can come back. When there are—'

'Now,' she interrupted. 'We must speak.'

Alarm warred with surprise inside him. 'Has something happened? Is there a problem?' He didn't know what he could do to help, but he certainly had more resources than her. Or at least more friends in London whom he could call upon.

'There is no problem,' she reassured him. 'But I would say my piece.'

Ah. Yes. He deserved no less. He squared his shoulders and faced her, part of him dreading her words, part of him praying she destroyed him. Indeed, if she took a knife to his chest, he would allow it. He felt that guilty for his actions.

'I am a foreigner in this land,' she began, her tone hard. 'I am here because a stranger took pity on me. I went with him because there is no home for me in China. Grace and I have no one but him. Do you know what happens to women who are alone in a strange country? With no money, no food?'

'You are not alone!' he said, the words coming out with the force of a vow. 'I would help you. Others—'

'Do you think I trust you now?' she scoffed. She looked at him, then stepped away. She was pacing off her fury, moving back and forth in the narrow foyer as she spoke. 'I have seen what it takes to survive,' she said. 'You think it is easy for a girl to spread her legs for coin?'

'Of course not!'

She glared at him. 'That is the easiest part of it. Five minutes and it is done. But the beatings, the disease, the pregnancies, bringing another reviled child into the world.' Fury burned in her eyes. 'Do you know the terror of that? Of starvation? Of fighting with rats for food?'

He shook his head. He could not comprehend the way she was raised, and it made him sick to think of it.

'You risked everything when you told our secret. If he had reviled us, if he had cast us aside, where would we go? What would we do?'

He swallowed, feeling the magnitude of what he had done. In his desperation, he had risked her life as surely as if he'd shot her with a pistol. That it had turned out well was merely luck and a measure of Lord Wenshire's goodness. He could have easily tossed them aside. And then what would she and Grace have done?

At the time, he'd imagined that they'd turn to him

for salvation. Even then, he wanted to stand by them. But his rash words had risked everything, and he could not be more ashamed.

He wanted to say something. He wanted to express the depth of his shame. But what words could he offer that would mitigate what he had done?

'I am beyond sorry,' he said miserably. 'I—'

'How can I forgive you after what you did?' she asked. 'How can I look at you without thinking of what could have happened?'

Obviously, she could not. Indeed, he doubted he could look himself in the mirror and not think the same things.

'I do not ask for forgiveness,' he finally said. 'I see that is impossible. But how can I make this better for you? What can I do to make you feel safe? Your father loves you. Your sister will be a duchess. You need not fear—'

'And yet I keep food secreted away in my bedroom. I have items in a satchel that I can sell.' She stepped up to him. 'I lived in fear all my life. I was finally feeling secure here and with one sentence, you ripped all that away!'

'Lu-Jing!' he cried, daring to touch her hand. She whipped it away from him, but he stood there nonetheless with his hand outstretched. 'Do not let me— or anyone—tear away your peace! You are not alone. Declan will see to it if no one else.' He dropped to his knees before her. He wasn't even sure why except that he had no right to stand tall before her. 'I was ten thousand times a fool, but you are safe.'

She looked at him, tears shimmering in her eyes. 'I trusted you,' she whispered. 'I loved you.'

She could not have hit him harder if she'd stabbed him. It was even worse because he knew he deserved the wounds. 'I will go,' he finally whispered. 'You need never think of me again.'

Then he stood without looking at her. He grabbed his hat, and he left. He heard the door shut behind him and knew that whatever his future held, it would not include her. It could not.

That knowledge destroyed him.

The reason was obvious. It wasn't even a surprise to him. And yet, the truth of it echoed in his mind over and over as he walked the streets of London.

He was in love.

He loved Lucy.

Lucy might very well be his one true love.

And if he were a baker or a sailor or the lowest bootblack, nothing would stop him from pursuing her. But he would be an earl someday, and some things were expected of his title. Chief among those requirements was to support the estate and the people who lived upon it. Not just his family, but the tenants, the village and of course, his blighted parents.

He could not stop thinking about what she'd said or that he could not convince her that she was safe. She had people who cared for her now. People who loved her, including him. And even if he could never speak of it to her, could never show her how much she was valued, the truth of it was all around her.

She was loved.

And he...

He...

He wanted to drown himself in self-pity. He was alone. No one cared for him. No one protected him.

Except that wasn't true, was it? Just like her, he had friends. A great many of them. And the protection of his title, if nothing else.

In fact, many of them would be all too willing to help him ease the pain of a lost love. They thought he mourned Grace. He did not need to correct them.

So he sought them out. What else could he do? And they brought him in, plied him with drink and let him grieve however he willed. Since he refused to gamble, they gathered in other haunts, their own bachelor accommodations, and even Carlton House with the Prince Regent.

Yes, he got royally drunk with Prinny himself. And when he got sick of talking about lost loves and incompetent fathers, he turned the conversation to commerce. It wasn't a polite thing to discuss money like this. But they were all drunk, and men liked to talk about making money.

So he did. He told them all what he had learned aboard *The Integrity*. He said he knew he could find more markets for English goods. He could find things other than tea to bring back from the Orient. He could do these things, he said, if only he had a ship, investors in his cargo and a roof to cover his sisters' heads.

By morning, he had all three. Or at least the coin to see it done.

This time, he swore as he cleaned himself up, he wouldn't fail. His only wish was to see Lucy one last time before he left.

One month later, he got his wish, though not at all in the way he intended.

Chapter Nineteen

It did not take Lucy months to feel safe again. It was as if saying her piece had transformed her. She expressed her pain and her fears. She saw the shame in Cedric's eyes, and she felt all the wrenching agony of a love destroyed.

Tears and pain followed. She drenched her pillow in a tidal wave of tears. But in time, the storm passed. She slept. She ate. And soon, she could breathe again.

She stopped hoarding food. She put away her satchel of trinkets and did not think of it again. Cedric was right. She was safe. Her father had not abandoned them. Grace was going to be a duchess. And whether it was her father, Grace or the Duke, she would be cared for.

She would never starve.

That was so momentous a shift that it took her some time to adjust. It helped that she was now officially 'out'. She could go to parties with Grace and their new friend Phoebe. Finally, she was able to meet all those men who were supposed to fall at her feet. And since

Grace was now engaged to a duke, the three of them were invited everywhere.

She tried not to be aware of Cedric. She didn't listen when gossip reached her ears. If he were at a party when she arrived, he immediately departed. And if all those men asking her to dance weren't distraction enough, she also helped with the plans for Grace and Declan's wedding.

And yet, she learned what Cedric was doing anyway.

He was gathering investors for a ship and cargo. Everyone was talking about how experienced he was now that he had spent so much time working on *The Integrity*. Prinny was said to be so impressed that he invested, as well. And once the royal invested, others joined.

She heard other things, too. Things that she didn't understand. Cedric was touting the wonders of a children's book? And he knew of a man who could repair canals for a moderate price. Indeed, for a man who existed on the edge of society, she heard a great deal of what he was doing.

She didn't care. She was meeting eligible bachelors. And they were very exciting…for a time. Dancing was fun. Living life as a pampered woman was fun. But all too soon, she became bored. The men did not have a twinkle in their eyes like Cedric. They did not ask her about her interests. What they did want to know was exactly how much money was in her dowry.

In that way, they were exactly like Cedric. And she couldn't have despised them more.

And yet, she still dressed in fine new clothes, smiled brightly at Grace and the Duke, and then pretended to love every moment of it. Including the night they went to the theatre.

It was hard to hear among the crush of people. The Duke had a box of his own, so that helped. It lifted them up above all the people milling about on the floor.

She'd never been to the theatre before. Never seen actors on the stage performing a tale. Most everyone here knew the stories they acted. It was part of their English heritage. But she didn't know them. Neither did Grace. And so they watched with rapt attention at the beginning.

But the language of the tragedy was in a form of English that was hard for her to understand. There were words she couldn't follow about kings and queens she'd never heard of before. And though she enjoyed it, the strain was significant.

She needed a break. Indeed, her sister did, too. And so when Lucy indicated she needed to find the ladies' retiring room, Grace went with her. The chatter here was equally loud and soon the two sisters escaped to walk slowly down the hall back towards their box.

They'd barely made it up the stairs when she heard his voice.

Cedric.

He was laughing with a couple, the sound light if

not exactly happy. They were talking cargo and coin, what would be purchased and sold for profit. Her interest piqued, her head lifted, and naturally she wanted to listen to the conversation. The exchange of goods always interested her. But it was Cedric's voice that drew her most. There was a new quality to his speech that interested her.

They rounded the corner and saw each other. She was acquainted with the couple, Lord and Lady Deforte, who were of an older generation. The man was genial, as far as she remembered, but the lady was a known gossip. Her eyes lit up when she saw Lucy and Grace, and she immediately waved them over.

'Why it's the Misses Richards! Come here! You must join us. No, no, Lord Domac, don't go. I'm sure it's all water under the bridge now. No need to run away.'

What a shrew! Barely one month had passed since the disaster at Almack's. Lady Deforte was looking for gossip. She wanted to see how Grace and Cedric interacted so she could tell everyone about the way he still pined for her. But his gaze was on Lucy, and hers on him.

'You look well, my lord,' Lucy said as she and Grace performed their curtsies.

'Thank you,' he said, his voice rough. 'You look…' He shook his head. 'Astonishing.' He turned to Grace. 'You both do.'

'What a delightful thing to say,' Lady Deforte gushed. 'What exactly seems to astound you, my lord?'

He smiled winningly at the lady. 'Only that such beauty surrounds me tonight. I fear with the three of you ladies here, no one will watch the stage. All will watch you as if you were Helen of Troy directing the way of their hearts.'

The lady pinked and giggled. Cedric was always able to flirt, but now Lucy saw how smoothly he turned a shrew into a blushing girl. Odd that she wasn't jealous. Indeed, she was pleased that he need not suffer any sleight or jab from the woman.

Meanwhile, Grace was looking towards their box. 'A pleasure to see you three again, but—'

'Have you heard?' Lady Deforte interrupted. 'Lord Cedric is getting together a ship and cargo. Prinny himself has invested!'

'That is excellent news—' Grace began.

'What is the ship?' Lucy interrupted. 'What choices have you made for cargo?' She knew she shouldn't ask. She should walk away. She'd burned him out of her heart, hadn't she? And so why would she need to know his particulars? But she did want to know. Indeed, she wished him well for himself and his family.

'I haven't found the right ship yet,' he said. 'Everything seaworthy is either too expensive or full of holes.' He flashed a chagrinned expression to Lord Deforte. 'I mean that quite literally. Wood rots. And if it's the wood beneath your feet, that's a big problem.'

'Yes, yes,' Lord Deforte said. 'I'm very interested, mostly because Prinny wants me to be interested. But that doesn't mean I'm going to help you out blindly. Come see me tomorrow afternoon at my club. We can discuss the particulars then.'

Cedric grinned, his cheeks flushing to a healthy colour. Indeed, now that she was this close to him, she saw that he'd lost weight, but the slight tightening of his body was offset by the gleam in his eyes. He was pleased. And that made his natural charm all the more handsome.

'But we're missing the end of the tragedy,' Lord Deforte continued. 'Come along, my dear. Our business here is done.'

'But—' his wife interrupted.

'Lord Domac, I'm sure you can see these ladies back to their box, yes? You know it's never good to have tension among families. Makes Christmas awkward. And all those christenings and Easter.' He shook his head. 'Best make one's apologies immediately and move on.' The last words were aimed at Lucy and Grace. Clearly the man thought that they were the ones punishing Cedric, and he was doing his part to see that they forgave him.

Cedric, however, was quick to reassure the man. 'Both Miss Richards have been exceedingly gracious to me.'

'Good, good. Then go with them and see what the Duke can do to help you out with your boat problem.' He arched a brow at Cedric. 'And then come talk to me tomorrow and tell me what you've arranged.' Then he gently, but firmly, steered his wife through the door of a nearby box.

Which left the three of them together, awkwardness increasing by the second. Until Cedric smoothed it over, not with charm, but honesty.

'I am so sorry,' he said. 'I didn't know you would be here, and Prinny commanded me to find Lord Deforte. So I had to come here, but I'll leave—'

'You couldn't have known we were walking back from the retiring room,' Lucy interrupted. 'And you needn't run away.' She glanced over to Lord Deforte's box. 'Won't he expect you to talk to Declan now?'

Cedric winced. 'I'll make something up. You needn't—'

Grace set her hand on his arm. 'We are going to be family now. You cannot run out every time we walk in.' She glanced at Lucy. 'Shall we walk together back to the box?'

'Yes.' She fell into step beside her sister. Neither of them gave their hand to Cedric, and he didn't offer his arm. She saw him twitch to do so but then stopped himself. Nevertheless, he walked beside them with all appearance of courtesy. So she smiled at him. 'It's true then? Prinny has invested in your venture?'

'Yes and no,' he said. 'He's promised money, but not how much. He's put his voice to my project, which is a significant help. But it will be for nothing if I cannot find the right ship at the right price.'

Grace nodded. 'Good ships are hard to find.'

'They're *expensive* to find,' Lucy corrected.

'But I'll find it. Never fear.'

She didn't. He had a strength in him when he spoke that hadn't been there before. He'd always had determination to succeed, he'd always been willing to work for it, but this time he seemed to have a clear vision. One that he believed in. One that seemed to guide him in a good way instead of a destructive one.

'How are your sisters?' she asked. She knew the pressures he felt. Just how desperate was he?

His expression softened. 'My youngest sister, Lilianna, has written a children's book. Several, actually, and I have found a publisher for her. It will take some time for the books to be printed and sold. And I have let it about to my friends that it will make an excellent holiday or birthday gift.'

So that was why there was talk about books for children. He was preparing the *ton* to buy the books. 'That will be good income,' she said.

He nodded, clearly pleased. 'I hope so, though it will take time. And I know the publisher personally. He will not take advantage of her.'

'That is most excellent.'

He smiled as he looked directly at her. 'It was your words that made me think of it. You said that money is made in slow, careful inches. I used to think like a gambler, in large wins and losses. But it is the small, steady progress that works best.'

That was true. And her heart warmed that he would remember her words. 'Windfalls happen, too,' she said.

'Sometimes a generous man goes all the way to China to save a pair of orphan girls.'

He smiled. 'Your father is the best of men.'

'He is. But what of your other sisters?'

They were outside the Duke's box, but they lingered there. Or rather, Cedric and Lucy lingered. Grace waited silently, her eyes and ears missing nothing, but she didn't interfere in their conversation.

'I found my future brother-in-law some work. He's an engineer who understands canals, and I know plenty of people whose canals need repair.' He rubbed a hand over his face. 'I leave in two days for their wedding. That's why I had to find Lord Deforte tonight.'

'Yes, I understand. You could not give them dowries, but you found a way for them to have income. Income is better, I think.'

'It's slow money, but yes. They will survive. Indeed, I think Eric's money will outpace mine. At least until the repairs are finished.'

'You are finding your way,' she said. 'I am happy for you.'

'As are you,' he said. 'You're quite the sensation this Season.' He glanced at Grace. 'You both are. But now that you are engaged, every good man I know has asked about you. And many of the bad ones, as well.' His voice darkened at that, but he needn't have bothered warning her. It was that moment Declan stepped out of the box, likely looking for them.

'I am taking care of them,' the Duke said, his tone equally dark.

Cedric straightened. 'Yes, I know. But I've warned several others off, just in case.'

The two men held gazes for a long moment. Lucy didn't understand what passed between them, but it was significant. And in the end, Declan gave his cousin a slow nod.

'Come see me after you return from the wedding.'

Cedric stiffened. 'You... How—'

Declan lifted his hand. 'I know about the wedding and the reason for it. I didn't beforehand, but—'

'You cannot tell my parents. Cora doesn't want them there and I agree—'

Declan held up his hand. 'I won't tell anyone. But I am sending a wedding gift,' he said. 'It should be enough to finish any repairs and properly furnish their home.'

Cedric's eyes widened for a moment. And then his breath left him in a long, slow exhale. 'Thank you, Declan. That is very generous—'

'It's for Cora. It's for them all, really. I should have been watching them closer. And for that, you have my apology.'

Cedric nodded, clearly overcome. Declan's lips curved. Not quite a smile, but there was warmth there nonetheless. 'You're family, Cedric. I can be furious and still not abandon you.'

'I am sorry,' Cedric said as his gaze took in all three of them. 'It will not happen again.'

'I know,' Declan said. 'I hope you make a go of the shipping venture,' Declan added. 'The last thing you want to do is take Prinny's money and fail.'

'I have no intention of failing,' he said, resolve in his tone. 'But it is a risk.'

Lucy spoke up, not wanting to see him waver. 'Every venture is, but if we never tried anything, Grace and I would still be in China.'

'And for that,' Declan said as he pressed a kiss to Grace's hand, 'I am truly grateful.'

As was Lucy. For all that she had lost her dream of marrying Cedric, she would not change anything in her life. Leaving China had been a gamble well worth taking.

And perhaps, she thought, it was time she took another one. Cedric was not the man for her, but she would earnestly open her heart to the other men courting her. She would stop comparing them to Cedric, she would stop thinking of eradicating him from her heart and honestly spend time with her suitors.

She would stop hating men for abandoning or betraying her and allow herself to truly search for a husband.

Chapter Twenty

Two months changed everything and absolutely nothing.

Lucy threw herself into the social whirl and Grace's wedding preparations. She learned with her sister how to hire servants and manage a staff. Lucy would only manage her father's small household, but her sister was to be a duchess. Together they undertook a lady's education in a very short amount of time. And Lucy shuddered to think of how Cedric's sisters managed such a thing on a very tight budget.

And she let herself enjoy the men who courted her.

Except none of them stirred her the way Cedric once had. It was damned depressing. Especially since she saw him at her sister's wedding. He was so handsome in his English finery that he took her breath away. And when he looked at her, she wanted to leap across the room, straight into his arms.

She couldn't. She didn't feel that way about him anymore. And yet, when he at last came to greet her, she nearly melted when he complimented her dress. It was a form statement, said by nearly everyone here. But he held her hand longer than anyone else did, and he looked in her eyes when he said she was beautiful. Then he added one more phrase.

'I'm awed by you.'

There was such feeling in the statement, such intensity when he said it, that her emotions nearly swallowed her whole. She tried to respond, but had no words. And then the moment was lost. His attention was caught by someone else. He turned away from her, and she was left wondering if she was reading too much into his words. If she was hearing what she wanted to hear or if there was something between them still.

Did she want that? Did she want him?

Yes, a thousand times yes. And also no.

And so she turned her attention to the next guest and kept her mind and heart strictly under control.

He left immediately after the bridal breakfast and she saw him no more that day. Or the next. Or for the next month.

At least the wedding was beautiful, and her sister seemed ecstatic. Husband and wife disappeared soon afterwards on a honeymoon trip while Lucy settled into management of her father's tiny home. The first thing she did was dismiss her annoying chaperone. The next thing was to find a doctor for her father.

He was ailing, his cough continuing, and she very much feared for his life. He, on the other hand, made plans to visit his parents' graves on a family estate owned by his older brother. And he did not want her to join him.

'Not this time, my dear,' her father said. 'I need to have words with my brother, and those had best be done in private.'

'He will not approve of me,' she said quietly.

Her father shrugged. 'He doesn't matter. I do.' He took her hands and pressed kisses into them. 'It is sooner than I wanted, but you are out now. Next Season you will have the gentlemen clamoring for your hand.'

It hadn't waited for the next Season. 'I am well content.'

'I'm glad. But know that I plan to put a substantial amount into your dowry.'

'Father—'

'We have to wait until the next ship returns to figure out exactly how much.' Then he grinned. 'Or perhaps I should say you will decide. I am very pleased with how you managed the accounts for *The Integrity*.'

'Thank you, but—'

'No, no. Leave a man to dote on his only remaining daughter.' Then he sighed. 'If I could, I would go back there and bring out a dozen more of your kin.'

By kin, he meant all the other half-white Chinese orphans raised at the temple. 'You are too kind.' She meant it. All that travel would kill him. And yet, she couldn't love him more for the good heart he had.

So she closed up their small London place and went

to stay with the honeymooning couple. She saw the love between the two of them and her heart ached. And every time she saw their tender looks, she thought about Cedric. And she wondered when her heart would begin to heal.

What a change two months had wrought. Her sister was a duchess and blissfully happy. And how everything ended up the same. Lucy was yet again hanging on, an extra piece of baggage intruding on her sister's life.

What was she going to do with the rest of her life?

Then came the morning that she and her sister were drinking tea in the parlor and the Duke sauntered in with a big grin on his face.

'What has you so happy?' Grace asked as she extended her cheek for a kiss.

'I have finished with my solicitor, my banker and my steward, not to mention my valet and your maid.'

Her sister frowned. 'Why would you be talking to my maid?'

'Because we need to go. Now.' He tugged her upright. Lucy had already set aside her tea. She would find another book to read. Thankfully, the Duke's library was extensive.

'No, no,' the Duke said as he turned to her. 'If you will join us please?'

Lucy nodded, confused but all too happy to have something new to do. Her sister followed more reluctantly. She wasn't as delighted by surprises as Lucy was. Nevertheless, they climbed into a carriage and headed away.

Soon the familiar scents of the docks filtered through the air. Grace smiled, having spent much of her youth aboard ship. Lucy, on the other hand, wasn't as excited as they neared *The Integrity*. The ship stood proud, though there were still some repairs to be done. And Captain Banakos waved a smiling hello to them.

One other person was there.

Cedric.

Lucy's heart squeezed painfully tight at the sight of him. He looked good, though there was still a leanness to his face. And his clothing didn't fit well, but his shoulders were squared and his expression...

Well, it was guarded as hers would be.

'Why is Lord Domac here?' she said, her voice coming out as a strangled kind of squeak. 'I will not—'

'Oh, I remember now!' her sister cried. Then she squeezed Lucy's arm. 'Don't worry. You will love this.'

She wasn't so sure. Coming face-to-face with Cedric again was something she wanted to prepare for. But there was no time as the Duke helped them exit the carriage. And then they all climbed aboard *The Integrity*.

The greetings passed quickly enough with Cedric glaring at his cousin. Honestly, she couldn't blame him. If she felt discomforted by the situation, he had to be furious. After all, the two men had reached an accord in the last month. To be summoned like a servant was humiliating.

'Sorry, this has been abrupt,' Declan said by way of apology. 'I've been occupied with other matters.' He waited as his wife stopped inspecting the ship and turned her attention to him. 'I shall make this quick, shall I?' Declan continued. 'Miss Lucy Richards, your father and I have discussed things and have come to an arrangement. The repairs on *The Integrity* are underway. It will take another month at least, but then she will be ready to set sail with a new cargo.' He leaned towards her with a mischievous grin. 'Would you like to choose it?'

Her heart leapt into her throat. Was he truly trusting her with an entire cargo? Then the Duke turned to Cedric.

'I'm willing to give you a portion of that cargo, cousin. I'll let you supervise it, sail with it and sell it in China as you had initially planned. Any profit will be allotted to you and your sisters' dowries evenly.'

'What?' Cedric gaped at the Duke.

'One condition though,' he said as he turned to Lucy. 'She will be the one deciding on the cargo. She will be the one to set the price. And you will work under Captain Banakos and her. Prove your mettle and we can discuss the next sailing.'

'You want me to be her lackey?' Cedric asked, bristling.

'Yes,' the Duke answered. 'For the next two months. If you want the boat.' The Duke's expression softened as he stepped closer to Cedric. 'I am trying to help.

You hurt us all deeply, but you are my cousin, and I care for you.'

'I apologise, Declan. Truly, but—'

'I didn't know about the roof. If I had, I would have taken care of it.'

Cedric nodded. 'It's done—'

'I know. I also know you've been looking for a boat—'

'I have investors. I don't need—'

'But there's none better than this one.' His gaze lifted to *The Integrity*. 'You chose well with this.'

Cedric's jaw firmed, but he nodded.

'I want you to have your chance, Cedric. But you risk a great deal—for all of us—if Prinny's investment goes sour.'

'I can do it.'

'I hope so. This is your chance.' He looked back at Lucy. 'But if she wants to punish you, I'll allow it. You certainly deserve it.'

Cedric's gaze turned to her, and she didn't know how to respond. Her heart still ached for him and for his pain, and yet all her darker emotions remained.

'She's not vindictive,' Cedric said in an undertone.

'Lucky for you.' Then the Duke squeezed his cousin's arm. 'If you don't want this, just say so. I mean it to be a help, not a punishment.'

The two men's eyes met and held. And then Cedric grimaced.

'I cannot leave my sisters without help. I found them

a banker and a new steward. Men who will treat them well and not be so easy on my father, but—'

'I'll see to their care while you're gone. I swear it.'

'They're damned independent.'

'It's a family trait,' the Duke said with dry amusement. 'They'll be safe. Even the new babe.'

Lucy jolted. One of his sisters was pregnant? She hadn't known.

'Simon was born last week,' Cedric said, a pleased flushed to his expression. 'A healthy boy.'

The Duke grinned. 'Congratulations, Uncle.' Then he turned to Captain Banakos. 'I trust you will treat my cousin as he deserves?'

'That I will, your grace. That I will.'

Then the Duke grabbed Grace's hand and pulled her off the boat. Apparently, he had other plans for his wife, and they pertained to the sleek pleasure craft docked alongside. On the side of it, *The Duchess* was written in bold letters.

While the three of them stood gaping, the Duke swung his wife up into his arms and carried her up the gangplank. And once aboard, they paused long enough to wave a cheery goodbye.

'They're sailing on the evening tide,' Captain Banakos said.

'What?' Lucy asked. She was still trying to understand what the Duke had asked her to do. Manage the entire cargo? By herself!

'Yes, sirree,' the captain said with a grin. 'He asked

me to see you got home safe. But for the moment,' he cast a sidelong glance at Cedric. 'I expect the two of you have things you want to discuss.'

Then with a broad grin and a very loud chuckle, the man tipped his hat and withdrew. Leaving her face-to-face with the one man she'd never wanted to see again.

Chapter Twenty-One

Cedric could not stop staring at Lucy. He hadn't spoken with her in two months, beyond two sentences at his cousin's wedding. In that time, she'd seem to grow. She stood taller and didn't look on the verge of running anymore. It was a subtle change. She was a strong woman before, but now there was a subtle calm presence about her that was new. As if she could indeed command a fleet of ships.

It looked good on her.

And it required him to be the one who spoke first.

'You look lovely,' he said. 'You're wearing colours now that you're out. It suits you.'

She said nothing. Of course not. Lucy was never one to show how she truly felt. Not at first. 'I behaved abominably. I cannot tell you how much I regret it. I think back and I cannot believe I did it.'

He had apologised before, but some things needed to be repeated.

'Lucy—'

'One of your sisters had a son?'

'Yes.' He shoved his hands in his pockets. It was the only way he could stop himself from reaching for her. 'You were right. They found ways to survive. Cora is married now, and the babe is healthy.' Not to mention legitimate. 'If I can get dowries for my other two sisters, they will have the life they ought to have had from the beginning.'

'So you no longer fear for them?'

He arched a brow. 'I didn't say that. But I have helped all I can. Now I need to have a successful cargo.'

Her gaze went to *The Integrity*, but she said nothing. Just as well, he had more to say.

'You know,' he began as he settled onto a barrel. 'It doesn't matter what Declan decreed. I was coming to you anyway. I needed your help.'

'My help?' Doubt laced her tone.

'Yes. I have investors. I have a cargo planned. But I cannot negotiate like you do. And you have a better understanding of the buyers than I do. You *should* set the prices.' He looked up, hope lacing his tone. 'I thought we might work together, but now I accept Declan's offer. With gratitude.'

She was silent a long time, studying him. He tried to be as open as possible with her. No artifice. No attempt at charm. Eventually, it worked.

She scrambled onto a barrel set near to him. Not within touching distance, but close enough for discussion.

'You have changed,' she said.

'For the better, I think.'

'Or you have learned how to lie more convincingly. I cannot tell.'

'Of course you can,' he said. 'Of everyone, you have always seen me clearest.' He wanted to touch her but knew better. She was too wary, and he had not apologised enough for what he had done. 'I will do whatever you want. I swear it.'

She stared at him. 'You are not a humble man.'

He was now.

'You are a brash man with joy in his step and confidence enough to let another shine.'

He wasn't sure he was that man still. 'I have had my confidence knocked aside.'

She snorted. 'No, you haven't. You have found investors. That is no small feat.'

It had been exhausting, difficult work, but he knew the English *ton*. He knew how to talk to them. He knew how to persuade them to stoop to commerce. After all, if a future earl could work, then they had no excuse.

It helped that Prinny thought him the most brilliant of fellows. He just had to live up to the promise.

What he didn't have was a boat. He'd spent the last two months looking for one in between trips home to help his sisters and to greet his new nephew. Declan was right. None matched *The Integrity*. And as much as he made it sound to others like he had a couldn't-possibly-lose cargo, he wasn't sure about it. Which is why he'd been planning on talking to Captain Banakos. And to Lucy.

'Punish me however you want. I deserve it. But after you're done being angry—which you have every right to be—then I hope we can talk. I hope you will give me advice.'

She didn't even speak. She looked at him, her dark eyes liquid with thoughts he couldn't fathom. But in the end, she nodded.

'We can talk?' he asked.

'Yes.'

Relief poured through him. He hadn't completely destroyed what was between them. She didn't completely hate him yet.

'What do you want me to do first? Tell me and I shall do it.'

Her feet kicked out a bit, thumping the barrel as she sat in silence. It might have been a childish motion if it didn't draw attention to her shapely calves and ankles. It also told him that she was relaxing around him. Then she said the most wonderful thing.

'Tell me what you have been doing.' Then she threw him an arch look. 'Tell me what you have promised the Prince.'

They began to talk. Or rather, he talked and she listened. He loved that she understood what he was trying to build. Not just understood but helped with his dreams. She rarely interrupted him, but when she did, she asked something important. She made quiet suggestions, and he quickly learned to think about her words before he spoke again.

It was a kind of rhythm of discourse that he didn't have with anyone else. It helped him settle his racing thoughts and taught him to think with something more than just his passion and excited dreams.

And every time he chewed on her words or worked with her ideas, she flushed with pleasure. Bit by bit, he watched her blossom. It was such a simple thing to listen to her words, but she became more animated every time he did it. And how beautiful she was when he engaged with her thoughts.

That made for a good discussion. And when the captain finally came up top, they were both arguing without heat in a way he had never experienced before. Imagine having a disagreement without anger or insult! It didn't solve the question about which cargo went where, but it also didn't require embarrassment or groveling.

'It's time for the lady to head home,' Captain Banakos said when the two of them paused long enough for him to get a word in edgewise.

'But there are things we still need to decide,' Lucy said as she looked up at the late afternoon sky.

'True,' Cedric said, 'but they are not our decisions to figure out. They are yours to ponder.' He took a deep breath, startled to realise how easy it was to swallow his pride when it came to her. 'I have stated my case. You get the final decision.'

She looked at the captain as he nodded. 'Aye, miss. That's what the Duke said.'

Then he watched with pleasure as a slow smile spread across Lucy's face. 'Then I will make the decision,' she said. 'Tomorrow. At teatime.' She looked to Cedric. 'Would you care to join me?'

Such a demure invitation, just like a true society lady. 'I would,' he said, his heart beating a little faster. 'With pleasure.'

And so they set another rhythm between them. Teatime. The most polite time of the day where rules of behaviour were strictly observed. He could not importune her. She could not act anything but proper. Especially since there was always a chaperone in the room with them.

And yet, he could think of no better way to spend his time.

Chapter Twenty-Two

Lucy had never felt happier. She had work thoughts to occupy her mind and Cedric to hash them out with at tea. She had the excitement of commerce without the fear that had dogged her night and day in China. And, at times, she had sweet moments of laughter when Cedric met her eyes over a shared moment.

It never mattered what they were sharing. They connected over victories and disappointments alike. The moment their gazes locked together, she would feel an electric charge shoot through her body. Her breath would catch, her skin would prickle and need would bloom in her womb.

It was passion, romantic desire, or maybe it was simple bodies in proximity. But every time she won his smile, she felt her world brighten. And every time he relaxed in her presence, showing her either happiness or frustration, she felt the burden of anger ease inside her.

He was no longer the moody companion she'd met on *The Integrity*. Neither was he the angry, frightened man who had pursued her sister. This Cedric was a man of singular focus. He wanted to make their next shipment a financial windfall, and he worked tirelessly to see it accomplished.

So she worked with him instead of against him. And their time together was even better than their interludes aboard ship.

And yet the happier she became, the more she fantasised about that long-ago time. She remembered their kisses in the moonlight. She relived his touch in his cabin. And she pretended that they had not stopped. That he had opened her completely and thrust inside. That he had filled her as a man fills a woman because she could think of no one else who completed her so perfectly.

Their skills in commerce complemented each other. He charmed the investors. She calculated the money. And together they argued over the space in the cargo hold and the merits of each buyer or seller.

It was a complicated process as deeply stimulating as how he had opened her thighs and brought her to completion. And most nights, she found herself reliving one of their discussions while imagining his body between her thighs.

It was a tortured, twisted thought process that left her aching in a way that she couldn't satisfy herself. She wanted him. She loved him.

And maybe it was time to have him.

She might never get the kind of marriage her sister

had with the Duke. Cedric was not in a position to offer for her hand. Her father had said as much. And though she had forgiven his hurtful actions, her father had not.

So she was not destined to be Cedric's bride, but she would have her moment of perfection with him nonetheless. Because he had helped her find her confidence and her place in this world. She was manager of *The Integrity* now, plus her father's three other merchant ships. And she wanted to share that with Cedric in the only way she could.

In her bed. Because she loved him.

And so she made her plan.

She arranged to see Cedric on the boat. The repairs were done, and the cargo nearly loaded. Indeed, the ship was set to sail in three days. And, because the opportunity had presented itself, she asked Captain Banakos to inspect a new ship her father was considering buying. There wasn't money for it at the moment, but it was a possibility for the future.

Which meant that the captain was nowhere near when she and Cedric took a last tour of *The Integrity* and its hold. They talked with the ease of long friends, laughing together when needed, and worrying together because so much depended upon what they'd done here.

Finally, she led him to the tiny room that had been his berth so long ago. She noted the new mattress she had installed there, and then she looked in his eyes. She could see by the sudden flare of his nostrils that he was remembering what they'd done here. And when he shoved his hands into his pockets, she knew he wanted to touch her but was holding himself back.

All she need do was convince him that restraint was no longer necessary. And since she had never been coy once a thing was decided, she stretched up onto her toes and pressed her mouth to his.

He resisted. She could feel the tension in him neither giving in nor doing any of the things she dreamed about. Then he set his hands on her waist. Oh, to feel him touch her again! Inspired, she teased his lips with hers, and he met her tongue to tongue. They played together, at the edge of his lips, penetrating neither one's mouth.

And then, to her shock, he set her away from him.

'Did you arrange for Captain Banakos to be away?' he rasped. 'And did you plan to be here without your chaperone?'

She smiled. 'I did.'

'So we can do this?'

'Yes.'

'Because you want it?'

'Yes.' She lifted her face to his. 'I want it with you.'

'Has your father changed his mind? May I marry you?'

She dropped back onto her heels and shook her head. 'He was very angry at you.'

'As well he should be. What I did was unforgiveable.'

True. Except... 'I forgive you.'

She felt the impact of her words. His body tensed

then released, and the shimmer in his eyes made her stroke his cheek.

'You are not the man you were.'

He didn't seem so sure of that. 'I don't want to hurt you ever again. If this venture doesn't work…' He gestured vaguely around them at the boat and their cargo.

'Then you will find another way.' All through this, his determination had never wavered. 'But I don't want to wait.'

'Neither do I,' he said, and she thought for a moment that they were of one mind in this. She thought he would take her to the new mattress, and she would feel all those things again. How she ached for him!

But he did not.

'I must prove myself to you.'

He already had.

'And to your father.'

She rolled her eyes. 'I have lived without a father nearly all my life. What need have—'

He pressed his hand against her mouth, silencing her with a fierceness she didn't expect.

'Never say that again,' he said, his expression gentle despite his harsh tone. 'He is the best man I have ever met. He is the reason you are in England with a home, fine clothing and a dowry.'

'I don't have one yet,' she said. 'He won't dower me until next Season.' Resentment bubbled up inside her.

'And…' he said quietly, 'I must prove to myself that

I am worthy of you.' He spoke with such severity, not directed at her, but at himself.

'Isn't that my decision?' she pressed.

'It is,' he said. 'But it is also mine.'

She stared at him, seeing that he was determined. She felt the heat of him pressed against her, and yet he still held himself back.

'I have decided what I want,' she said firmly. 'I want you.'

'Why? I have brought you nothing but pain.'

So many answers to that. Because he saw her, fought with her, and surrendered to her. Because he daily struggled to honour his family responsibilities at the cost of his own happiness. But in the end, there was only one answer.

'Because I love you.'

He kissed her then with such fierceness that she became breathless. He thrust his tongue inside her, he stroked the inside of her mouth and he pulled her hard against his whole body. She felt his heat and his hunger, matching it with her own.

But that was all he did. He kissed her until she couldn't breathe, and then he pulled away, dropping his forehead against hers as they breathed together.

'I cannot say I love you,' he finally whispered.

'What?'

'I cannot tell you that until I have proven myself. God, I wish you understood this. I want you.' He ground himself against her as if she couldn't feel how thick he was, how hungry they both were. 'But you wouldn't respect me if...' He groaned. He couldn't even say the words.

'If you made love to me?'

He nodded. 'I wouldn't respect myself if I took your virginity now. And I don't think I can stop myself.' For proof, he slid his hands down her sides, his thumbs grazing across her breasts while she gasped in reaction. 'I will not dishonour you,' he said, his words harsh.

'I don't feel dishonoured,' she snapped. 'I feel...' What? Frustrated. Hungry. And precious. What other man would deny himself when she stood there offering everything? No other man but Cedric. 'You are so frustrating!'

'I know,' he said. 'Believe me, I am feeling very annoyed with myself.'

His cock was hot against her pelvis, the pressure sweet as she pulled herself higher against him. He groaned at the feel, but no more than she. How did he set her blood on fire so quickly?

'I decide,' she whispered. 'You do not make my choices for me.'

He looked in her eyes. Their gazes held for a long time, and she thought for a moment that he understood. But in the end, his expression turned fierce.

'You decide for you, but I am part of this equation.'

'Yes,' she whispered. 'Yes, you are.'

They were still standing face-to-face when she felt the buttons on the back of her gown slip apart. His hands were clever as always, and soon her dress sagged then slipped off her shoulders. But this was not China. She wore almost as much below her gown as above. The dress slipped away, but beneath that she wore stays atop her shift.

He looked down, his gaze hot as he stroked his finger across her chest. He skated to the edge of her shift, teasing the ribbons there, but not pulling them.

'I have dreams about your breasts,' he murmured. 'I remember how they feel in my hands. Your nipples enchant me.' The edge of his thumbnail cut over the fabric to her tightened nipple. He scraped it there while her breath caught with every pass.

'I think about your legs,' she said. 'I watched you climb the ratlines, the way your muscles bunched before you jumped from one to the other. The way you caught yourself, swinging while your shoulders hunched, and you pulled yourself up.' She shook her head. 'I watched you a thousand times. I can still see it.'

And she could, her eyes closing as she remembered him in the sails. Him behind her in his bed. Him with his hands on her breasts and his body surrounding hers. How he'd made her body sing.

How she wanted to feel it again.

She reached for the ties to her stays. She could undress herself as easily as he did. She could—

'No.'

'What?'

'I cannot touch you like that and stop. I cannot…'

'I want it.'

He released a long shuddering breath. 'I get to choose, too. I will not ruin you.'

'But—'

He cut off her words with a kiss. He cupped her face, he teased the roof of her mouth, and then—

He swept her up in his arms. She gasped and clutched his arms, anchoring herself to him as he set her down in the berth. There was room there for them both, but he did not set her longwise. And he kept her face forwards while he gently set her down.

'Cedric—' she began, but he shook his head. She wasn't sure what she wanted to say anyway, so she fell silent as he knelt before her.

'We can do this,' he said, his voice tense.

She didn't know what he meant, but she didn't care. In this, he knew what he was about. And she was his willing partner.

His hands skimmed down her legs, quickly cupping her feet before inching his way up her calves. She wore stockings and slippers, but they might as well not have been there for the heat she felt at his touch. Strong fingers, large hands and the mesmerizing squeeze as he steadily rose up her legs.

Her knees fell open and her toes curled. Then the cool air hit her thighs as her skirt bunched over his arms. Would he touch her there again? That spot between her thighs?

'Have you explored on your own? Have you touched yourself?'

He held her gaze as he asked, and she couldn't imagine lying to him for all that it made her cheeks flush.

'Yes,' she said, her voice hoarse.

'And did you think about me?'

'Oh yes.'

He grinned. His hands rolled over the top of her thighs and his elbows slid between her knees, pressing them open. Her skirt sat well above her knees, and he took his time rolling it even higher until her intimate place was fully exposed.

He teased his fingers across the skin above her stockings. He let his thumbs trail across her mound. And while he was still grinning at her, he let his fingers delve into places she had only begun to explore.

'It is better with you,' she said.

'Don't forget that,' he said, pride in his tone.

And then, to her great pleasure, he thrust a thumb inside her. In it pressed, thick and sweet. She groaned to feel it, her back arching. It wasn't her most sensitive place. She had learned that spot well. But this was good, and she loved it.

'You like that,' he said.

'Don't preen.'

'I'm appreciating.'

His other thumb joined the first, pushing in, widening even as she squeezed.

'Ah,' he said happily. 'You are strong.'

She squeezed him again, and he responded by stroking his thumbs upwards. He separated her folds, he pushed upwards, and then he rolled across that sensitive place.

Sensation shot through her body. She arched off the berth, her head thrown back.

'Pinch your nipples,' he said, his voice rough.

Her breasts were flattened beneath shift and stays, but she knew how to please him. While she held his gaze, she pulled her breasts out, showing them to him while she moved them in a way she liked.

And he liked.

His eyes grew dark, and he licked his lips. She pretended his mouth was on her breasts, sucking as he once had. And while lightning shot through her body from breast to womb, he stroked her nub. Her belly clenched, her legs trembled, and her muscles tightened around… around…his fingers?

She hadn't the awareness to understand what he was doing. Two fingers? Three? Pushed inside her, stretching her while she undulated above him.

So close.

So exquisite.

And then he stopped. She strained forwards, but his hands were on her thighs. She couldn't move where she wanted. She couldn't force him to continue.

Her hands fell away from her chest. She gripped the mattress as she strained forwards, but he held her off.

He held her still, and she nearly sobbed as the tension hovered, hovered, and then began to fade.

What was he doing? Why—

He pressed a kiss to her knee. And then another to the top of her stocking on her inner thigh. She was so open, so hungry that there was room for him there. Room for him to trace his tongue higher.

Further.

There.

His tongue pushed in where his fingers had been.

She didn't know what to think. The act was so intimate, so different, she couldn't at first comprehend it. But then she lost herself to the sensations.

He tasted her everywhere. He held her open as he explored her. Fingers, tongue. Sweet heaven, he was everywhere.

She lost track of what was his tongue, what were his fingers. She lost herself to the feelings. And then he pressed upwards. He found her most sensitive place. He licked her while she gasped.

Her belly coiled even as her back arched. She wanted more, more, more of whatever he did. Strokes and presses while she cried out. His fingers spread her wider and he blew cool air across her swollen flesh.

He played her body until she lost all control of herself. He built the tension in her, then paused. He held her at the edge with a caress, a taste, a tease. She could not tumble over, she could not get what she wanted, and he clearly loved the game.

'Cedric,' she gasped. 'Cedric!'

He didn't answer. Or if he did, she couldn't hear it over her own whimpers.

And then he paused again. He waited as her breath eased enough for her to whisper.

'Please.'

'Always.'

Then he opened her with his thumbs, pressed his lips to her flesh, and sucked.

Sensation.

Lighting.

Yes!

The waves crashed over her. Release burst through her, saturating her body with bliss. And all through it, she knew he was watching her. She knew he was pleasured by the sight of her ecstasy. And if she missed it, she was reminded as he pressed kiss after kiss to her thighs.

Tiny presses of his lips while she lay boneless and open on the settee. Whispers of words she couldn't hear against her skin while she remained spread before him like a banquet.

Until he stopped.

She felt him pull back. She watched as he used his handkerchief to clean them both. And then he rocked back on his heels as he gently pulled her knees together.

'Remember me,' he said. Then he flashed her an expression filled with regret. 'Forgive me.'

She frowned, straightening her clothing as she

pushed herself upright. But it was too late. He was already backing away.

'Cedric?'

'I'll understand,' he whispered.

'What?'

'I'll understand if you don't wait for me. Your father is right. You are young.'

She grabbed his shoulders, turning him to face her. 'I know my own mind.'

He wasn't listening. 'I will return, I swear it. I'll come back with a full cargo and enough coin to make you proud.'

She touched his cheek. 'What if I am already proud of you?'

He smiled as if she had just gifted him with life itself. 'That's why I need you,' he said. He pressed a kiss to her lips, then abruptly left the room. He waited for her up top, his gaze fixed outwards to India and China. And when she came up to speak to him, he shook his head.

'There is a hackney waiting for you. Do you see it? It will see you safely home.'

'But—'

'Do not ask me to break my honour, Lucy. It is the only thing I have left.'

She looked at him, knowing now that the risk she wanted to take was not in bringing him to her bed. That was a thing of pleasure and joy. The risk she must do was to speak her heart.

'You are abandoning me,' she said quietly. 'It doesn't

matter why you are going. I feel abandoned.' Just as she had when Grace left her to become a navigator. When Ah-Lan left her to learn his trade in China. And now, again, when she remained behind while he left.

He looked stricken. His jaw went slack as horror crossed his face. But even though she'd bared her heart to him, she could not change his mind.

'I want to become worthy of you,' he said as he touched her face.

'You are—'

'I must prove myself, Lu-Jing.' He flipped around to look back at London. 'I have failed so many times. Don't you see everything at stake here? My sisters' dowries, my investors, the Prince Regent! I cannot disappoint them. I can barely look at myself in the mirror without recounting my failures.'

'Count your successes instead. You found work for your brother-in-law. The first children's book is out and doing well.' She had purchased a copy herself and thought it wonderful. 'You found investors who believe in you enough to give you their coin. What is that but a myriad of success?'

He nodded, but his gaze did not return to her face. 'One more, Lu-Jing. One more success and I shall return to you. If you are still unattached, I will drop to my knees before you, I will shower you with treasure and I will marry you.' He turned to look at her. 'I will do this. But I will not say I love you until I can feel worthy enough to stand by your side as your husband.'

She sighed. There was no changing his mind. Not without breaking him.

Three days later, he left with their full cargo. He meant to seek a market along the way in Africa or India. Then he would fill the hold on the return trip with the tea so loved by the English.

While she remained behind to silently fume.

For nineteen very long months.

Chapter Twenty-Three

Nineteen months later

God, she'd changed.

That was Cedric's first thought as he made his achingly slow progress into Almack's. He was ill, weak and defeated, but he needed to see Lucy one final time. And so he'd donned clothing that did not fit anymore, spent his last coins getting a hackney and he'd blustered his way inside.

He'd heard the gasps at his entrance. He doubted anyone recognised him. Honestly, he didn't even recognise the man in the mirror. But she did. And as her eyes widened in shock, he looked at her and wondered if she had changed or if his memory of her had grown dim until this moment when the reality of her was so overwhelming.

Strong. Beautiful. Standing tall in a way she'd never done before except when they were together. He swallowed. During his absence, she'd truly adapted to English society. And here he was feeling as un-English as it was possible to be. Future earls are supposed to swagger when they enter a room. They are meant to have refined clothing and a perfumed scent.

He'd long since lost the knack of a swagger, and his clothing had been stored for the last nineteen months without anyone to care for it. As for perfume, his scent was that of the ocean and the lye soap he'd used. But he'd gotten into Almack's, and so that meant something. He was still accepted into polite society.

He was supposed to be returning buried in wealth with the words *I told you so!* on his lips. He'd held on to that thought with the grip of a drowning man.

But as the months wore on, as storms raged against their tiny ship, and as his body ached from constant work, his thoughts had changed to fantasies. Hot and erotic ones, but also quiet, soothing caresses. As the return trip had gone on interminably, she became an angel in his thoughts. He threw all his feelings, both good and bad, at her. His rage burned her. His pain flowed like a river to her. And when those were depleted, he sent her his tears and his regrets.

But now that she was here across from him, old patterns kicked in. He bowed to her and requested a dance as if he were again the spoiled peer he'd once been. A man who had never faced starvation, death or even true disease.

She gaped at him. That was no surprise. He was a pale shadow of who he'd once been. But then, he saw her rally. She straightened to her full height and smiled. The expression was tentative, and her shoulders were pulled in from tension, but it was a smile nonetheless.

Then she spoke.

'L-lord Domac. Welcome back to England. I had no idea you had returned.'

'Just docked. I barely had time to dress before coming to see you.'

'You came to Almack's straightaway?' He heard the incredulity in her voice.

'I knew you'd be here.' Then he held out his hand to lead her into the next dance. She had already stepped to his side, but then a damned coughing fit gripped him. He tried to suppress it, but that never worked. Indeed, it made it worse. All too soon, he was pressing a handkerchief to his mouth and praying he could remain upright.

He was excruciatingly aware of the people who drew back from him in horror. No one wanted to be exposed to disease. But unlike them, Lucy came closer. She set a hand on his shoulder, riding out the spasms like a flower atop the waves. And when he was done, she said something. He had no idea what. He heard her polite tone more than the words. And when he looked up, he saw her expression tighten.

Did she fear him? Or fear for him? Hard to tell.

Finally, he sorted through her sounds to remember a word. Lemonade.

'Lemonade would be welcome,' he said as he straightened to his full height.

He held out his arm, cursing it for shaking. She set her fingertips on it, then she gently steered him towards the refreshment, pausing only to apologise to Mr. Somebody. He couldn't remember the boy's name.

'I am sorry I shall have to forego our dance,' she said to the interloper. 'Lord Domac and I have some mutual interests that I am impatient to discuss.'

Mr. Whomever didn't take the rejection politely. He grimaced in distaste and then squared his soft shoulders as if for battle. 'Then I shall escort you to Hyde Park tomorrow,' he said. 'As recompense.'

Upstart puppy. She didn't need to do anything he demanded. Cedric opened his mouth to say something derisive, only to feel his lungs tighten up again. Damn it, if he forced words out now, he would cough instead. He held his tongue, and to his shock, he discovered that Miss Richards did not need him to defend her at all.

'Goodness,' she drawled. 'I don't believe I've ever received a ruder invitation. And believe me, I have received many. Sir, you are dismissed.'

The fop openly gaped at her, as did several others who were listening. Cedric, too, was momentarily stunned. He couldn't remember Lucy ever speaking so pointedly to anyone. Good God, it set him back on his heels. This was not the woman he remembered, and the dissonance was jarring. And yet a moment later, she was grace personified as she allowed him to move them—at his pace—to the refreshment table.

They said nothing. She was likely waiting for him to speak, but he did not trust his throat yet. He refused to descend into another coughing fit, but as usual, his refusal meant nothing.

He began coughing as the footman poured the lemonade.

She gathered their cups and gestured to a pair of chairs. The seats were occupied, but at her harsh look, the ladies jumped to their feet and placed themselves two steps away. Close enough to hear everything.

She sat quickly, still balancing the cups in her hands, then smiled politely as he all but collapsed beside her. It took him a moment to catch his breath. He tried to smile as she passed him his lemonade, but he doubted the expression looked anything like normal.

'Cedric,' she said sotto voce. 'Why have you sought me out? You could have sent me a message. I would have come to the ship.'

'I will not be there,' he said with as much strength in his voice as he could manage. 'I have been gone nearly two years. I must find out how my family fares. And if…' He swallowed unable to finish the thought. He needed to know if there was any money left in his estate or if his father had impoverished them all. If his sisters were dead of starvation while his mother survived on bitterness and her sister's charity. And had his young nephew survived? The first years of life were the most precarious.

'Your parents live much as they had before you left.'

He wasn't sure if that was for the good or ill. He did not wish for pain to befall them, but they were both miserable people who poisoned everyone around them.

'My sisters?' he asked.

'All well. We visited them for Simon's first birthday. And your brother-in-law has made a name for himself repairing canals. Your friends sing his praises.'

That was a relief. He remembered that Declan had promised to watch over them, but to hear the truth of it eased his mind.

'Thank you,' he said. 'I will rest easier now.'

She stiffened at his wording. Did she know he believed he was going to die soon? He had seen illness take a quarter of their crew. So far he'd survived, but that was out of sheer stubborn willpower. He'd never felt worse in his entire life.

'And what of you, my lord?' she asked.

'I fare exactly as you see.' He was sick, impoverished and holding on to his pride by a thread of determination. And wasn't that a shock? He didn't think he had any pride left.

Meanwhile, she shifted uncomfortably, twisting to face him more directly. 'My lord,' she began, but then hesitated. 'Cedric,' she tried again, but he cut her off rather than hear pity in her voice.

'You mean to ask about our cargo. I shall tell you. Good profit for you and for the Prince—'

'That is excellent, but—'

'I haven't the skill with the account books that you do...' He had to pause to take a breath. 'But even my review tells me you did very well.' By contrast, his own corner of the hold, the place where she allowed him to choose everything, had done less well. He'd made sure every inch of profit went to his investors, the Prince being the most important. They would have a solid return.

He, on the other hand, had spent his personal profits along the way. Extra expenses he hadn't counted on. And other special purchases he didn't regret. But the end result was not the windfall he'd hoped for.

'You win,' he said. 'My choices did not ever do as well as yours.'

'What game did I win?' she returned, her tone losing some of its gentleness. 'I asked after you, my lord.'

He looked at her, and his head bobbled with dizziness. He heard the censure in her tone and added it to his list of sins. He was handling this badly, but damnation, what did she want? After two years, he hadn't nearly enough to prove his worth to her father. Two years! And now he just wanted to lie down and die.

'Cedric,' she whispered urgently. 'You are not well.'

He flashed her a wan smile. 'Oh, how you flatter me,' he drawled.

He watched frustration knot her features before

smoothing back down. He'd always admired that in her. She was always so calm, but this close to her, he could see every shift of her features. Even when it indicated annoyance.

At least she wasn't indifferent to him. It would have destroyed him if she'd forgotten him completely.

'You are such an ass,' she muttered under her breath.

He would start braying if he could trust his voice.

'Let me be clear,' she all but hissed into his ear. 'I do not care about the cargo. I never measured your worth by your coin.'

She was right. It was he who measured and counted every penny and thought himself a failure if another had more than he did. 'I'm sorry,' he said.

At least he thought he did. Perhaps it was more of a mumble as she ducked her head to look him in the eye. He hadn't even realised his head had dipped until he faced the floor.

'You're sweating with fever.'

Was he?

'We must get you home.'

'My home is in Kent.'

She huffed. 'Well, that's not going to work.'

Neither was this. Neither was the way they were fighting each other. Which—now that he thought on it—was exactly what the two of them did. They bickered.

He straightened up in his chair. He forced himself

to stand as if braced against a stiff wind. She matched him, though she was shorter than he.

'Miss Richards,' he said formally, 'do you not remember our last conversation before my departure?'

Her expression turned wary. 'I do—'

He didn't let her finish. 'You told me to prove myself to you. And so I departed.'

She snorted. 'Those were not my words. They were *yours*. You said you would prove yourself to everyone.'

'And now I am here, standing upon all that I have left, my honour and a sliver of pride. There is c-coin. P-prinny will be pleased. But n-not enough to show your f-father.' Damn his stuttering tongue. 'I failed,' he repeated. 'And so you are right to discard me.'

She rolled her eyes. 'Lord Domac, only you could make a Cheltenham tragedy out of a middling cargo.'

Damnation. How could she see him so clearly and so completely wrong at the same time? He was making a dramatic pronouncement. Of course he was. Because after this, he would slink off to Kent never to be heard from again. 'At least, give me my exit scene,' he muttered.

'Exit? You've only just arrived. And, as usual, you are making all the decisions without considering anyone else.'

Was she joking? 'All I do is think of everyone else,' he choked out. It was hard because his vision was beginning to swim.

'Then you are thinking all the wrong things!' she

snapped. No, it wasn't her voice that snapped. It was her fingers. *Snap! Snap!* Beneath his nose. 'Cedric!'

He lifted his gaze to hers. Or he tried. Why was his head so heavy?

'Fetch the carriage immediately. We'll take him home.'

Was she talking to him? 'Kent is a very long way.'

'Your head is a very long way away.'

'Wha—?' He couldn't finish forming the word. His mother hated that.

He heard her sigh. Then her face dropped to be directly in front of his eyes. Her forehead was crinkled with concern. That made him smile. She cared for him.

'So enthralling,' she whispered. 'Just like when we first met. What is wrong with me that you are so damned mesmerizing?'

'Such big words,' he said, hearing the words slur but unable to fix the problem. 'Where'd you learn them?'

'From you!'

'Are you ill?' he muttered and didn't know if he was asking her or asking himself.

She rolled her eyes even as she slipped an arm beneath his shoulder. 'Come along,' she said. 'I'll explain everything.'

Would she? He doubted it because nothing made sense these days. The only hope for it was to close his eyes and pray that tomorrow was better. That was how he'd survived at sea.

Wait. No, that was absolutely not how he'd survived.

Every night he'd closed his eyes and envisioned his powerful, righteous return to England. And once there, he'd wallow in his wealth, his rightness and his brilliance. He was the man he sought to be. A man worthy of her.

Oh, bloody hell. That was an impossible dream now, and the act of giving it up utterly destroyed him. He was nothing without that hope. Better to pass out than face that reality.

So he did.

Chapter Twenty-Four

Cedric woke with a groan, his head pounding and his throat dry. He could barely tell that he was on dry land with the way his vision swam, but he knew the sounds of an English household. Knew, too, that he was in London by the distant cry of the hawkers.

He was probably in his cousin's house, he thought, and slammed his eyes closed. Better to remain in the dream of when he and Lucy had first met than face the reality of his life now.

But the more he remembered the carefree whimsy of his first nights on board *The Integrity*, the more he realised what a fool he'd been. He'd imagined her a timid flower drifting on the world's whim. In truth, she was a tiny, clever dragon, quietly gathering the world's riches. She would lead a man to wealth beyond measure. If he weren't dying, he'd move heaven and earth to marry her. But since he was, he planned to wish her well and expire with her name on his lips like a romantic figure of old.

Getting to see her one last time had been his singular focus for weeks now. Having achieved that, he could go to his final rest. He let all the strength go out of his body, allowed his lips to shape her name and dropped into death.

Right now.

He was dying...now.

Oh hell.

He was thirsty. He tried to ignore it. He'd gone without drink so much of the voyage. But to have clean water at hand and ignore it? That was a travesty. And he really wanted that drink.

He forced himself to sit up, his head swimming worse than in the storm that had cost them months to repair the ship. Too embarrassed to ring the bell for help, he reached for the water, but his hand was shaking too much. He was going to spill the precious liquid all over. Oh hell.

And while he was bracing his head and his hand, he had the errant thought that he might not be dying. What if returning to Mother England brought him back to life?

How terribly inconvenient.

If he wasn't dying, he'd have to get strong again. He'd have to deal with his still crumbling estates, his dowerless sisters and his horrid parents. The very thought of that had him praying for death.

It still didn't come, but something else did. Some-*one* entered the room and immediately began cursing.

'Good God!' exclaimed a female voice. It was spoken in Chinese, so he knew it was Lucy by more than the cadence of her voice. 'I was gone for five minutes!'

'I'm fine,' he lied, though it sounded more like a grunt, so she could be forgiven for not heeding his words.

She plumped his pillows and helped ease him back under the covers.

'Why didn't you ring the bell for help? I set it right there beside the bed.'

Wasn't the answer obvious? Proper English lords did not ring the bell when they were dying. They were supposed to already be surrounded by beautiful ladies who bathed them in their tears. And if they weren't dying—which, apparently, he wasn't—then proper boys got their own drink of water.

'Don't sigh at me like that,' she continued. 'I've been harassed for three days now by ladies inquiring after your health. You're the talk of the *ton*, and I'm in the envious position of getting to spoon broth into your mouth as I pray for your survival.' Her tone was sarcastic, but not cruel.

Had she been spoon feeding him? God, that was tedious work. He'd done it himself with ill sailors. Did he remember her by his bedside? Maybe, but it was too much work to recall. Especially when the memory of their first meeting lingered in his thoughts.

'You used to be shy,' he said. It wasn't an accusation. Merely a memory.

'I'm frightened. My sister says I get shrewish when I'm frightened.'

He relaxed against the pillows, his body sagging like a sack of meal. 'I don't mean to be a bother,' he muttered.

'A lie if there ever was one,' she retorted, a teasing note in her voice. 'You enjoy being the centre of attention.'

That wasn't true. Or it wasn't exactly true. He liked it when people noticed him. And if he couldn't be a jolly good fellow, then he was a jolly awful bother. Good God, his thoughts were a jumbled mess.

A string of Chinese words melded into his thoughts, confusing him even more. And then she spoke, her voice a great deal more tender.

'How do you feel now? Are you hungry? You really need some food.'

'Did you pray for me?' Where had those words come from?

'I did,' she said as she rang the small bell at the side of the bed. 'I prayed that you would choose one direction or the other. Life or death.' She cupped his face and gently lifted his chin until his gaze met hers and she smiled that radiant smile of hers. 'I am pleased you chose to live.'

He blinked as he tried to focus on her face. Actually, he'd tried to choose death, but obviously God had other plans. He wasn't arguing. If she were part of the plan, then he would be exceedingly grateful.

'Don't leave,' he said. 'I might die if you abandon me.'

'See? Alive and well. You're flirting again.'

'You used to like it.'

She arched perfect brows at him. 'Who said I don't still?'

He looked at her. With his eyes focusing again, he saw changes in her. He'd made a study of her, so he noticed differences both small and large. They'd been apart for nearly two years, and he saw a new woman before him.

Her face was fuller now and her eyes seemed less haunted than before. She was no longer a curious rabbit who ran away if one moved too fast. She looked like a woman now, one who could fit into the highest reaches of society. But then he'd always seen the poise in her, even when she'd hung on his every word as he taught her English. He supposed the difference was that she no longer hung on his words as if he set the moon and the stars in the sky.

'How long?' he asked, forcing himself to focus. 'Since Almack's?'

'Three days.'

He winced. Had she been by his side all that time? 'Have you slept at all?'

Her expression softened. 'You will oblige me now by eating. Cook took great pains with her soup. She would like more than stained bedsheets for thanks.'

He glanced at the bedsheets and noted the dark splotches. The sight sickened him. Why wasn't he properly insensate so that he didn't have to face the millions of tiny humiliations that came with illness?

A footman arrived with a tray of food. Honestly, he didn't feel like he had the strength to eat. His body felt too heavy to move. And yet, when she gathered his hands in hers and pressed them to the sides of a small cup, he worked with her rather than against her. It was the least he could do to ease the problem he had become.

At last, he got that drink. Better yet, it was broth and she was holding his hands as if he were precious porcelain.

'A little more, Cedric,' she chided gently. 'Drink a bit more.'

He did so because she wanted it. And when he finally collapsed back in exhaustion, she gently wiped the drips from his mouth.

He winced. Now he was a drooling fool when he had a beautiful woman in his bed.

'It is only pride,' she said softly. 'Haven't you had your full of it?'

'Not pride,' he murmured. He'd given that up long ago. He took a deep breath and gathered the strength to explain himself. 'I had such high hopes.'

Everything he tried to do, everything he'd fought to accomplish for himself, for his sisters, even for his blighted parents, had ended up as wasted effort. He'd made good for Prinny and his other investors. He had that much. But his own profit was negligible. And now he could barely feed himself.

What was that except failure?

'Heaven does not count our failures,' she said. 'Neither does love. Only pride keeps count. Pride measures win and loss. Arrogance points to success while misery dwells on loss. Have done with that, Cedric. Life cannot be measured on a balance sheet. And neither can you.'

Spoken like a woman with a full dowry and a brother-in-law who was a wealthy duke. He didn't begrudge her that. He knew she'd come from nothing. To be so cared for now was merely her due. She was worthy of such prosperity.

'I meant to be worthy of you. To show your father that I could provide for you.' He closed his eyes. He knew that no proper father would accept an impoverished man for his daughter.

Misery welled up inside him. He had worked so hard. He'd done everything right. He'd toiled until his hands bled. And then he'd worked at night with a quill until his vision swam.

'Never mind,' he heard her say. 'You'll see the truth of it when you're feeling better.'

Or she would. When she had time to look at the books. When she could see what he had done while he had command of the ship. For a first-time captain, he hadn't been so bad. But he hadn't been great either and they'd lost so much in that storm.

At least Captain Banakos had survived his illness.

The man was available for her next attempt. That, too, was a success. Cedric hadn't sunk the ship while he'd been in command. Maybe that should be his epitaph: *Here lies Cedric. He didn't sink the ship.*

She touched his hand, then stroked upwards to wrist and forearm. It was a casual gesture, done to pass the time as he fell asleep. And yet, it didn't feel casual to him. He felt her caress like a balm on his soul. Failure he might be, but she was still here. She sat with him, helped him eat and even touched his sun-weathered skin.

His mind centred on that caress. He focused on it, he breathed with it and he used it to silence the misery that threatened to overwhelm him.

Could she be right? Could all his mistakes be the result of pride?

Absolutely not. His mistakes came from ignorance and greed. And from thinking he could outwit the weather.

And what was that but pride?

Oh hell. He couldn't think anymore. It was too exhausting.

Thankfully, she began to sing. It was a Chinese song, one he had heard before with no understanding of its meaning. But that didn't matter. He found it more pleasing because he had no idea what the words were. And because it was her who sang.

Finally, he slept.

Chapter Twenty-Five

Lucy waited until Cedric's breath was deep and easy. She'd spent a lot of time in the last three days listening to the cadence of his breath and wondering if it would end. She'd spooned in broth whenever he stirred and prayed it would help. It wasn't until his fever broke last night that she'd begun to hope. And now that he'd woken and taken shaky sips of soup, she began to believe he would survive.

It wasn't a hundred percent. Not by a long shot. She knew that illnesses could turn on a whisper. But for now, she held his hand and felt a quiet reassurance run like a steady current between them.

It had always been thus. From the first moment they'd touched hands, she'd felt a connection between them. It made no sense. It certainly wasn't any sign of a future between them beyond the contentious relationship they already had (no matter what Phoebe said). But it was reassuring nonetheless.

And so she held his hand and she breathed peace into

her heart while silently damning him for bringing terror back, as well. Terror that he would die. Terror that they'd never share a kind word between them again. Terror that she hated him and terror that she didn't.

As usual, he was making her head spin.

She heard the knocker sound and dreaded the interruption. Her sister, Grace, was often indisposed with morning sickness, which left Lucy to cover the social duties. Given that Grace was a duchess, those tasks were myriad, and Lucy struggled to fill them all, especially since she preferred to watch from the shadows. But then she heard the telltale sound of Phoebe's delightful laugh, and her fears melted away.

Phoebe was the one Englishwoman Lucy adored. She would be happy to while away some hours with her friend while Cedric slept.

Still, it took her a moment to quietly disentangle her hand from his. She noted again how strong his hand had become. There'd been a softness to him when they'd first met. Honestly, it was a pleasing look. Men with sharp angles often had sharp tempers, and Lucy would not have warmed up to him so quickly if he'd been cut in harder lines.

Now his hand looked bony. She knew there was strength in him from the callouses that roughened his palm. And yet, his fingers still appeared long and elegant, emphasizing that he was an educated man. He even had a bump on his middle finger from where he gripped the quill.

How she wanted that fullness to return to his body. She stroked his arm one last time, pretending she could caress health into his body. Then she forced herself away.

Her steps picked up speed as she made it downstairs and heard her sister's voice. Good! Grace was feeling better this morning. She found both women in the breakfast room. Grace was nibbling on dry toast, her skin tinged with green, but her eyes were bright. And better yet, she was chuckling at something Phoebe was saying.

'You'd think it was obvious!' Phoebe continued as Lucy walked in. 'You cannot call me an encroaching mushroom one night then seek to invest in my brother's newest venture in the next. My father might ignore such slights—'

'Oh, I doubt that!'

'—but my brother can be vindictive when someone insults me.'

'He's a good brother,' Grace said as she set down the toast. 'Though, to be fair, Lady Wilma didn't care about investing. That was—'

'Her family. Well, she had best understand now how the world works. Things are changing. Money isn't just for the peerage anymore. I swear she pines for the days when the lady of the castle was worshipped hand and foot.'

Grace frowned. 'Did that really happen?'

'No. As I understand it, castle ladies worked very

hard and had a special kind of courage. Not that you could convince Lady Wilma of that.'

'That's exciting!' Lucy exclaimed as she gave Phoebe a quick hug. 'I want to hear all about these courageous castle ladies.'

Phoebe returned the embrace only to pull back with a frown. 'Goodness, you look pale. How are you faring?' She squeezed Lucy's shoulders. 'Has it been awful?'

Lucy bit the inside of her cheek, appalled by how quickly tears flooded her eyes. She could remain calm—downright placid—against all kinds of slights. Indeed, by the time she was eight, nothing could bring her to tears except to physically break her bones. But one soft look of concern from Phoebe, and her body began to expel emotion in a tsunami of symptoms.

'Oh dear,' Grace murmured. 'Oh no. He's gone?'

'What? No!' Lucy cried, trying to explain, but she couldn't get the words out. Damn it, why was she crying? He was going to be all right!

'I'll ring for the doctor,' Phoebe said. 'Maybe there's still hope.'

Lucy grabbed her friend's arm before she could touch the bell-pull. 'Don't,' she whispered.

She needed to pull herself together. She knew of only one way to bring her emotions to heel, one technique that always worked. She'd learned it from Ah-Lan, and it had always served her well.

Taking a shuddering breath, she used her method of last resort. She spat out the longest, filthiest stream of curses she could utter, partly in English, but mostly in Chinese. It was a long string of words, slowly losing strength as she lost breath.

And when she was done, she looked up to see both women staring at her with mixed expressions of shock and humour. The humour, of course, came from Grace, who understood her better than most.

'He's better, isn't he?' her sister asked.

Lucy nodded as she pulled out a handkerchief to wipe her eyes.

'Better?' Phoebe asked, her expression filling with relief. 'Is that how the Chinese tell someone good news? With a string of curses?'

'No,' laughed Grace. 'It's how Lucy does it because she is an odd one even among us half people.'

'Don't call yourselves that!' Phoebe cried. 'You are a full person no matter who your parents are. Mixed race, orphan or cit—we are gloriously wonderful women, and I shan't hear a word against any of us.'

And that was why Lucy adored this feisty English beauty. She never seemed to see the lines that people drew between each other. As the daughter of a wealthy banker, she could have grown up as spoiled as Lady Wilma. Instead, she judged people on how kind they were. From the lowest beggar to the King and Queen themselves, she measured them on that stick alone. And she held herself to the highest standard of all.

'Here. Have some tea,' Phoebe said, offering Lucy

her own cup. 'I haven't touched it, and it always settles me.'

Lucy looked at the tea and winced. Phoebe liked her drink sweet, but that much sugar made Lucy's teeth ache. Thankfully, Grace was already pouring her a new cup.

'Thank you,' Lucy murmured to her sister as she took her seat.

'Now I can chatter, if you like,' Phoebe offered. 'Or we can wait in polite silence. Whatever you prefer.'

Lucy snorted. 'As if you could wait in silence.'

'I can!' the girl protested, and she crossed her arms and pressed her lips together.

Grace and Lucy waited, sharing matching looks of amusement. Phoebe was generally irrepressible.

Sure enough, the silence lasted less than two minutes.

'Very well, then. We'll talk about something else.' Phoebe pointedly turned to face Grace. 'Tell me more about the baby. Have you felt it kick yet?'

'Not yet,' Grace answered as she dropped a hand to her barely protruding belly. 'Soon, I hope.'

Silence.

'Has the Earl visited again?'

Lucy tensed. 'Not since the last time.' Cedric's father had demanded to see his son on the second night. They had let him in, of course. No one wanted to deny a father access to his ill son. But after one look at Cedric, he turned away, clearly disgusted. And then, to everyone's shock, he demanded the money from the cargo.

She'd denied him, of course. She knew the truth of the man, but he would not be denied. Indeed, he threatened violence until she told him who was the captain of Cedric's ship. As if Cedric had been the owner.

The information was common knowledge, so she told him if only to get rid of him. And once gone, she'd barred the door to him until Declan returned. No servant liked denying an earl, even if the man was an unruly, violent blackguard.

'Declan should be home soon,' Grace said. 'He'll take care of it.'

Lucy hoped so. She did not relish another confrontation with the man.

And that was it. That was the extent of the conversation outside of Cedric. And so, after another long minute's silence, both women turned to her.

'Come on,' Grace said with a gentle smile. 'Tell us what happened.'

'His fever broke,' she answered with as little inflection as possible. 'Last night. And this morning, he woke up and was completely lucid. I caught him sitting up on the edge of the bed.'

'What?' Grace said, abruptly leaning forwards. 'I thought we had a footman in there night and day.'

Lucy shrugged. 'I sent him to bed. No use in both of us losing sleep. But then I was hungry sometime after four. I ate some bread, stopped at my bedroom to get a new book, and...' She shrugged.

'Fell asleep?' Phoebe asked. 'It's no wonder. You've been at his side night and day.'

'No,' she said, shaking her head. 'Well, yes, but not for long. Oh, I don't know. I'd already been in to see him, but then...' She was babbling. 'It doesn't matter.'

'Of course it matters!' Phoebe exclaimed. 'You're running yourself ragged for him. Everyone's talking about it.' At Lucy's pointed look, Phoebe flushed pink. 'Everybody but me, of course. There are bets on whether you'll marry him before he dies just for the title. I heard it from my brother.'

And when neither Grace nor Lucy said anything, the girl lifted her hands in surrender.

'I didn't make the bets! I'm just telling you what's going on. And how everyone thinks it romantic that he came to Almack's just to apologise to you. It's remarkable, you know. Men don't do that kind of thing. And yet he did.' Phoebe's words ended with a sigh that seemed to come from her toes. 'It was very romantic.'

'It was terrifying,' Lucy retorted. 'I thought he'd died. And he still might.' She purposely kept the wail from her voice, but it hovered in the back of her throat.

'No, he won't!' Phoebe declared as she gripped Lucy's hand. 'He'll get better and better, and then he'll propose because he's madly in love with you.'

Lucy's heart squeezed, wishing it were true. 'I don't think love was what he felt.' Lust, yes. Desire for how she could help him? Of course. But love was a complicated emotion, and Cedric was a complicated man. Only he knew what he wanted now that he was back.

'He once told me he couldn't say he loved me. He couldn't!'

Phoebe frowned. 'Why not?'

'He doesn't think it's honourable to love a woman when he has no money. He's trying to be worthy of me.'

Grace frowned. 'Have you disparaged him for that?'

She shook her head. 'You know I haven't.' She'd known good and bad men with all different levels of money. So long as they had food and shelter, she could be happy.

'Then—'

'Men!' Phoebe huffed. 'They don't understand us, do they?'

The three sipped their tea in silent agreement while her sister watched her with a steady, concerned gaze. In the end, Grace spoke, her words soft but no less jarring.

'Men are all idiots sometimes. Why does this man haunt you?'

That was the very question she'd been asking herself for the last three days and nights of worry. They'd been apart from one another for nearly two years. In that time, she'd met scores of gentlemen, many more accomplished than Cedric. And yet if they disappeared from her life for a week, she'd completely forget them.

Only Cedric made her breath catch and her heart soar. He didn't even have to be near. She'd spent countless hours remembering him, reliving what they'd done and wondering how he fared.

'He thought I wanted to talk about the cargo,' she complained. 'He is upset that it didn't do as well as he wanted.'

Phoebe frowned. 'I thought you looked at the account. You said Prinny will be pleased.'

She had to do something while sitting by his bedside. So she sent to Captain Banakos for the account book.

'Yes, yes. His investors will be happy. There were losses because of the storm, but not too bad. The biggest cost was in repairs to the ship because of the damage.'

'Then why does he think it failed?'

She threw up her hands. 'I don't know. All he talked about was how he was a failure. That he didn't have enough money. That all his hard work has amounted to nothing.'

Her sister smiled gently at her. 'Meimei,' she said, using the Chinese endearment for little sister. 'He has been gravely ill. What does any person think about when they believe they are dying?'

Lucy didn't answer the question, but Phoebe did, her voice bright. 'I'm miserable when I'm sick. I think about everything bad that's ever happened. All the things I didn't do right or all the ways someone has hurt me. Everything and everyone is awful, especially me.'

Lucy looked down at her tea. Her head was thick, her body achy and her every thought was consumed by Cedric. Why him? When she'd met so many other nice men.

'I used to love him,' she finally said. 'I used to dream about the time we could be together.'

Phoebe leaned forwards. 'And now?'

She shook her head. She didn't know how she felt. He could be so damned aggravating! She'd imagined their reunion a thousand times. Never had she thought his first words to her would be about money!

'You're tired,' Grace said. 'You haven't slept in days. He's not the only one who cannot think straight in such a state.'

'It's not about thinking!' Lucy huffed. 'It's about what we feel for each other.'

'And what do you feel?' Phoebe pressed.

Frustrated. Confused. Anxious. Tired. And so damned happy he was alive and back here with her.

'I think I will go back to the sickroom. He shouldn't be left alone.'

'No,' her sister said as she set down her teacup. 'There is a footman with him. You need real sleep.'

'Every time I close my eyes, I think…' She pressed her lips together, unwilling to speak the words aloud.

'About him?' Phoebe pressed.

'That he might die.'

Her friend nodded. 'Did you get him to drink the herbs I sent? Did you put it in his broth?'

'I did. I think it helped. It's so hard to say.'

'He'll keep getting better,' Phoebe promised. 'You'll

see. He'll get stronger. You'll get some rest. Everything will be better by tomorrow.'

She hoped so. In truth, a part of her knew it would be so. He was on the mend now. But the rest of her was still a tight knot of anxiety.

'If he wakes up and talks about money again, I think I shall strangle him!'

Her sister chuckled. 'Perhaps we should warn him about that before you murder him.'

Phoebe snorted. 'We should leave a note by his bed.'

'And perhaps,' Lucy said, 'we should all talk about something other than him!'

The two women obliged her and changed the topic. They spoke about which gentleman were interesting this Season. Answer: not many. Worse, Lucy already knew the men were not for her. None of them set her heart beating. None of them consumed her. And none of them were Cedric. For good or for ill, he was the one she must deal with now.

Chapter Twenty-Six

Cedric opened his eyes to sunny weather three days later. The birds were chirping as this neighbourhood was too nice to have too many hawkers about at first light. A maid had already been in to open the window to let in a fresh breeze, and Cedric relished the scent of England in spring, even if it was London and not the countryside.

As he'd slept, he'd hoped to hear Lucy come in. She hadn't. And a quick glance about the room showed him a ginger-haired footman named Scottie.

'How is Lucy?' he asked as he had every time he'd woken.

'Miss Richards is still sleeping.'

Was there a bit of censure in his tone? As if he didn't like Cedric referring to Lucy by her given name. Well, he wasn't. Lu-Jing was the girl's given name. Lucy was what he called her now, and the lovesick footman could bloody well accept it. Yes, that was the primary thing he'd noticed about the boy. He seemed completely lovesick for Lucy.

'She was here in the middle of the night,' the man continued. 'Checked in on you and we chatted for a moment.'

Ah. He'd thought that was a dream. 'You slept here last night?'

'Right on the floor beside you. I promised Miss Richards I wouldn't leave your side, and I didn't.' Oh, such pride in the boy's tone.

'Scottie,' Cedric said as the boy helped him sit up. 'Tonight, you will sleep in your own bed.'

'I'll let Miss Richards decide that,' was his response. 'And now, it's time to choke down—'

'The tea.' He held out his hands and was pleased to see they didn't shake. And when he received a half-full cup, he took a tentative sniff. Not as bad as yesterday.

'No honey?' Cedric asked.

'Not in the tea, my lord.'

Of course not. He did as he was bid, choking down the stuff as if it tasted palatable. It did not. But then, he needed the liquid, so he did not argue when Scottie poured him another half cup.

'I've got toast for you this morning,' he said. 'With a thin bit of jam. You'll love it.'

He likely would. Even a thin covering of jam was more than he'd had in months.

'What I'd love more, Scottie,' he said as set down his teacup, 'is information. What have I missed?'

'Missed? Shall I get you a newspaper?'

'That would be excellent.' Assuming he could stay awake to read it. 'But I mean about, um, my family. I haven't seen Declan since I got here.' Or had he? He'd been unconscious so much of the time, it was hard to know.

'His Grace has gone north. It's spring planting and with the duchess feeling so poorly, he agreed to do the visit alone.'

Cedric straightened as much as he could manage. 'Does Declan leave her alone often?' Their marriage was still young. Had it had grown cold already?

The boy snorted. 'The Duke dotes on his wife. So much so that some people say it's unnatural. And the cook, Mrs. Timley, was beside herself. Bad enough that Her Grace couldn't keep any food down, but the moment she got sick, the Duke was put off his own food, as well. The two of them were wearing each other out, and Mrs. Timley couldn't help but cook everything all the time just in the hopes that one of them would eat.'

'What? Why wasn't the duchess eating?'

'Oh! Well, that's because she's in a family way, my lord. Feeling poorly because of it. But she's getting better now. Miss Phoebe has a right talent for herbs.'

'Grace is pregnant,' he said, startled to feel no rancor at that. Two years ago, he had believed Declan had stolen her away from him. But he now realised it had been his pride that was hurt by her defection. And his bank account. 'Is she happy?'

'Happy, my lord? She's smiling all the time when she's not getting sick. She looks right eerie sometimes, the way she's pleased. And the smells don't bother her anymore so Mrs. Timley says the babe will grow proper now that she's eating. And the Duke will be back by Monday, what with the government in session.'

Ah. Good. He'd get a chance to talk plainly with his cousin soon. 'So Grace is happy and Declan's returning on Monday. Good.' And wasn't that a surprise? He looked forward to seeing Declan when he'd spent most of his life dreaming of punching his cousin in the face.

'And what of Lucy?' he asked, trying to be casual. 'I assume she'll return to her father's home soon. Still, you must know how she's faring. Is there a suitor?'

'Her father, my lord?' There was a stiffness to the man's face that made Cedric focus more sharply. He'd been doing his best to be casual, but now he frowned.

'Yes. How is Miss Richards's father?'

'Thank you, Scottie,' interrupted a voice—her voice. 'I believe I shall help his lordship finish his breakfast.'

The footman had just settled into a chair by the bed to help Cedric, but he leapt up like a frog the moment he heard Lucy's voice.

'M-miss Richards! I didn't realise you were... I mean, I thought you were—'

'Scottie, would you please get me some toast as well? I see the honey pot is here. That's wonderful.'

'And tea, Miss Richards. I'll get you a fresh pot—'

'Oh, I suppose. Phoebe has declared that I'm to drink something special, as well. Bring up whatever she says.'

'Yes, Miss Richards. Right away, miss.' He gave her a quick bow and all but clicked his heels together before dashing out the door. Cedric stared after the man, feeling unaccountably annoyed with the boy.

'Was he escaping my question,' he asked. 'Or trying to please you?'

'Both, I assume,' she said as she settled into the chair beside him. 'How are you feeling?'

'How is your father?'

'His cough overcame him nearly a year ago.' Her voice was soft and composed, and Cedric's stomach sank as much from her expression as her words.

'A year?' he whispered. Her father had passed a year ago and he hadn't known.

'His cough got worse after the wedding. I thought that summer would help but...' She shook her head.

'I'm sorry,' he said. 'I had hoped...' He thought back over everything he'd done in the last year. 'Everywhere we stopped,' he murmured. 'Every port, I looked for medicines and a way to send it back.' It was where much of his money had gone. It was why his investors made money, but not him. Because he spent his portion. But her father hadn't received any of them. 'Too late.' It was a statement, not a question.

'It was kind of you.'

'It was useless.' He closed his eyes, but his fingers

reached for her hand and squeezed. 'I'm so sorry. I know how much you loved him.'

'Thank you.'

'I should have been here. I would have gone to the services with you. I would have...' He shook his head. 'No. I would have just made things worse. We always fight. You needed comfort, not...' Him. She wouldn't have wanted him there.

'We always fight?' she asked.

He opened his eyes. 'Don't we?'

She didn't answer at first. Instead, her eyes grew pensive, and then she shrugged. 'Sounds like you're fighting with yourself. I've barely said a word.'

He stared at her, his mind hopping around in confusion. Was she chastising him? Accusing him? Or just stating a fact? He didn't know, and all his guesses were turning his brain to mush.

'Lucy...' He said softly.

'I gave those medicines—the seeds and the formulas—to Phoebe. She has an interest in these things.'

Phoebe? The blonde?

'She is working with a doctor.' Her expression softened. 'That tea may have saved your life.'

He frowned as he looked at her. 'I meant them for your father.'

'And they may save many lives here in England.'

He hoped so. He certainly couldn't argue that he felt better today than he had in a long time. And yet he didn't really care about the medicine. He wanted to know how she fared. 'Have you met someone, Lucy? Do you have an understanding with anyone?'

She frowned, her mouth opening in surprise. She might have said something then, but her words were cut off when Scottie reappeared. He was carrying a tea tray and a beaming expression, as if doing his job was a thrilling accomplishment.

'Thank you, Scottie,' she said calmly. 'You can wait outside now until his lordship requires more help.'

Spoken like a British lady when dismissing a servant. She had perfect intonation, perfect delivery. She'd grown so much from the skittish girl he'd first met. And in that vein, he found his voice, speaking like the self-important peer he'd once been.

'I'll need a shave, Scottie. Do find what I need and come back in a half hour. I trust that you can keep your hand steady or that you will find someone else.'

'Er, yes, my lord. Right away, my lord.'

'Good man,' he lied. He actually thought Scottie was a young puppy with too much lustful imagination. But that was because Cedric was an old man with a lustful imagination. 'Shut the door as you leave.'

'No, Scottie,' Lucy interrupted. 'Leave it ajar. But you may go find what you need.'

'Yes, my lady,' the man said with a quick bow.

'Miss Richards,' Cedric corrected. Lucy wasn't a lady, not officially. She had no title, so her proper address would be Miss Richards. But it wasn't Cedric's place to correct the boy. Especially since Cedric didn't have the right to call her by her given name either. There was no formal engagement between them. So if he took liberties with her name, then why couldn't the staff as well?

The servants followed the master, didn't they? And he was being an ass.

He saw Lucy's arch look at him. She knew everything he was thinking. It didn't help that the boy coloured red up to his ears and bowed himself out while leaving the door wide open. Cedric ran a hand over his face, feeling the rough skin, the patchy scratch of his beard and the sharp jut of his bones. A scarecrow probably looked better than he did.

And why the hell was he wasting his time with Lucy? Medicines and overeager servants weren't important.

'Pray tell me what you've been doing since I left. Caring for your father, obviously, but since then?'

She shrugged as she poured her tea. 'Much as I did before. I help my sister. I go to parties.'

She fell silent and he frowned at her. 'You barely did that before. Your interests were in your father's boats and cargo. In how the accounts were managed. You wanted more investors to reduce your risk.'

She set her teacup down as she studied him. 'You remember that?'

He gaped at her. 'Of course I remember.' Some of their happiest and most frustrating times were when they argued about such things. It had been a daily discussion between them, and he longed for such ease with her again.

'Tell me what you decided. Tell me how it went.'

She was quiet for a bit, then she spoke, slowly warming to her topic. 'It went badly,' she said. 'With my father so ill, no one would invest with us. Even Declan tried to help, but you were the one who could bring people to the venture. You were always the one they believed in. Not my father and certainly not me.'

He shook his head. 'I never hid your involvement. But each person cared about a different thing, had different reasons to invest with us.'

She nodded. 'You understand that. I never did. And so without you, we floundered.'

'You didn't sail?' he asked. He knew now how risky shipping could be, but without sailing a cargo, she would have no income at all.

'One ship. The others wait for investors.'

'I can help you,' he said, warming to the possibility. 'My investors will be pleased. I can get more.'

She bit her lower lip even as she looked down at her hands. 'So you intend to sail again?' Her words sounded casual, but he could see the tension in her body.

'I understand the business better now. And there is joy in the work,' he said. 'But I want to be England for a while.' He wanted to be with her.

'A while?' she pressed.

Maybe forever. 'I am a good sailor now, but not a gifted one. My skills are best used here with the investors.' He had gone all around the world. Twice! Only to learn that he was happiest at home. Hopefully with her.

'I would be grateful for your help,' she said.

He smiled, feeling some of their rapport return. He ached to touch her, but he didn't dare yet. She was still reserved with him, and he did not want to rush her.

'Cedric,' she began, her voice tentative. 'I have looked at the ship's account.'

He tensed though he didn't want to. She should be pleased by her profit.

'Why did you spend so much silver in China? The tea was not that expensive.'

Trust her to find the one thing he wasn't anxious to tell her. But it was in the account book, so he knew he couldn't hide it from her. 'I only took from my share. It was not debited from anyone else.'

'I know,' she said. 'But what did you buy?'

Information. Knowledge so that he could understand her better.

'Cedric?'

'Captain Banakos did not tell you?'

'I haven't asked him. I'm asking you.'

There was no real secret. And it was something he wanted to tell her. And yet, the words were difficult to confess. It felt too vulnerable to confess how desperately he had missed her. And to what lengths he had gone to learn more about her.

He had done so willingly, though he hadn't expected to give so much silver. He'd miscalculated the cost of the bribes and, of course, hadn't expected the storm or the expensive repairs.

'What did you do?' she pressed.

'I went to the temple where you were raised. I wanted to see it. I wanted to know who you were before.'

She stared at him, clearly understanding the magnitude of what he had done. It was difficult for Cantonese to slip into the Thirteen Factories district. It was near impossible to smuggle a white man from that district into Canton proper.

'Why?' she whispered. 'If you had been caught…' She shook her head. 'If you had been betrayed, you would have died horribly! Do you know what could have happened to you in a Chinese prison?'

Probably not. But he'd had to see it himself, where she had come from, how she had lived. Her world was so alien to his experience, but he understood things better now. And he had seen the other children at the temple, her sisters and brothers, so to speak. Many of mixed races like her. Others with obvious deformities. Children who were not wanted and had not been killed at birth. Children who survived on the charity of the temple.

'They asked about you,' he said. 'I told them you were doing well.' His gaze slid away from her. 'They wondered if I had come to adopt more children as your father had.'

'The children at the temple will not have good lives in China,' she said. 'That is why I had to leave.'

He had not realised the depth of her problems in China. Not until he'd seen it himself. 'I wanted to take them back with me. I wanted to adopt them all. I gave them all the silver I had instead. I made them promise to use it to feed the children.'

She said nothing, and when he looked at her face, he saw shock and understanding.

'When we first met, you gave away your last coin to a pickpocket.'

He frowned, not remembering but believing her nonetheless. 'I suppose it was foolish of me.'

'It is what first drew me to you. You are a kind man, not a selfish one. Thank you for caring for my other siblings. It is good that they know someone cares.'

'I hope they will honour their promise.' He had no way to ensure that the monks spent the money on the children.

'They will do it. They care, too. Otherwise, none of the half children would survive.'

That was good to know. And good that she understood that he couldn't see those children, know they were half-starved and reviled, and not do anything for them. And, of course, he hadn't expected to spend the rest of his money on ship repairs.

She touched his hand, showing him with a simple caress that she understood him. And that she was grateful for what he had done. Pleased beyond measure by that, he shifted until their fingers were entwined.

'What are your plans now?' he asked.

She frowned. 'Plans?'

'Yes,' he said, stretching for the right words. 'Your plans. You have money now or will soon, thanks to the cargo.'

'I had money before. My father's estate filled my dowry.'

Right. 'Well, now it's bigger.'

She nodded. Why didn't she speak?

'I mean, it's May, right? You're in the middle of the Season?'

'Yes.'

'Are you engaged? Did you find someone to marry?'

She carefully set aside her teacup, making pains—he guessed—to show that there was no engagement ring on her finger. 'I have not selected a husband. Why should I? I am content here with my sister, and I look forward to my niece or nephew.'

That made sense. Indeed, many unwed sisters lived such a life on their relative's generosity. 'You are happy then?'

Her lips curved and her gaze grew abstract. 'I am happy.' Then her eyes sharpened. 'Are you? Do you have plans?'

'God, no. I thought I was dead. It's disconcerting to have survived.'

'Hmmm.'

Damnation, she knew how to be inscrutable when she wanted. She stood, as regal as a queen, and he could do nothing but gaze in amazement at her. She'd always been lovely, but now she had a maturity that had been lacking before. A strength in herself that made her stunningly beautiful. She would age into a goddess.

And then, while he was still caught up in his fantasy of her as Juno or Athena, she abruptly bent down and pressed her mouth to his.

Never, in his entire life, had he been surprised by a kiss. That was because he was the one who orchestrated the dance. Always. Except with Lucy. She'd never said what he expected, never done as he thought she would. She was kissing him, and he scrambled to catch up.

Her lips touched his, warm and wet from her tea. And when her tongue stroked across his flesh, he felt a roar in his blood that hadn't been there since he'd left England. But it was back now, and it wanted her.

He pressed into her kiss, trying to deepen what she'd started. She allowed it for a moment, but only a moment. It was as if she sank into him long enough for her to remember him and for him to realise her presence with him.

Then she pulled back.

He caught her arm, but only barely. So when he tried to hold her close, she slipped away. And then she stood there, waiting while her breath steadied, and his heart kept pounding.

'Lucy—' he began.

'Do you remember our time on the ship? Just before you left?'

How could he forget? How many times had he relived the taste of her? The feel of her coming apart beneath his mouth?

'Yes,' he rasped.

'Now you know how it feels to begin something, to open to something you want, and then have it disappear. For nineteen months!'

He winced. 'I had to prove myself.'

'And have you? Do you feel like a worthy man now? Do you know what you want?'

He paused before answering. He knew the question had more significance than it appeared. There was a finality behind her eyes that told him so much rested upon his answer.

He sat up and thought about everything he had done, everything he was. He knew not to count the money. Coin was the least measure of a man, but it was the way the world counted. If he chose to look at himself by the world's standards, he would fall short.

Instead, he chose to look at himself the way Lucy measured a man. Or perhaps the way he now thought of other people.

He held to his responsibilities, for good or for ill. He cared for his family and for the children of strangers. He could be foolish with money, but he was gaining ground there. He balanced accounts, he calculated what was necessary and what was excess. He'd made mistakes there, but he owned them. And he apologised when he was in the wrong.

'I am a good man,' he realised. The words were spoken in a whisper at first, but then he looked straight at her and spoke with strength. 'I am a good man.'

'Yes,' she agreed. 'You are.' And then she folded her hands in front of her. She looked almost demure though he knew there was a dragon beneath that quiet exterior. 'There's something else you should know.'

He was still reeling from his own realization, but it was easy to look at her. Easy to wait for whatever blow was coming.

'I looked at the account book. You made a miscalculation.'

He winced. Good God, now what? How much had he lost?

'You don't own *The Integrity*,' she said. 'Declan does.'

'I know,' he said, weariness entering his tone.

'So the costs of the ship's repairs fall to Declan. Not you.'

He frowned. Was that true? He'd been the man on board, the one handling the accounts alongside Captain Banakos. As Declan's representative, of course he paid for the repairs. So he'd applied those expenses to his own tally. But he didn't own the boat.

He didn't own the boat!

'I spent… The repairs…' He blinked, mentally reviewing the costs.

'They will all be returned to you. Cedric, you have made an enormous profit on this venture. Enough, I think, to cover the expenses of a Season for both your sisters. And to give them a modest dowry.'

He gaped at her. 'I have money?'

'A very great deal.' And with that, she turned and left the room.

Chapter Twenty-Seven

Why had she kissed him? What was wrong with her?

Over the past nineteen months, she'd lived without his peculiar brand of absolute confidence in his own opinions. She'd gloried in the fact that she didn't yearn for his touch anymore. She barely thought of him, except when his extraordinarily touching gifts arrived. Medicines from all over the world, sent with detailed instructions and often with seeds to grow her own plants.

Every time they'd arrived, she'd grieved anew at her father's death. She'd passed the entire package over to Phoebe who had an attic set up as a London greenhouse. And she'd tried again to shove Cedric into a forbidden part of her memory.

She'd stopped reliving their amazing first kiss. Or rather, that had been true before he showed up at Almack's. What else could she do during the endless hours sitting by his sickbed? She remembered…everything. His kisses, his kindnesses and his awful betrayal, not to mention all their fights. Then he admitted to visiting the temple where she'd been raised. As if, oh, by the way, I wandered past the Thames the other day. Except she knew that it was no easy feat for a white man to step inside her temple.

He would have bribed someone to take him. And then bribed the monks to keep quiet about his visit. That didn't include what he'd given the monks to feed the children. And Cedric had done it just to understand her a little better. To see where and how she was raised. And to wish that he could save all the abandoned children there.

God, how she wanted to hate him for the chaos he brought. Not among others. In truth, her brother-in-law Declan created a bigger stir when he argued politics in the House of Lords. No, Cedric's chaos churned up all her emotions. She could not remain placid when he was around. Her blood surged and her thoughts ran in every direction.

Until she found herself kissing him.

Damn the man for making her heart flutter. And he had the gall to ask her what her plans were. Her plans? She planned to fall in love with a boring Englishman! She planned to dance and laugh all through the Season. And she certainly did not plan to kiss him!

Why did she feel half-dead when he was gone? Why did he make her heart beat and her mind soar? Why was it always him?

And why was she still fighting the draw between

them? Her heart had decided on who it wanted. She loved him. If he wanted her, she would go to him. But now that he knew he was wealthy, now that he knew that he had enough money to establish a good future for himself and his family...would he still want her?

Did he love her?

Chapter Twenty-Eight

Cedric slept with the memory of her kiss on his lips. He also held to himself the realization that he was a good man. He didn't even remember that he had money now until he woke later, and even then it was an afterthought.

She'd kissed him. And he was a good man.

So he was filled with hope, which was why he woke with a smile and an erection. Clearly, he was getting better if his body could plague him with desires that were impossible to satisfy. The sun was barely up, but the servants were about. Specifically Scottie who groaned on the floor soon after Cedric opened his eyes.

Cedric looked at the poor lad who was rubbing his neck as if it pained him. 'You've had a hard time of it, haven't you?' he rasped. Damn, his throat was dry.

'My lord! You're awake.' The boy sprang to his feet with the alacrity of youth.

'I am.' He winced at the continued rasp and reached for some water. Scottie was there before him, pouring a full measure which Cedric greedily consumed. 'Here's what I need,' he said when he finished. 'You will help me clean up then fetch me some breakfast. And then off to a real bed for you. I won't cripple my cousin's staff.'

'I'm not crippled—'

'You're not to argue either.'

He sat up by himself this time, poured his own water and grinned when he didn't spill it. He was on the mend.

Lucy didn't visit, which was a disappointment. But she did leave a packet of letters for him, which he greedily consumed. They were letters from Cora to Declan, and every word was a miracle to him.

The sale of Lilianna's books had gone very well. Thanks to his friends spreading the word—and a surprise approval from Prinny—her tales had become all the rage. She was happily penning more tomes and pocketing the cash to save for her coming out.

That was such amazing news. After all his worry, Lilianna had made her own dowry.

Simon was growing up healthy and strong. Cora and Eric seemed happy, especially as he was getting work throughout England. And even Rose had begun thinking about her future. She hadn't made any decisions yet, but she was determined to accompany Lilianna for her Season.

Better yet, Declan and Grace had promised to sponsor them, and Cedric couldn't be more pleased. Adding in the money he'd earned, his sisters were well set for their future.

His family was doing well. He could breathe easier. Indeed, he could look to his own future. He could even build upon what he'd begun, finding investors again for *The Integrity*'s next trip.

That night, he slept better than he had in his entire life.

'Cedric? Cedric, are you awake?'

He opened his eyes to see the mid-morning sun. Had he slept so late? He inhaled deeply, turning to see Lucy at his bedside.

Best sight ever.

'Cedric?' Lucy whispered. 'I did not want to wake you.'

'You didn't,' he lied. 'I am never asleep if you want to visit.'

She rolled her eyes. 'You will always flirt, even when on death's doorstep.'

He frowned. 'Am I on death's doorstep?'

'No, thank Heaven. But are you well enough for a visitor?'

He grinned. 'I am always well enough for—'

'Not me,' she interrupted.

Oh. 'Who?'

'Me,' came a male voice.

Father.

He winced. So many emotions flooded him. Anger,

hope, love and disappointment all churned together. It made his whole body freeze as he tried to parse what he should feel and what he should say.

'My lord,' Lucy said as she addressed his father. 'I told you I would let you know—'

'He is my son. I will not be stopped again.'

Cedric frowned. 'You stopped him before?'

'He has been here twice since you returned to England. Once after you first arrived, then again two nights ago.' Her tone hardened. 'He was in no fit state for us to answer the door.'

'Kept me from my own dying son!'

Lucy's tone was tart. 'He was sleeping, not dying. And you were not kept away. We do not let drunks into the ducal household.'

'And you,' his father said, 'you conniving, thieving bitch—'

Cedric didn't think. Life aboard a ship had changed his reactions. Refined argument was rarely possible there, and violence had to be stopped immediately. So he did what a sailor would do when woken from a dead sleep by a man threatening something—or someone— he cared about.

He grabbed the water pitcher and threw the contents straight at his father. He nearly lost his grip on the pitcher itself, but habit had him keeping the makeshift weapon in hand.

His aim was true. Lucy remained dry while his father was abruptly drenched. If he were aboard ship,

Cedric would follow up with a knife to his father's throat. But he didn't have a knife on him. Instead, he spoke with as much strength and authority as he could muster. Which, it turned out, was quite a bit.

'My apologies, Miss Richards. My father is unwell.'

'Why you impertinent whelp—'

Cedric surged up from the bed. It was awkward, which meant he didn't have full power. But he was standing at his full height within seconds. And since he was taller than his father, the man backed up in shocked surprise.

Lucy didn't say anything. He heard her gasp as she shrank back. He hated that she was witness to this, but he was too committed to stop now.

'Please excuse us, Miss Richards,' he ground out. 'My father and I must discuss appropriate behaviour.'

'Uh... I...'

'Lucy,' Cedric said, his tone softening. 'Go.'

Her chin firmed as she gave him a quick nod, and then she swung the bedroom door wide. At her gesture, the butler and a very large footman entered the room. He also heard the heavy tread of another rushing up the stairs.

Very good. But he knew that he needed to be the one who put the Earl in his place. Otherwise, the man would huff and puff about uppity staff and never learn the lesson he needed right now.

'Are you in control of yourself?' he asked his father.

'Are you mad?' his father sputtered.

'Extremely,' he answered, his voice deadpan.

He watched his father's eyes dart about the room. He was now outnumbered four to one as Lucy stepped out of the room and a second footman entered. 'Cedric,' he said, his expression shifting to concern. 'Get back in bed. You are not well.'

'Actually, I'm feeling better than I have in years,' he said with grim cheer. 'I never thought I'd hear my father insult a lady in her own home.'

'You heard nothing of the sort,' his father snapped. 'I believe you have a fever. Pray lie back down. This is unseemly.' Then he snapped his fingers at a footmen. 'You there. Hand me a towel. My son has spilled his drink.'

The footman obeyed because that's what servants did when addressed by an earl. Cedric backed up, giving his father room to wipe off his wet face and hair. Thank God Cedric had woken early that morning and cleaned himself up. He was even wearing a freshly laundered night shirt.

How civilised when he was feeling decidedly uncivilised.

'Do you know,' he said as sadness gripped him. 'I had to learn how to discipline unruly sailors. First with my fists and later with a whip.' His gaze found the Earl's. 'It's awful to do such a thing to my own father.'

Not just his father, but an earl. That used to mean something to him, but all he saw now was a sad man who'd never had to earn what he had. His father had spent his life gambling and drinking when he could have done anything. What a waste! Meanwhile, his father waved at the men who stood guard in the room. 'Go on. He's under control now. No need to protect me.'

Cedric snorted. How like the man to pretend that Cedric was the one in the wrong.

'Go on,' he said on a sigh. 'Pray ask my cousin to visit me as soon as he is available.' He had no idea if Declan had returned or not. Probably not given that the Earl felt like he had free rein to burst unasked into bedrooms. But it was a good reminder to his father that the Duke was due home at any moment. 'And bring me some fresh water, if you please.'

'Right away, my lord,' intoned the butler. 'And I'll fetch you some luncheon. Jones, Hillard, remain in the hallway in case his lordship needs an extra pair of hands.' He didn't mention which lord, but the meaning was clear enough. There would be no violence from either father or son.

'Father, why don't you wait outside with them? Unless you wish to aid in my toilette.'

'Oh, good God,' the Earl huffed.

Cedric arched a brow at his father. 'You're the one who burst uninvited into my sickroom. Either help with my care or wait until I'm done.'

'You're not that sick. And it is my right—'

'I need the chamber pot.'

'Imbecile,' his father muttered. But then he stomped out of the bedroom and slammed the door behind him.

Cedric winced at the noise but managed to quickly set himself to rights. He pulled on a bed-jacket and took a seat by the window. It was a power position, forcing the other person to act like a supplicant as he stood hat in hand. Indeed, his father had used it on him dozens of times. But this time, the position was reversed, and Cedric was human enough to enjoy it.

'Very well,' he called. 'You may come in.'

The Earl stomped in, curled his lip in disgust when seeing his son, then dropped unceremoniously onto the bed.

'Well, I'm glad that's out of the way. Damned unpleasant to be treated this way. This was once my home. Used to run wild here, pinching the maids. Don't know what's gotten into Declan, allowing that foreign girl into his bed.'

'Stop insulting the ladies of this household!' Cedric snapped.

'Don't be daft. You don't know what she's been doing with your money. I tried to get a look at the account. She said you would manage the money, but you can't do anything from a sickbed. She's probably draining the account as we speak, but I won't let her get away with it. Never you fear.'

Cedric sighed. 'She is taking exactly what is her due, Father. Hers and Prinny's.' Not to mention his other investors.

'Good God, the sickness truly has gotten hold of you.

Cedric, listen to me. You're my son and heir. I'll take care of things. That's what a father does for his son.'

Such beautiful words. They were tinged with warmth, too, and all the protective notes that were so absent during his childhood. He knew they were a lie, and yet he couldn't help but respond to it.

'Father,' he said softly. 'I kept the account. I know exactly—'

'We need the money, son. And you deserve it. It wasn't her working herself near death, was it? All she did was have her servants carry you here and feed you a little broth. You deserve that coin, son. Every penny of it.'

'What I deserve from this venture is mine alone. I will handle my affairs.'

'Course it is!' His father pushed to his feet. 'You've been too ill to understand. I'll have a talk with Declan. We'll see it done proper. It's his ship. He won't see all that profit go to a foreign girl. Not over his own cousin and uncle. Mark my words. You deserve that money. And I'll see that it goes where it's needed.'

'And where's that, Father?'

'To the estate, of course. It's where all our money goes, isn't it? The canal needs repair and something happened to the roof. We lost a bunch of pigs to the heat. Damned farmers. Can't keep a bunch of hogs alive. Say they can't make the rent. Claiming all sorts of folderol.'

Something happened to the roof? Cedric gaped at

his father. This was the man who had loomed so large when Cedric was boy. But now all he saw was a weak and slightly ridiculous old man.

'When was the last time you were home?'

'What? Why does that matter?'

'I saw the roof restored before I left.'

'What? Oh. Well, good then. But I told you about the pigs, right? So you see, it's a good thing that you've come home. That shipload of goods is just in time. I'm told we can get an advance on the sale right away. We just need Declan to write the cheque. I thought I'd do it tomorrow after he's been home for a night. Catch him in a good mood after a night with his wife, if you know what I mean.'

Hard to miss his father's crude wink. 'Yes, I know.'

'That's settled then. And don't you worry. I'll handle all the details.' He grinned as he clapped his hands. 'Good to see you getting better, son. I'd thought you'd died, you know. When your ship didn't come back. But here you are, getting stronger every day—'

'What's your favourite gambling hell these days, Father?'

His father's sallow skin flushed. 'What?'

'Where are you headed now?'

'Oh, just to my club. Got a few mates who enjoy faro.'

'And then where? Which gaming hell?'

'I don't go to them anymore,' he said. 'Too many card sharks. Skin a man alive if they could.'

Cedric's eyes widened. Had his father finally done it? Had he given up gambling? 'You don't play anymore?'

'Not in that pit of vipers. No, no, there's a few friends of mine. We get together of an evening and talk.'

Of course they did. 'Cards or dice?'

'Well, son, you know a gentleman plays whatever comes his way. A little bit of everything, just to keep the mind sharp.'

His mind might be sharp, but his body and clothing weren't. 'How far in the duns are you?'

'Not at all! Not at all! Son, I promised you, didn't I? Before you left. I said I'd change and I have.'

Cedric wished he could believe it. 'Then why do you need the profit from the ship?'

'For the estate, boy. Didn't you hear me?'

'What about your bills? Your tab at the club and the coin to the tailor?'

His father laughed a little too loud as he answered. 'Well, I'll admit to being a bit behind at the club. But there'll be plenty from your boat. Declan will see to—'

'Declan won't be paying you anything, Father. I told you. This venture is mine. I will dispense the profit to those who pledged a stake. Which you did not.'

'Don't be ridiculous. I see how frail you are. Nearly died. Don't tell me you've been gone for nearly two years and have nothing to show for it. You're not that stupid.'

Well, he'd thought he was exactly that stupid. How odd to realise he wasn't. Either way, his father had nothing to do with it. 'Declan won't give you a penny, Father.'

'Don't be stupid!' His father invested such disgust in that last word. As if that was a bigger crime than lying, stealing or gambling away their entire family's wealth.

'Remember what you promised me before I left? Remember how you said you'd stop gambling, stop bleeding the estate dry. You promised me you'd do it.'

His father lifted his chin. 'By what right do you question me? I'm the Earl of Hillburn and your father!'

Cedric stared at his father, seeing the man more clearly than before. Not the wastrel or the man with pride in a title that he had done nothing to maintain. He'd seen all that before. But what he saw now was a soul who was untethered to anything but gambling. There was no person he loved, no work to keep him focused.

Cedric hadn't understood that before. He hadn't known then how work built up a man and how love could keep him going when all else failed. His father had none of that, and that was a pitiful life.

Good God, the man probably didn't know he had a grandson. That's how disconnected he was from anyone who might care for him.

'How have you changed, Father?' he asked softly. 'What is different in you from two years ago? Five years? Ten?' Just how long had the man been lost?

'What the devil are you talking about?'

'Growth. Maturity.' He smiled to himself. 'Love, Father. Look at what a life devoid of love has brought you.'

'You're ill, son. Best lie back down and leave it all to me.'

Never.

'I have it under control, Father. It was my investment, my labour and I am of age. I will speak to Declan.'

The Earl puffed out his cheeks. 'Don't let him run roughshod—'

'I have whipped men. I have beaten them into submission, and I have faced the coldest, cruelest storm it has ever been my misfortune to endure. Never fear, Father. I will speak with Declan.' Then his tone softened. As frustrated as he was with the man, the Earl was still his father. He still needed to make an offer even knowing the man might never take it. 'Let's both of us go home soon. We can see…' He almost said *your grandson*, but that wasn't his secret to tell. Nor could he mention the books that Lilianna had published or the children that Rose taught. 'Um, let's see what Cora has done with the place. She's a remarkable woman, you know. They all are. There's good food there and—'

'Pigs, Cedric. Just pigs and crops. Nothing else.'

'Your family is there, Father. The people who love you.'

His father shook his head. 'Ah, but I haven't any gifts to bring them, you know. They like that kind of thing, and I can't show up without it. You know that.'

Cedric looked at his father, feeling a thought struggling to be born. Something important, but he couldn't quite grab hold of it yet. 'They—we—don't care about that. We don't expect it. We want to see you.'

His father rolled his eyes. 'Don't be childish. Of course they expect it. I can't go home until I've got the presents in hand.'

Cedric looked at his father, seeing the man's absolute certainty that he couldn't visit without some sort of show of wealth. That money was all his children cared about. Which, of course, was ridiculous. They wanted a father, not his coin.

'They don't want your money. They want you.'

'See how little you know your sisters. All they talk about is the repairs that are needed, the roof that has collapsed. That's all they think about.'

Maybe he'd thought the same, too. But that's not what he'd seen when he'd gone home. He'd seen a happy family, one where he was included.

'Maybe they want to show you what they've accomplished,' he offered.

'All the more reason I can't go empty-handed.'

They stared at each other in silence, each seeming to take a new measure of the other. Cedric felt himself strengthen as he realised how wrong his father was about his family. But the man wouldn't see it, and Cedric now understood why.

His father tied money and love together. He could not have the latter without the former. And so had Cedric. But they were both wrong! Love and money had nothing to do with one another. They might both be necessary, but they were not intertwined. Indeed, they should never be intertwined!

'They want love, Father. Not money.'

'Don't be a child, boy,' the Earl said, standing up. 'I'll come back to visit you in a couple days. See what you've worked out.'

'As you wish,' he said, his mind still on this new revelation. And from it came a new feeling. A wonderful feeling.

Hope.

He could have what he needed. He could have love; he could give love and it had absolutely nothing to do with how much money he had. Certainly, he still wanted to support Lucy. He wanted to help his sisters and build for the next generation. But that had nothing to do with what he felt for Lucy.

And it should have nothing to do with how he expressed his love to her or how they shared what was between them.

Meanwhile, his father was headed for the door, but there was one more thing he had to make clear to the man. One more thing before he could lay his heart out before the woman he adored.

'Father,' he called, then waited until the Earl looked at him. 'If I ever hear you saying one rude comment, one hateful word about Miss Richards or her sister, you will not see a penny from me.' Since his father equated love and money, then he would have to meet the man where he was. Whether or not there was coin to be shared, the rules needed to be absolutely clear.

His father's face crinkled in confusion. 'The foreign girls?'

'The Duchess of Byrning and her sister, Miss Lucy Richards. One word, Father, and I will whip you before I give you a penny.' Then he dismissed his father in the exact way the Earl had done to him for so many years. 'I believe we understand each other.'

He saw emotions chase across his father's face. There was a moment when the man thought to defy him. Several moments, in fact, but Cedric had learned how to stand strong against any defiance. And his father must have seen it.

The Earl left without another word. Which left Cedric alone to ponder the huge shift—the excellent shift—in his relationship with his father.

Chapter Twenty-Nine

Lucy listened intently outside Cedric's bedroom door. His father had left the house ten minutes ago with nothing beyond a polite nod in the hallway to her as he passed. She had waited until the front door closed behind him, then headed straight for Cedric. But what was she going to say to him? That she had never been more thrilled than when he had drenched his own father in her defense?

She'd been terrified of the possible violence, but the knowledge that he would fight for her still rocked her to the core. All her anger, all her frustration with him melted away at that moment.

He defended her. He fought his own father for her.

And now she loved him even more than ever.

Unable to keep herself away, she knocked quietly on his bedroom door. There was no answer, and the silence worried her. So she twisted the doorknob and peeked inside, half afraid of what she would find.

No dead body, thank Heaven, but what she found

was akin to a death. Cedric sat in his chair completely immobile. For a man who was constantly moving—he was even a restless sleeper—this absolute stillness frightened her.

'Cedric?' she whispered. And when he didn't seem to react, she quietly crossed the room to his side.

Still no reaction, but this close she could see that he breathed. And given that there were no obvious wounds, she decided her best choice was to sit beside him and wait. He would come back to himself eventually, and then they could talk.

'I've changed.' Cedric's voice was low and, as far as she could tell, his gaze never lifted off the floor.

'What?'

'I see it so clearly. What he has been missing all his life. And what I want in mine.' He looked up, his eyes bright with the sheen of tears. 'I swear he'll never hurt you. And if he says one word against you or your sister, then tell me. I will cut him off. I swear I will—'

'Cedric,' she said as she sank down before him. She pressed her hand to his cheek, searching for fever. 'Slow down. How do you feel?'

He took her hand and brought it to his lips for a kiss. 'I feel…clear-headed, I suppose.' He brought her hand down to his lap and she happily left their fingers entwined. 'I see what my father has been missing all his life. I see why he turned to gambling and why it never fills him. Win or lose, he can't stop playing.'

'What?'

'Love, Lucy. He has no love. Not of work, nor of his own family.' How it hurt to say it, but he knew the truth. 'Have you ever seen gamblers deep in play? They aren't happy, and yet they can't stop themselves.'

She smiled at him. She had no idea if what he said about his father was correct or not. But she saw the spark in Cedric's eyes, and it pleased her so much that warmth filled her heart. Finally, he was returning to the man she remembered. The one who had hope and a ready smile no matter what happened. But now it was even better because she didn't read any desperation in him. Only determination.

Then his gaze intensified. 'You shouldn't be on the floor in front of me.'

'I don't mind,' she said as she pressed a kiss to their joined hands. 'I like it when you smile at me.'

'Then I shall always wear a smile for you.'

He would do it too, she realised. Just because she liked his smile, he would put one on for her no matter what he truly felt. 'I like honesty between us.'

His expression shifted, his gaze softened and she felt his fingers tighten around hers. 'Have you truly forgiven me?' he asked. 'For all the other things. I was angry and desperate and—'

'An idiot.'

'Yes! A complete idiot.'

She chuckled. 'I cannot hold a grudge against every person who makes idiotic mistakes.'

'I don't care about anyone else. I care about you.'

She smiled. 'I have forgiven you.'

'Then marry me, please.'

She jolted, shocked by his words. 'What? But—' She pressed her hand to his cheek.

He caught her hand then pressed a kiss into her hand. 'I'm not sick. This isn't a fever, and I can wait if you want. But I understand what I need now and it's you.'

She shook her head. 'You have always wanted me, Cedric. We have wanted each other.' But he'd refused her so many times.

'I didn't think I was worthy of you. I didn't think you could possibly want me. Not unless I had money to support you, money to take care of my responsibilities. Money for love.' He closed his eyes. 'I've been such an idiot.'

'You have plenty of money now.'

'It doesn't matter.' He looked at her, his eyes twinkling with merriment. 'Don't you see? It never mattered!'

He was trying to tell her something. She wanted to shake him until he said something she could understand. But he had to find the words his own way. And so she held silent and watched as he gently wrapped her hand in his.

'Money for love. That's what my father taught us. That money was the only way to love. When he was flush, he rained gifts upon us. We felt loved. And then he left, looking for more money. Somehow, I thought the two were the same.'

'I've never cared how much money you had.'

'I know,' he said. 'But I never believed that was true.'

'But you do now?'

He caressed her face. 'I believe that love is entirely separate from money. That I need love. And without it, I will be as pitiful as my father. I will chase coin until I am as lost and empty as he.'

Her heart was beating hard in her throat, and her hands felt weak where he clasped them between his. She saw the change in him so clearly. The revelation had turned him inside out, and she was at last able to touch the heart of him. The man who needed love.

But did he love her?

'Cedric,' she said, her voice a hoarse rasp. 'I am so happy for you.' That was true. It was glorious to see someone she loved so transformed.

'But you don't believe me,' he said, his expression tender.

That wasn't it, but he didn't give her time to explain.

'This has nothing to do with money. Your dowry or anything like this is entirely separate. Here, I'll prove it to you.' He looked up, over her shoulder at someone else behind her. 'Cousin, you have control of her affairs, yes? After Lord Wenshire's death, you are her guardian?'

Lucy twisted around to see her brother-in-law, Declan, in the doorway. He had clearly just arrived as he was standing there with his mouth ajar. Grace was beside him, her expression soft as she held his hand.

'Good morning to you too, Cedric,' Declan said with a slow drawl. 'I am pleased to see that you are alive. I have been in contact with your sisters during your absence. I can give you details about—'

'I read the letters. Thank you,' Cedric interrupted. 'Do you have guardianship over Lucy?'

'Yes, but—'

'Then here is the marriage contract I want. Set all her funds into an account that she manages.'

'Are you feverish?' Declan stepped further into the room. 'No bank will allow that.'

'They will allow it, Declan. You're a duke. I'll be an earl. If we tell them so, it will be.'

'Cedric, this is not necessary,' Lucy said, her voice low. And yet, even as she spoke, she wanted to hear the rest. She wanted to know what he would give up for her.

'I don't want her dowry. She will manage it better than I will anyway.'

She squeezed his hands. 'I could not have gotten the investors you did. I could not have filled the cargo hold on my own.'

He looked back at her, and his mouth curved into a smile that heated her all the way to her toes. 'I am good with the investors. That's what I bring to the business then.'

That's not what she wanted in her marriage. 'Cedric—' she began, but he was moving, straightening out of his chair. She went with him. How could she not when he still gripped her hand? And then, when she thought he would stand before her, he sank down. 'Cedric!' she cried, alarmed. But a moment later, she realised he'd gone down on one knee before her.

'I love you, Lucy. From the very first, I have dreamed about you, wanted you, fought with you and adored you. No woman has ever consumed me as you do, and I never want it to end. You have made me a better man, and please God, will you stay and help me be worthy of you? It is all that I have wanted these last two years, and I swear I will make it someday. I'm already figuring things out—'

She pressed a shaking hand to his mouth. Finally, he had said the words. All this devotion, and all she cared about were his first words. He loved her. *He loved her!*

And she loved him.

'I don't care about the money,' she said as she touched his cheek. 'I can always make money. But that's not what I want.'

'Then what?' he said. 'Tell me, and I will get it for you.'

She smiled. 'You, you idiot. I have always wanted you.' Then she matched his pose, sinking down to the floor until she knelt before him. 'I love you, Cedric. I have since I first heard you laugh in the marketplace. Such a strange Englishman, but I couldn't look away. I still can't.'

He stared at her, his eyes wide and his breath quick. 'You love me? After everything, you love me.'

'From the very beginning. Through all our fights and

your absences. I have never stopped loving you. And yes, I will marry you.'

He touched her face then, cupping her cheeks in the tenderest hold. As if she were the most precious thing in the world. Then they kissed. Slowly at first. Sweetly and with reverence.

But she didn't want to be revered. She wanted to be loved. And so she deepened the kiss. She opened to him, and he responded with fervor. Love and lust collided inside her, igniting an inferno. He seemed no less affected, and if her sister and brother-in-law were not standing there, she would have given him her all.

But Declan stopped them, gripping Cedric's shoulder on one side while Grace tugged at her sister on the other.

'Enough, enough,' Declan declared. 'Do not debauch my sister-in-law in front of me!'

Cedric looked up, his expression clear. 'I meant what I said,' he stressed. 'She needs control of her dowry.'

'I know,' Declan said. 'I would not approve of this match otherwise.' Then before either of them could react, he held up his hand. 'If it's what you want, Lucy, I will not interfere.' He glanced at his wife. 'I have found such joy in my marriage, why would I deny my cousin his?'

Lucy didn't answer. She was too busy being lifted into her sister's arms. They hugged each other tight, both stunned how their lives had turned out. Two half-Chinese orphans had found love.

Then as soon as she was released, as soon as Declan finished pressing a kiss to her cheek, she was pulled back into Cedric's arms. He held her joyously and a little possessively, which fitted her needs perfectly.

And when she looked up into his eyes, he said the words with her.

'I love you.'

Epilogue

They were married three weeks later in a small family ceremony in a cathedral that easily matched the size of the temple in Canton. Cedric wanted a large wedding, announcing their love to the entire *ton*, but Lucy didn't. Not because of the expense, which would have been exorbitant, but because she had never been one to show her treasures to the world.

She wanted Cedric to herself, quietly, in the sweetness of each other's arms.

So he agreed. After all, he'd promised to agree to everything she said. She knew it wouldn't last. They enjoyed their arguments too much, but they had both found their strengths and a new power in working together.

Which is what she told him as he carried her to bed their first night as a wedded couple. 'I am never as bold as when I'm with you,' she whispered. 'You make me believe I can do anything.'

'And I am never so strong as when you look at me like that. As if I am the answer to your dreams.'

'You are.'

'And you are.'

He kissed her as he set her on her feet. He teased her mouth, her cheeks, and her neck as his fingers unfastened her gown. She moved as quickly as he, matching his hunger as she helped him out of his waistcoat and more.

She loved how he touched her; his caresses were reverent, adoring and absolutely too tender for what she wanted right now. So she kissed him, putting her feelings into action. She had waited too long for this. She would not be denied now.

But he stepped back, his chest heaving. 'Lucy, I want you. But we don't have to do this tonight. It's been a long day for you—'

She didn't know if he was teasing her or not. Either way, she grabbed his arm as she climbed up onto the bed. 'We have waited long enough, don't you think?'

He grinned. 'I do.'

'And so do I,' she said, echoing their wedding vows.

He wasted no more time on denials. He stripped out of the last of his clothing and she was pleased at the sight of his body. He no longer looked wasted. Indeed, he looked virile as he climbed upon the bed.

He caressed her breasts and he teased her nipples in the way she remembered. And then he spread her knees when her body grew too demanding to wait.

She gripped him then, using arms and legs to pull him on top of her. She wanted him in her body as deeply as he was in her heart.

He waited a moment. An eternity of patience. Then he pierced her. Deep and hard he thrust into her, and she welcomed it. She was open for him, hungry and so happy that a worthy man wanted her.

She would have spoken her love then. She would have cried it out to the heavens, but she hadn't the breath. She had only the sight of him above her. His eyes seemed to see only her as his breath shortened and their bodies moved together.

They built together. Steadily, powerfully, and in perfect rhythm. And when the climax came, she knew it was only the beginning. So many peaks they would climb together. So many things ahead for them.

'I love you,' she cried, as her body condensed and expanded around him.

'My love,' he whispered as he poured everything he had into her.

And, unknown to them, that night they began a family. One that would grow stronger with each passing day.

Some hours later, Lucy turned in his arms and murmured sleepily into his ear. 'I forgot to tell you.'

'Hmm?'

She took a deep breath, loving the scent of him. 'You know all those medicines and plants you sent back for my father?'

'Yes. All the ones that arrived too late.'

'I gave them to Phoebe,' she reminded him. 'She's been growing them according to the instructions.'

She felt his exhale along the side of her neck and shivered in delight. 'I hope it works,' he grumbled. 'They certainly cost me enough to get the seeds.'

She pressed a kiss to his lips. 'She's going to open an apothecary shop with a doctor she's been working with. They're going to sell your medicines.'

It took a moment for her words to penetrate. And when they did, Cedric straightened up enough to peer at his wife. 'What did you say?'

'They're going to make medicines and hopefully, a fortune from it.'

'Huh,' he said. 'Good for them.'

'Yes, but that's not what I wanted to tell you,' she said as she stretched beside him.

'It's not?' They were both getting distracted as she moved her legs alongside his.

'You need to use your influence to get people to try their medicines.'

He lowered his mouth to her neck, nipping in a way that made her breath catch. 'Easy enough, but why?'

'Because you get a portion of every sale they make. They were your seeds after all.'

He lifted up to stare at her. 'They are your seeds, my love. I sent them to you and your father.'

'And I am gifting them to you on our wedding night. Because I love you.'

His expression brightened and his gaze filled with love. 'I am the luckiest man alive,' he said.

'I agree,' she quipped, 'because you have made me the happiest woman alive.'

'God, I love you,' he said. And then he set about proving just how much he did. Every single day—and night—of their lives.

* * * * *

If you loved this story, be sure to check out the previous instalment in Jade Lee's Daring Debutantes miniseries

The Duke's Guide to Fake Courtship

And look out for more stories by Jade Lee, coming soon!

MILLS & BOON®

Coming next month

CINDERELLA'S CHARADE WITH THE DUKE
Jeanine Englert

'I would like to extend your offer of employment not only as Millie's governess, but also as my fake betrothed. I think a Lady Penelope Denning would do nicely,' he said, his words rushing out. 'But if you prefer another name, I am open to such possibilities. Do you think you could do that?'

She could have sworn he said something about pretending to be his betrothed, but surely she had misheard every word. 'I am sorry, Your Grace. I do not think I understood you properly. I would love to remain on as Lady Millie's governess, but that last part... Did you say you wish for me, an orphan from Stow, to also pretend to be your betrothed as some other person entirely?'

A beat of silence passed and then His Grace sat back in his chair, his hands sliding down the curved wooden armrests before covering the painted gold flowers at the ends. He met her gaze. 'Yes, Miss Potts, that is *exactly* what I wish for you to do.'

Not even Ophelia would have anticipated this request. Hattie was torn between the shock of silence and the wild laughter of disbelief and confusion. He stared at her and waited.

She asked the only thing she could think of. 'Why?'

'A fair question,' he replied.

This whole scene was ridiculous. Why would *this* man need a woman like her to be his pretend betrothed? He was a duke, he was handsome and had all the time and wealth in the world at his disposal. He could find an eager wife in the time it would take him to blink.

He paused in front of the portrait of the late Marchioness and faced Hattie. 'In the simplest terms, Miss Potts, I cannot take a new bride, but the *ton* will give me and my daughter no peace until I am adequately…unavailable to help quash the rumours they create to sell their gossip sheets. I cannot ask a woman of high Society to fill such a role as they all know one another and will talk about such a ruse and embarrass me.

'So, my hope was that you being from Stow and far removed from here and someone who cares for my daughter and whom my daughter adores would help me with this…endeavour.'

'You mean lie to everyone?'

'Yes.'

Continue reading

CINDERELLA'S CHARADE WITH THE DUKE
Jeanine Englert

Available next month
millsandboon.co.uk

Copyright © 2025 Jeanine Englert

COMING SOON!

We really hope you enjoyed reading this book. If you're looking for more romance be sure to head to the shops when new books are available on

Thursday 23rd October

To see which titles are coming soon, please visit
millsandboon.co.uk/nextmonth

MILLS & BOON

MILLS & BOON TRUE LOVE IS HAVING A MAKEOVER!

Introducing

Love Always

Marrying a Royal
Nina Milne
Suzanne Merchant

Summer with the Billionaire
Rachael Stewart
Justine Lewis

Swoon-worthy romances, where love takes centre stage. Same heartwarming stories, stylish new look!

Look out for our brand new look

OUT NOW

MILLS & BOON

LET'S TALK
Romance

For exclusive extracts, competitions and special offers, find us online:

- **f** MillsandBoon
- **X** @MillsandBoon
- **◉** @MillsandBoonUK
- **♪** @MillsandBoonUK

Get in touch on 01413 063 232

For all the latest titles coming soon, visit
millsandboon.co.uk/nextmonth